HER FORBIDDEN HIGHLANDER HUSBAND

CLAN MACKINLAY SERIES

HER FORBIDDEN HIGHLANDER HUSBAND

CLAN MACKINLAY SERIES

ALLISON B. HANSON

This book is a work of fiction. Names, characters, places, and incidents are the product of the author's imagination or are used fictitiously. Any resemblance to actual events, locales, or persons, living or dead, is coincidental.

Copyright © 2021 by Allison B. Hanson. All rights reserved, including the right to reproduce, distribute, or transmit in any form or by any means. For information regarding subsidiary rights, please contact the Publisher.

Entangled Publishing, LLC
10940 S Parker Rd
Suite 327
Parker, CO 80134
rights@entangledpublishing.com

Amara is an imprint of Entangled Publishing, LLC.

Edited by Alethea Spiridon
Cover design by LJ Anderson/Mayhem Cover Creations
Cover photography by PeriodImages
rpeters86/GettyImages

Manufactured in the United States of America

First Edition November 2021

At Entangled, we want our readers to be well-informed. If you would like to know if this book contains any elements that might be of concern for you, please check the book's webpage for details.

https://entangledpublishing.com/books/her-forbidden-highlander-husband

To my family, both by blood and by bond.

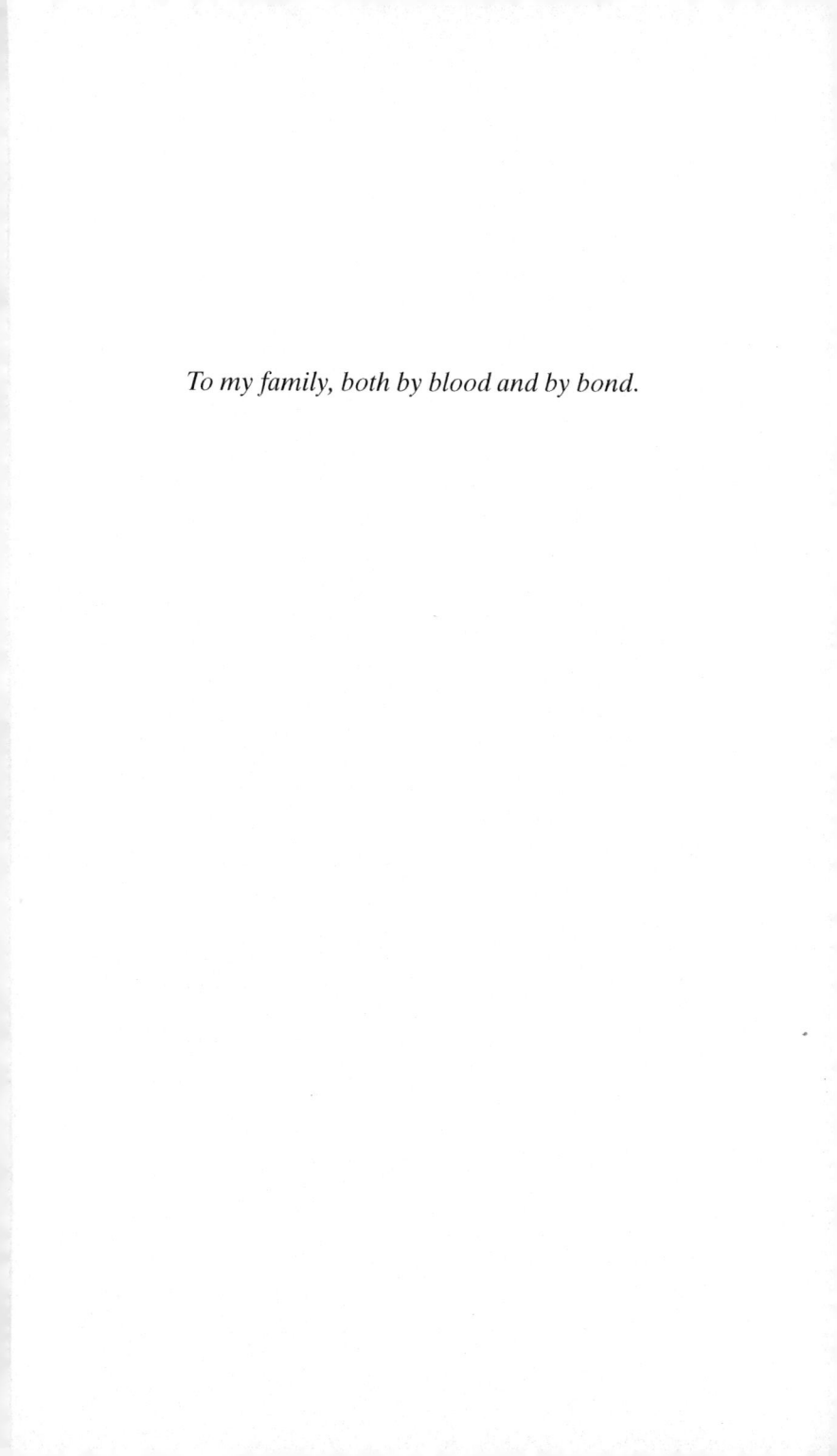

Chapter One

May 1664

Standing outside the laird's study, Evelyn Stewart took a deep, steadying breath before knocking. A summons from her father could mean anything from a request to have the maids change his bedding, to a lecture on her shortcomings for hours on end.

It all depended on his mood, which hadn't been good of late. Last year, after assisting with the defeat of the McCurdy clan, her father and his men had come home to find the MacDonalds had taken the opportunity of their absence to raid the cattle. The laird blamed Evelyn, since she was in charge while the men were away. In his mind, she should've done something to stop them.

Had Evelyn known before the cattle were gone, perhaps she might have tried. But she hadn't. Just as her father wouldn't have been aware, either, had he been there, but that didn't matter. She had failed him, yet again. In truth, his disappointment in her had started years before, after she'd run away and returned ruined and useless for his plans.

"Come in," he bellowed.

"You summoned me, Father?" Evelyn asked. She bowed before him hoping this might be the time he returned to being the father she remembered of her youth. He scowled, which didn't bode well for the rest of her visit.

"Sit."

She took her seat, obediently. *Obediently* was the way she did everything when it came to her father, ever since he'd accepted her back into his home.

While she wasn't happy with the way her father handled everything, she had no right to complain given her position. She'd shamed him and wouldn't give him further cause to throw her out of the clan. She couldn't afford to be put out.

"I've made an arrangement with the laird of Clan Morgan."

Ev blinked, trying to remember having met any of the Morgans. She didn't even know where in the Highlands they resided.

The laird must have caught her confusion. "Their lands are in the northernmost part of Scotland."

"And what do they offer?" She smiled at his smile. He was pleased she was aware of the politics involved in clan dealings. Everything in the Highlands was acquired through barter or alliance with another clan. Everyone needed something and had something to give in exchange.

Unfortunately, his pride in her was short-lived. It had been this way between them since she'd returned three years ago. Their relationship, once tender, was now strained beyond measure.

"They have the means to restore our stock of cattle, since you sat by as the MacDonalds ran off with our herd last year." Of course, he had to take the opportunity to remind her of her failure yet again. Even if she'd been in the castle at the time of the raid, there weren't enough remaining warriors to fight them off. Rather than try to defend herself, she sat silently and waited for him to continue.

"The Morgans will even deliver the cattle to us before autumn. It would take us many more years to get our stock back to what it had been before the MacDonald vermin attacked us."

"And what will they take in trade?" She wondered how many barrels of whiskey her father planned to part with. She hoped once the trade was complete, she wouldn't have to hear how she'd let him down again.

"You."

She choked on a breath. *"Me?"*

"The Morgan laird needs a wife for his heir. We've arranged it so you will marry when they bring the cattle south at summer's end."

"But I am ruined." How desperate were these Morgans?

"About that. While it's true your maidenhead is no longer intact, there's no reason the bridegroom or his father need know that. Their clan is too far away to have heard what happened, and by the time they arrive it will have been more than four years."

As if her virginity could grow back after four years. She bit her lip, trying to rein in her terror, but couldn't help herself. "Father, I—"

He cut her off with a slice of his hand. "You are perfectly able to perform the role of wife to the Morgan heir and eventually become mistress of Clan Morgan. You've been raised for such duty your entire life. We'll not let an unfortunate incident a few years past get in the way of that."

"An unfortunate incident…?" Evelyn seethed but bit her tongue. It was much more than that. It had changed her life forever, yet her father continued to brush it aside. He wanted to pretend it hadn't happened, and now he was making her play the part of the virginal bride when she couldn't be further from it.

"You'll remain chaste until they come for you."

She might have been offended by his assumptions; however, she was numb to the things her father said to her by now. Once she'd been his most prized possession, a daughter he was proud of. But when she ran away and was captured by five McCurdy deserters, she became soiled, and no longer worthy of his affections.

"Of course," she said, consenting to his terms of remaining chaste. That was one thing that was easy to agree to—she had no interest in touching or being touched by a man for the rest of her life.

Just the thought of it caused panic to return as if it was happening all over again. She could almost feel the cut of the rope on her wrists and smell the foul scent of sour ale and rotting teeth.

"That is all." Her father dismissed her with a casual wave of his hand.

This hurt her the most. The way he cast her aside as nothing. Gone was the father who shared stories of his youth and planned a great future for her. The man had loved Evelyn's mother to distraction and often spoke of Evelyn finding a man who would worship her as he had his wife. That dream had died at the hands of five monsters.

"Yes, Father." She left his study feeling weighed down by her impending fate. But it was only just early May and the Morgans wouldn't arrive until September at the earliest.

She had time to come up with a way out of this. She'd spend every waking moment focused on that task. One thing was certain, though.

She wouldn't be marrying anyone.

Chapter Two

Liam MacKinlay stepped into his chamber and smiled widely, just as he had for the past year. It was a silly thing to be so happy to have his own room.

It wasn't grand in any way, but it had a large, soft bed long enough for his tall frame. A stand with a washbasin stood next to the door, and in the corner there was a trunk that still remained mostly empty, since he didn't have many things to fill it.

He'd hung his few articles of clothing and his weapons on the pegs in the wall. It wasn't much, but it was his.

Growing up an orphan, he'd slept wherever it was convenient. Davinna MacKinlay, the current laird's late mother, had given him a bed in her solar when he was small. Later, when he'd joined the ranks of warriors, he simply bedded down in the hall with the rest of the bachelor soldiers of the clan.

However, for the last year Liam had been the war chief, and the war chief was given his own quarters that he could share with a wife.

Visions of a lass with golden-red hair and dark brown eyes came to him. Evelyn Stewart. The only woman he'd ever wanted for a wife.

Liam had already asked her father twice for her hand. Once, a few years ago, when Liam had escorted her home to her clan after she'd been found on MacKinlay lands as a prisoner to a group of beastly men. She'd not spoken much at all as Liam rode next to her during their weekslong journey.

He took up most of their time telling her stories to help keep her mind off what had happened to her. He'd earned a few smiles and fewer laughs, but he felt they'd bonded in a way. There was a night he'd had to wake her from a terror and she'd cried. She'd allowed him to hold her while she wept, and his heart was hers from that point on.

He'd offered for her on the spot when he'd delivered her to her father and wasn't surprised the man was too stunned to answer with more than a curt, "Go away."

Last year when Liam had been sent to secure the Stewarts' assistance, he saw it as an opportunity to ask again. He waited as they traveled closer to Dunardry. The night before they were to join the rest of his clan, Liam took a chance and was rejected once again.

Liam flopped onto his bed and reached out across the empty space, smiling despite the emptiness beside him. He now had a bed and a position that might help change the man's mind, for he'd already given Evelyn Stewart his heart. He wanted to give her his name. Rather the name he'd taken, since he didn't have one of his own.

It was time to take fate into his own hands. He got up and went to the laird's study. He hovered by the open door, appraising the man's mood. Lachlan MacKinlay was playing with his newest son, Andrew. The boy had been born hours after they'd returned from defeating the McCurdys. The babe stared up at his father adoringly.

Not wanting to intrude on the moment, Liam made to step out but bumped into Kenna in the doorway as she came up behind him and entered the room.

"Are you coming or going?" the laird's wife asked with a smile as she went to her husband and took the lad.

Liam bowed. "I can come back another time."

"Come in. What's on your mind?" The laird of the MacKinlay clan waved him closer.

Lachlan was like a brother to him, though much older. Liam remembered following him and his cousins around.

Kenna gave Liam's arm a squeeze as she walked by. He remembered when her hand would have circled his forearm, but now at twenty, he was much too large. Still tall and lanky, he'd filled out to the point he was nearly as wide as the laird.

Liam cleared his throat and stepped closer. "As you know, my laird, we approach a year since we took Baehaven and I became your war chief."

"And as *you* know, I've asked you many times since to call me Lach."

"Yes. Lachlan—I mean, Lach," he corrected quickly as the other man frowned. He was making a hash of it. "Very well. And a good day to you." Liam turned to leave.

"Liam?"

"Aye, my laird?" He squeezed his eyes closed but didn't attempt to correct his blunder yet again.

"I believe ye forgot to tell me the purpose of your visit."

"Of course. Perhaps another time." He bowed to the man he respected more than anyone. Nine years separated them, but Lachlan was a man while Liam often felt like he was still the boy chasing after him.

"Liam, take a seat," Lach ordered when Liam had almost made his escape. Once seated, the man waited a full minute before letting out a breath. "A laird and his war chief need to be partners. To strategize and plan together to protect the clan and ensure victory. We need to communicate with each other."

Liam knew himself to be a formidable warrior and a skilled war chief. He'd spent much of his life practicing, drilling, and studying battle plans. Aside from eating, it was all he really knew. In the few raids and battles he'd led over the last year, the laird had approved of his strategy.

Liam nodded in agreement but remained quiet.

"Will you tell me what you wanted to see me about?" Lachlan asked finally.

"Yes." Liam shifted uneasily. He'd never needed to ask anyone for something so personal before. "Last year, when the clan was joined by the Stewarts to defeat the McCurdys, I asked the Stewart laird for his daughter's hand—Evelyn." Even speaking her name made his heart flutter before dropping into the pit of his stomach.

"Aye. Bryce had mentioned it to me." The laird gave no hint as to what he thought of this.

Liam went on. "The man turned me down, she being a laird's daughter and me being a nameless bastard."

"He said that to you?" Lachlan's hands tightened into fists on the top of his desk.

"Nay. Well, not exactly like that, but it was really no surprise, and I don't take offense. It's true enough, I'm not worthy of her." He swallowed. "However, I still think of her. It's been more than three years since I've last seen her, but the burning in my chest is no better after all this time."

Lachlan fought a smile, but Liam caught it. "Ye wish to petition him again?"

"Aye. My hope is he'll allow it now that I'm a war chief and hold a more honorable position with my clan."

"I've not met a man more worthy than ye, Liam. I'd recommend you as a fine husband to my own daughter if I had any, and they were of age to marry. But, alas, my wife provides me my own army of male progeny." He smiled and Liam knew his complaint was in jest. The laird was proud of his four boys and in love with his wife. "Hugh Stewart would be a fool not to approve of you. For no one would treat his lass with more respect and honor."

Liam appreciated his laird's praise; however, it wasn't Lachlan's nonexistent daughter Liam wished to marry.

"You wish to ask my permission to go speak to him again?"

"Yes, my laird—Lach."

"I'll do so, if you will take a letter with you and present it to Hugh on my behalf."

"Of course." Liam stood and bowed.

"Do you wish any of your men to accompany ye?" It was a kind offer, but Liam didn't need any of his warriors to witness another rejection if it came to that.

"Nay. I'll be fine on my own. Thank you."

Lachlan gave a nod. "I'll have the missive ready when I see you off at dawn tomorrow."

"Thank you, truly. I hope the man accepts my offer this time."

"As do I."

Liam knew his chances were slim, but he needed to try once more. He'd never be more than war chief. If his position wasn't enough to impress the Stewart laird, he'd be forced to give up.

He'd thought of no one but her in all these years. While he didn't know her well, it didn't keep him from imagining what their marriage would be like. Her shy smiles and sweet disposition. She was an angel sent to Earth just for him.

Chapter Three

"Bloody hell," Evelyn muttered to herself as she entered the bailey with her head down.

She was late returning from the village. She could only pray her father hadn't taken notice. She wouldn't be able to stay silent through yet another scolding.

It'd been more than a week since her father's announcement about her pending marriage to the Morgan heir, but she'd hoped to have come up with a plan and a few alternate plans by now.

To date she had nothing. She was so distraught she didn't hear her name being called at first.

"Evelyn?"

She turned to see an angel standing before her. It could've been the way the sunlight seemed to come from him as she looked up into his smiling face. Surely, his white hair and pale blue eyes also caused her initial confusion.

"Liam MacKinlay?" she asked, unsure if it was really him. He'd been almost thin the last she'd seen him. A boy growing awkwardly into a man's body. But he was all man now. Except for his sweet smile and those dimples that made him look like the most genuine person she'd ever met.

He'd seemed that way when he'd escorted her home after her ordeal with the McCurdys. She'd been of no mind to talk, but he kept her thoughts busy with his wild tales so she wouldn't dwell on the hell she'd endured.

He'd provided comfort with his smiles as well as his arms on the occasions when the memories became too much and she'd broken down in tears. While she shied away from men, Liam had managed to gain her trust during their journey; she didn't remember if she'd even thanked him for his kindness.

When her father and their warriors had returned home after defeating the McCurdys last year, Evelyn wondered if Liam had survived the battle. She'd thought of him and was now happy to see he'd lived. So happy she hugged him without thinking first.

His large arms wound around her waist and held her loosely. She pulled away quickly and noticed Liam's smile had changed from one of friendliness to one with more intent.

She swallowed and stepped farther away. She shouldn't have touched him. She didn't want him to think she welcomed his interest. "Forgive me."

"I didn't mind." The smile widened and the dimples deepened.

Of course, he wouldn't mind. He was a man now. While he'd been an honorable one back then, deep down they were all the same, ruled by their pleasure. She didn't know the man he'd become.

"What are you doing here?" she asked, taking yet another step back to put more distance between them.

"I've come to speak to your father." The smile fell and something that looked like dread crossed his face. Whatever he'd come to speak to her father about was clearly not a cheerful topic. Not that it mattered to Evelyn. Unless he was here to offer a large herd of cattle for free, he couldn't help her.

"I'll take you to him." She turned toward the entrance to the castle, but Liam didn't follow her.

"Mayhap I could have a moment first," he said, looking almost ill.

"Are you well?" She reached for him but caught herself in time.

"Aye. I will be well. Just nervous is all. How have you been?" he asked and that sincerity she remembered was clear in his voice. Perhaps he hadn't completely lost himself to his male needs.

"Well enough." She shrugged, unwilling to burden him with her troubles. She had a roof over her head. Her father had allowed her to remain in her clan. Beyond that, she had no right to complain. Not that it would matter if she did.

"You look even more beautiful than I remembered," he said as if he opened his mouth and the words poured out without his consent. "Have you married?"

"Nay." She didn't mention the plans with the Morgans, since she still hoped to divert them before it was too late. "Are you ready?" She nodded toward the castle, wanting to get on with it.

Liam brushed the dust from his kilt and ran a hand through that beautiful hair that had just a hint of curl.

He'd once told her the old MacKinlay laird had given him the name Liam because it meant gilded helmet. The man had said when he'd spotted Liam walking across the field—no more than four—he'd thought he wore something gold on his head. Only to find out it was the boy's hair when he'd gotten closer.

Liam had shared the story with her on their travels. She'd noticed the way his hair glowed when the sun hit it and understood why the man would have come to that conclusion.

Liam fussed with his brooch and plaid as Evelyn led him through the hall and up to her father's study. She knocked on the door and waited for the man to bellow from inside.

She opened the door and stepped in. "Father, we have a visitor from Clan MacKinlay to see you. Will you allow it?"

"Yes. Send him in." He waved and a nervous-looking Liam offered her a strained smile and a formal bow before stepping into the room. "Close the door on your way out," her father ordered her.

She did as asked, happy to be excused without further comment, but curiosity kept her from returning to her chamber. Instead, she left the door cracked enough to hear what Liam had to say. If it was bad news, it'd be good to know ahead of time so she could prepare to hide from her father for a time.

...

Liam swallowed down his nerves and took the seat offered to him in front of the laird. He'd been deliberating in the bailey on whether he should just turn around and go home when he'd seen Evelyn.

She was more stunning than she'd been the last time he'd seen her.

Of course, the last time he'd seen her she'd been at her worst, shaken and distraught from her capture. She'd been thin and bruised. But through everything she'd endured, he'd thought her more lovely than any woman he'd ever known.

Now, healthy and radiant, she'd stolen his breath. He had no choice but to try again to win her hand.

He may have told her his intentions to marry her, but until he got approval from the laird, Liam didn't see a reason to ask her if she'd have him. But ask her he would, if given the chance.

He didn't need only the laird's permission, but he needed her acceptance as well. For he wouldn't take her to wife if she wasn't amenable.

With two impossible tasks before him, he decided to start with the part of his visit that was easiest. He drew the letter from his sporran. "I've brought a letter from my laird." With a bow, he handed it over to the surly man.

Without any reply or gratitude, the man broke the seal on the letter. Liam watched as the laird's eyes snapped back and forth as he read the page. An occasional snort escaped his lips and a grumble.

Liam wished he knew what was in the missive so he'd know what to expect. He knew very well many servants read their master's mail. It was easy enough to reaffix a seal if one had a mind to. But Liam had never done such a thing; he respected his laird too much.

While Liam wasn't much for writing, he could read well enough. But he kept his skills to his own correspondence, of which there was very little.

Liam cleared his throat when the man refolded the letter but said nothing for a long while. Had he forgotten Liam was still there? Had he fallen asleep?

"Your laird thinks highly of ye."

Liam blinked. This wasn't what he was expecting. "I believe so, sir. I've given him no reason not to."

"A faithful man is what he called you in this..." Hugh Stewart picked up Lachlan's letter and waved it around before tossing it to the side like rubbish. Liam's fists tightened at the disrespect, but he remained quiet. "I assume you're here to ask for my daughter's hand yet again, though I'm not sure why you'd bother, since I've already told you no twice already."

"Aye, sir, but if you'll hear me out..." Liam tried to swallow but it felt as if dust clogged his throat. "The last two times I asked, I had nothing to offer Evelyn but a warrior's pay. I come before you as the war chief of clan MacKinlay. I ask that you consider my request now that my position has been elevated to one of honor."

The man snorted again. Liam found himself hoping Evelyn didn't have a strong bond with her father so they wouldn't have to visit the old codger once they were wed. But he remembered, the few times she'd spoken during their travels. she'd worried her father wouldn't love her anymore.

Liam had assured her a father's love was not easily brushed aside. It was forever. His words were empty, since he'd never experienced such a thing for himself, but it had calmed her.

"Your laird offers an alliance on your behalf," Hugh reported.

Liam's eyes went wide. "I did not know."

The laird laughed. "Surely you read the letter along the way."

"Nay. I didn't."

"Ah, yes. The *faithfulness* he spoke of." The man spat the word, making it sound like a horrid thing.

"I congratulate ye on your advancement to war chief. And I appreciate the laird's offer of transporting goods once his ship is constructed. However, I'm in no need of such services, and I already have an alliance of peace with the MacKinlays, since we joined forces to take down the McCurdys. I'm afraid I'll have to decline your offer yet again."

"Sir, I understand I may not be able to offer anything of great value, but I swear on my life, she'll not want for anything. I'll make sure she's happy and treated like a queen all her life."

"Feel free to stay for a meal before starting your return trip home. You've a long journey ahead of you."

No offer to even stay the night within the castle walls. It was an insult, but one Liam expected.

"Aye. Thank you, laird." He managed to keep the bitterness out of his tone, but it was a hard thing. He'd been rejected again.

Evelyn Stewart was not to be his.

Chapter Four

Evelyn jumped back from the door when she heard footsteps coming closer. She rushed down the hall and watched from the corner as Liam exited the laird's study and rested his head against the wall.

"Bloody hell," he mumbled and stood taller. With a deep breath she could hear from her hiding spot, he turned and left.

Shocked to her core, she hurried to her chamber and shut the door. Liam had asked her father for permission to marry her. From what the laird said he'd done so three times, each time earning a rejection from her father without him even asking her.

In truth, it wasn't her decision to make. It was a laird's right to decide for their children without consulting the parties involved. It was the way of things, but that didn't mean Evelyn had to like it.

She *didn't* like it at all. She especially didn't like the way her father had treated Liam when he'd come all this way to offer for her. The laird had hardly given him a shred of the respect Liam was due.

Liam was a kind man. He'd been wonderfully patient with her when he'd escorted her home, going out of his way to bring a smile to her face. In those days, she didn't think she'd ever smile again.

Not just because of what had happened, but for what she faced when she arrived home. She didn't know if her father would take her back or send her away.

Her father was going to marry her off to the Morgan heir at the end of the summer.

Evelyn paced her room a few times, thinking over her options. She didn't know much about the Morgans, though she'd heard a rumor the laird had killed his wife and she worried they could be monsters like the McCurdys. She didn't think her father would agree to marry her to such a clan, but he'd changed since she'd returned to him. He'd barely been able to look at her, let alone offer a kind word.

At least with Liam she knew she'd be treated kindly. And the MacKinlay clan had been friendly when she'd been there. She remembered Marian and her husband Cameron who had ended her torment by killing the McCurdys.

The laird's wife, Kenna, and even the laird himself, had been gracious hosts during her short, traumatic stay.

Another thought flitted through her mind, a dream she hadn't dared to dream in such a long time. The possibility took her breath away and helped make her decision.

She looked down to see the few things she'd collected from her room to take with her before she'd even finalized her plan. Her heart must've decided before her mind had a chance to catch up.

Tossing a few gowns and the only thing she had of value—her mother's necklace—into a bag, she rushed out of her room. Checking the corridor, she practically ran out of the keep toward the stables. She needed to hurry before

Liam left without her.

She'd been waiting for an opportunity to avoid marrying the Morgan heir. It was a pity she couldn't avoid marriage entirely, but at least she had a choice of husband.

And she chose Liam MacKinlay.

. . .

In the stable, Liam kicked the stall door, startling a few horses with his outburst. Their disgruntled whinnies and snorts had him apologizing to the beasts he'd upset.

It wasn't that he'd expected anything but another rejection; however, his heart was still reeling with disappointment and loss. He'd dreamed of a life with Evelyn Stewart as his wife. But, as it was with the dreams he'd had as a lad, it wasn't to be.

He often wondered what he'd done to be punished so. And from the time he'd heard the stories of God's wrath he'd tried to atone for whatever sin he still paid for. Being a warrior piled on the debt with the lives he'd taken, but he hoped killing to protect his clan was redeemed in some way.

"What did I do?" Liam's question was for God, but he spoke it to the white mare that had come to stare at him accusingly over her stall door. She didn't have an answer. Instead, she lifted her head a few times and snorted before pulling back inside to leave him alone once more.

Alone.

It seemed he'd been alone all his life. He had snippets of memories from a life he didn't know, a faceless man who'd lifted him on his shoulders. An older woman who fell asleep in the woods and didn't wake up when he called for her.

As a boy, he'd spent a lot of time on the battlements watching for his parents to come for him. He didn't know what direction they'd come from so he wore himself out moving from one end of the castle to the other. Occasionally, he'd fall asleep and Roderick, the old laird and Lachlan's father would come gather him up and carry him to the hall or the solar to sleep.

No one ever came for him.

He'd made sure never to cause a fuss or a bit of trouble so he wouldn't be turned out of Dunardry. While he'd known he didn't belong, it was the only home he'd ever had.

"I must've done some terrible sin in another life to deserve all the trials of this one." He held out a bit of apple to the mare he'd insulted and thought maybe she forgave him.

His own stomach growled, and he took a bite of the apple. The laird had offered him a meal, but he couldn't think of eating in the hall. What if he saw Evelyn? He didn't think he'd be able to stand it.

"Liam?"

He turned to see her standing before him as if he'd conjured her with his thoughts. His heart picked up and his stomach twisted. It was an unsettling feeling, one he felt each time he thought of her.

"Evelyn."

"Are you leaving already?" she asked.

"I—yes. My meeting with your father didn't go as expected. Or rather, it went as expected, but I had been hoping for a different outcome." He couldn't stop babbling. Where was his easy charm that had the maids at Dunardry eager to drag him off behind the kitchens? "Yes, I'm leaving."

She adjusted a cloth bag on her shoulder. It looked full to bursting. He reached for it, wanting to ease her struggle if only for a short time. It was a small thing he could offer during their last moments. She waved his gesture away and repositioned the bag.

He would need to tell her goodbye, and it would be forever. He looked about the stable, wishing for something that would give him more time with her. Every second was a memory he could hold onto when he returned to his home alone.

"I know why you're here," she said before biting her bottom lip. It did nothing to help with the twisting feeling in his stomach.

"You do?"

"Yes. I listened at the door. You seemed so nervous I thought you must be here to share troubling news."

He nodded and frowned. He was certainly troubled. "You should know, I would've asked you after speaking to him, if I'd gained your father's permission. And had you said no, I wouldn't have pushed the matter. It was to be your decision. I would never try to force ye into anything."

"I know that, Liam. I remember how kind you were when you saw me home. I was a mess. Skin and bones and more skittish than a rabbit in an open field. But you were patient and calm. When I needed a friend more than ever, you didn't push for anything more."

He smiled at her words. Perhaps it wasn't what he'd wanted to hear from the woman he'd hoped to marry. He might have preferred manly or striking. Maybe even courageous rather than kind. But he nodded in acceptance of her compliment because he knew, at the time, she hadn't needed him to be any of those other manly things.

As she said, she'd needed a friend and he'd tried his best to be that.

He'd offered her a shoulder to cry on and a distraction when she'd been overwhelmed. And he would cherish the moments he'd had with her for the rest of his life.

"It's because of your kindness that I agree to marry you," she said nervously. She adjusted the strap of her bag while he stared at her.

It was possibly the best thing anyone had ever said to

him and the most heartbreaking as well, for he knew it would never be.

"I'd like nothing more, but your father denied my request."

She nodded. "I heard. But I also heard you a moment ago when you said it was to be my choice. And I've chosen. I want to marry you, Liam. Right now."

"Do you mean elope?" he asked, slow to catch on to a plan she must have made before meeting him in the stables.

"Yes. We'll marry in the village. The minister doesn't know me. Then we can return to your home and Dunardry. I'm ready to go with you." She patted the bag.

Had he thought it full? He knew it carried everything she wished to take with her for their new life and it didn't seem near enough.

She'd packed her things and come for him. That bag, full that it was, held everything she was able to bring with her. He couldn't allow a laird's daughter to run off with a bastard and nothing more than a bag of her belongings. She'd surely hate him once she realized what she'd given up.

"I can't ask you to flee your home to be with me, Ev."

"You didn't need to ask." She frowned and looked up at him with her large brown eyes.

"I'd give you everything I have, but it's not much. It's not enough for someone like you." He'd planned to save her dowry and use every farthing for her. But to elope meant she'd have nothing but what he could provide. She deserved so much better.

"Did you change your mind?" She bit her trembling lip and he nearly pulled her into his arms to comfort her.

"I surely didn't change my mind."

"Then it was only my dowry you wanted?"

"Of course not. I don't give a damn about your dowry except to use it for you." He frowned. "Forgive my language."

Christ, he couldn't even act dignified. Why would she want to marry him?

"I want to marry you. If you want to marry me, why should anyone else stand in our way?" she explained simply.

She made a fair argument. Lachlan had always told him to make wise choices. It was what made the difference between a man and a leader. But he couldn't think straight with her looking at him like that. He could only want.

And hope.

"Let's go," he said finally. Whether it was a good choice or not, they'd find out later.

He knew only that he couldn't leave without her. He'd marry her and deal with whatever consequences came next.

Chapter Five

Not even a half an hour later, Liam found himself in front of a minister holding hands with his bride. She smiled up at him, and he was most certainly smiling back. He'd never been happier in his life.

True, it would've been better if the marriage had been approved by her father, but she'd approved of him herself, and she was the one who would live with him, so he tried to put his other worries aside.

He could only hope they'd be able to get off the Stewart lands and have the marriage consummated before they were found and forced into an annulment.

She looked him in the eyes when she spoke her vows, and he felt her words settle deep in his heart. When he spoke his response, he was just as sure.

"Those whom God has joined together, let no man separate." The minister spoke the final passage and Liam could hardly breathe. They'd done it. He was married to Evelyn Stewart.

"We're married now," she said quietly when the minister

walked away after being paid.

"Aye. Are you sure you don't want to let your father know you're leaving?"

"My maid will hide the fact I'm gone for a day or two. I'll send a note to my father once we get to your lands. It'll be easier that way."

Liam had faced down formidable warriors and didn't like thinking himself a coward, but in this situation, he didn't mind leaving the telling of her father to a letter. The man wouldn't be pleased to find Liam had disobeyed him.

At the moment, with his bride's hand in his, Liam couldn't care about the man's displeasure. Liam was much too happy to spare a thought for Hugh Stewart.

"I need to stop in the village before we leave," Evelyn said as she led him toward the stable. "We'll get the horses first."

It turned out the white mare who'd been flirting with him was Evelyn's own horse. Liam hadn't minded the idea of having her ride with him so not to be accused of horse theft, but she insisted on bringing her own mount.

What was one more sin added to the list he'd already committed today?

He followed behind Evelyn as she maneuvered around the cottages. She stopped at one and dismounted.

"Wait here. I'll be just a minute." She looked back at him with a wave before entering.

Liam waited, allowing her to have her goodbyes with whoever resided inside. The villagers looked him over as they passed, and he hoped Evelyn wouldn't be long.

The fewer people who witnessed them together, the more time they might have to make their escape. They'd need to ride hard to put as much distance as possible between them and the Stewarts.

When the door opened and his wife stepped out, he was

amazed once again that this beautiful creature had agreed to wed him.

She stepped away from the door and moved toward the horse. It wasn't until she was next to him where he waited to help her mount her horse that he noticed the child clinging to her skirts.

A little girl, not four years old, with dark hair and darker eyes. "Up you go, love," Evelyn said as she took the child by the waist and hefted her up into the saddle. Liam stared while Evelyn swung herself up behind the girl. He'd been so shocked, he'd not even helped.

"What is this?" Liam said with wide eyes as Evelyn took the reins and turned her horse.

"This is Gwendolyn, my daughter. Are we ready to go? We should try to put a few miles between us and my father before nightfall in case he notices I'm gone before I planned."

Her words melted together as Liam stared.

A daughter. His new wife had a daughter.

• • •

Evelyn knew it was beyond cruel to have tricked Liam into marrying her without telling him she had a child. But once freedom was a possibility, she found herself unwilling to risk it. This was her only chance to be a mother to Gwennie.

When Evelyn realized she was increasing after her time with the men who'd attacked her, her father sent her away to birth the babe. At the time, Evelyn agreed with her father and didn't want to see the child after it was born so she'd never have to look into eyes the same as the men who'd hurt her.

She feared the child would grow up to be like them.

But when her daughter was born, Evelyn looked at the screaming little girl and felt the hatred slip away. She knew she'd do whatever she had to do to make sure Gwendolyn was safe and loved.

Her father railed at her for naming the child after her late mother and continued to refer to his granddaughter as *the McCurdy bastard*. He'd forced Evelyn to give Gwennie to a maid in the village to be raised as her own so there wouldn't be talk.

The maid had been kind enough to allow Evelyn to see her daughter in secret over the last three and a half years. And Evelyn claimed every chance to sneak away to the village for a few stolen hours with her daughter.

While Gwennie was clean and fed, she was one of many mouths to feed, and it was clear by the way the girl clung to Evelyn at the end of the visits that Gwennie didn't get much attention or love.

Each time she had to leave her child it was as if she'd left another chunk of her heart in that cottage. But now, thanks to Liam, Gwennie was snuggled up to her in the saddle, and they'd never be parted again.

She'd apologize to Liam for deceiving him, but she had no regrets. Had she stayed with her father, he would've sent her off to the Morgans alone. His ruse to pass her off as a virgin bride would fail if anyone knew of Gwennie.

Evelyn had done the right thing, even if it felt wrong at the moment. If she'd told Liam the truth and he'd refused to marry her, she'd have but a few short months left before the Morgans came to claim her. Then she'd never see her child again. That was something she couldn't bear the thought of.

She turned in the saddle to see Liam was following and let out a breath of worry she'd been holding. He hadn't changed his mind. At least not yet.

It was clear from his frown he wasn't happy with her, but would his anger prove dangerous for her or her daughter? She didn't know him well. The boy she'd met had been kind, but what if this man was different?

When the castle was no longer within view, he nudged his horse and caught up to her. "Does Gwendolyn have a father who will miss her?" he asked from his place next to her.

"She has no father." She turned to look at him. "Cameron MacKinlay sent him to hell where he came from. Not that I'm sure which one it had been."

She saw Liam swallow and nod. She had no idea what he was thinking. He met her gaze and gave another nod. "Are you able to pick up the pace so we can put some distance between us and your father?"

She pressed her lips together, so grateful he wasn't yelling at her, but instead moving forward with their escape. She'd been wrong to doubt him.

"Aye," Evelyn answered before leaning closer to her daughter. "Gwennie, can you hold onto this very hard so we can go faster?" she asked as she pulled a sash from her waist and tied her daughter to her.

Gwennie gave a nod and squeezed her tiny fingers around the loop in the saddle.

"Hold on tight. We're going to race." Evelyn kept Daria, her mare, at a canter until the bindings were tested and then guided her horse into a gallop. She wasn't surprised to hear her daughter's giggles in the wind mixed with her own laughter.

They were free to be together. Yes, she had a husband she didn't know what to do with, but she'd deal with that later. For now, she and her daughter were safe.

Chapter Six

It was nearly impossible for Liam to hold onto his anger when he could hear the two of them laughing ahead of him. He kept up but stayed behind, guarding her—them—from anyone who might give chase from the castle.

He was glad for the hours they rode, for it gave him time to come to peace with their new situation. He'd dreamed of having a family one day, children he could love in a way he'd never had except from strangers.

After he'd calmed from the shock of Evelyn's secret, he saw this as an opportunity to repay those strangers by loving another child who needed him. He'd be a father—a good father—to Evelyn's daughter.

It hadn't been in question. He'd never mistreat a child or even be angry. Gwennie hadn't lied to him. He'd never take out any frustrations on her.

Now that he'd given it more time, he could even see why Evelyn had kept the truth from him. She no doubt feared he'd change his mind if he'd known before they were wed. If anything, her lack of faith in him bothered him more than finding out she had a child. Hadn't he proven himself years ago when he'd assisted her home?

When they finally stopped for the night, he reached for the little girl to help her down. But he couldn't lift her from the horse with Evelyn grasping her so fiercely.

"No. Don't touch her," she said, her voice a bit frantic.

He pulled his hands away, surprised by her reaction. "I was just helping you both down."

"We don't need help." It was clear by the way she struggled that wasn't true, but he kept his distance. With a look of confusion, he backed away farther, allowing her to handle the situation herself.

"Thank you," she said once they were both down.

Gwennie was nearly asleep so Liam quickly grabbed a blanket and spread it out in the area they would sleep so Evelyn could lay her down. He took another blanket from her pack and held it out so she could cover the girl.

"I'll make a fire and set a few traps, so we'll have food in the morning. When I come back, I'd like to talk with ye a bit."

She nodded and brushed Gwennie's hair from her face.

Liam collected branches and dried leaves to start the fire then added in a pile of bigger sticks and finally a large chunk of timber that would burn for a while.

After setting the snares, he came back, his questions near to erupting out of his mouth. He stopped at the sight of Evelyn stretched out beside the little girl, both asleep.

He took the spot next to them, wrapping his kilt around him for warmth. He'd purposefully waited to make this journey after the weather broke from winter to full spring. At the time he'd envisioned him and Evelyn sleeping together under the stars, making love, and celebrating their marriage each night on their way home.

This wasn't the way he'd imagined his wedding night, but they had many years ahead of them. Giving up this one night wouldn't be such a sacrifice.

Liam didn't sleep well. Mostly because his new wife was right next to him, close enough to touch, but he didn't dare to. Instead, he shifted with discomfort once more before finally giving up when the sun hinted at the sky.

He gathered the game from the snares and cleaned the rabbits he'd caught. After setting them to roasting over the fire, he turned around to find only Evelyn was still sleeping on the blanket.

Jerking up to his feet, he found the little girl right behind him. She startled but didn't make a sound. Instead, she watched him with big brown eyes. Her mother's eyes.

She wiggled a bit before heading to the bushes. He moved to follow and then realized what she was doing. He stayed back, close enough to help if she needed him, but far enough away to give her a bit of privacy.

He pulled out the piece of wood he'd been carving and continued working on it. When he'd started it was just something to do with his extra time, but now he knew who he would give it to.

Gwennie came to stand next to him, watching him pick away pieces of wood until it turned into the shape he wanted. When he finished, he held the wooden rabbit out to her. "For you."

She took it and watched him as if fearing he'd take it back. "It's yours. What will you name him?"

"Bunny," she said. It was the first time he'd heard her speak. She was a little older than Lizzy, Cameron and Mari's little girl, who was only three.

"That's a fine name for a rabbit."

"Mama sleeping."

"Yes. She's very tired. But she'll wake up when the sun touches her. Shall we watch?" He winked and to his surprise the little girl crawled into his lap.

Something about the situation struck a memory. A woman sleeping in the woods who didn't wake when the sun had come up. The thought might have made him panic, but from where he sat, he could see Evelyn's shoulders move with her breathing. She was fine. Just worn out from the hard ride yesterday.

"What kind of adventures do you think Bunny will go on?" he asked his new daughter. "Maybe he'll go down to the stream to get a drink and fall in."

She gasped, holding the rabbit closer.

"But then he'd climb onto a leaf that would carry him down the stream to the river and out to the sea, where he might make friends with a seal and hop on his back."

Liam took the rabbit and put it on the little girl's shoulder, making her squeal with laughter. He bounced it up to the top of her head and they laughed together as she tried to catch the rabbit.

"Don't touch her," Evelyn shouted as she rushed over and pulled Gwennie away from him. She pushed the girl behind her in a defensive posture that had him on his feet with his sword drawn, ready to fend off an enemy. But there was no one there.

He was the enemy in her eyes.

Gwennie began to cry and reached for the rabbit that had fallen in the dirt. He picked it up and held it out to her, causing Evelyn to jump.

"What's wrong with ye?" he asked his wife as he stood to tend to their breakfast. She took a few steps back, dragging a sobbing Gwennie with her. "Calm down. You're scaring the lass."

"I wouldn't blame you for being angry at me for not

telling you the truth of the situation," said Evelyn.

"Aye. I was angry with you for a good bit of the ride yesterday, but then I came to understand why you might have been hesitant to mention you had a child. Though, had you told me, I still would have wanted to marry you. One thing the MacKinlays are good at is making babes, and there are a bunch of them around. I'm fond of children. I hope to have a few of my own. So, it doesn't scare me to have one."

"She's mine," Evelyn said.

"I understand that but, since you married me, she's mine as well, and I'll see that she's cared for and protect her with my dying breath if called on to do so." He made sure his voice was calm yet stern. He'd not argue about his duty on this.

Evelyn bit her bottom lip and nodded reluctantly.

After the scare and seeing her mother's distress, Gwennie didn't come near him, instead hiding behind her mother and peeking at him only when he held out the food for them.

Rather than allow Liam to give Gwennie the food directly, so he might earn her trust again, Evelyn took it and fed her herself.

It was a mother's job to protect her children. He'd seen it well enough with Lady Kenna, Mari, and Dorie with her new little one. Liam wouldn't judge Evelyn harshly for wanting to protect her child. But it stung seeing the little girl afraid of him and unable to do anything about it.

As soon as they finished eating, they packed up and were off again until dark. That night, Evelyn moved her blankets on the other side of the fire from where he'd bedded down, as if she feared he'd launch himself on her.

He grumbled his displeasure at being left alone and falsely accused. Despite the fact he'd been thinking of being with her all day as he watched her fine arse bounce up and down in the saddle before him.

He started a new carving until he dozed off. By the time

the girl woke the next morning, it was finished. Gwennie was more cautious that morning, but when he held out the second rabbit, she rushed over to collect it.

"I'm sorry, lass. I know how to make only the rabbits. Anytime I try to make something else, it's a pitiful mess." He laughed and she smiled at him.

When Evelyn stirred, Liam backed away so she wouldn't panic at him being close to Gwennie.

And so it went on for the next few days as they made their way back to Dunardry. He'd not so much as kissed his new bride, though he'd longed to do that and more.

He'd added six more rabbits to Gwennie's collection. At this rate, the wooden ones were outproducing live rabbits, but they were working only to gain the trust of one of the females in his party.

He would give his wife time to adjust to their new situation and hope that eventually they'd be a family like he'd always dreamed.

Chapter Seven

Evelyn grew weary of being the fierce protector. Each time she saw the uncertainty in Liam's eyes as he backed away from Gwennie, she knew she'd hurt him with her distrust. But he'd not once complained or argued with her about Gwennie's care.

At the time she married Liam, she'd been desperate, but as was the way with decisions, very few were made without repercussions. She didn't know what she expected. She thought maybe he'd be angry to find she had a child. She thought he might take her to Dunardry and not want to have anything to do with her. That would have suited her fine.

But she'd landed the one man who actually wanted a family and didn't care if the child didn't come from his loins. She should've known the sweet man she'd met in her darkest hour years ago would have the patience to stay with her. Other than a few grumbles she couldn't make out, he'd not spoken an ill word.

Her new husband had shown nothing but kindness to her and Gwennie as they traveled, yet she made sure to keep distance between him and her child. He'd offered more than once to take Gwennie with him for a bit as they rode, but she couldn't allow it. Gwendolyn was *her* child. Her responsibility.

It was Evelyn's job to protect her daughter. She hadn't been there to do it for the beginning of the girl's life, but she would see to it from now on.

At night, she waited until Liam was settled before taking her daughter to the other side of the fire. It was colder compared to the first night when Liam had slept next to her, but she couldn't let down her guard.

They stopped midday for a quick bite to eat and a drink. The May sun warmed her face and arms, which had become chilled while riding in the hills. Her cloak was wrapped around Gwennie to keep her warm.

When they were ready to leave again, Liam came to help her mount as he always did. She made sure to tend to her daughter. But as she reached for Gwennie this time, her daughter cried out in pain.

"What is it, love?" Evelyn asked.

Gwendolyn held up her arms to be lifted, but again when Evelyn placed her hands on Gwennie's ribs she screamed. Evelyn bent to look, pulling up her dress to find bruises.

"It's from that bloody sash. In the hills it pulls on her too much," Liam said.

"She'll be fine. The land will level out soon enough." With a firm nod she adjusted her hold on Gwennie and put her in the saddle before getting up without his assistance.

"Evelyn," Liam said quietly, "I'm your husband, which means she's my daughter, too."

"Stepdaughter."

Liam waved his hand in disregard. "Step is an extra word that has no relevance. I'm Gwennie's father, and I'll take care of her the same as you. It's my duty." With that, he reached up and lifted Gwennie from the horse by her waist instead of her ribs and carried her to his horse. "I can ride one-handed and make sure she doesn't fall."

Evelyn expected her daughter to cry and protest at being carried off by a stranger, but she didn't even though Evelyn herself tensed. Over their journey and despite Evelyn's attempts to keep her away from him, her daughter had grown to trust Liam. They'd bonded in the mornings while Evelyn slept as he made her an army of wooden rabbits and won her heart.

She should've been happy her new husband cared so much for her child, and she definitely preferred that to how he might have felt considering her deception, but Evelyn still wasn't comfortable for her child to be out of her arms. It was so new.

Evelyn's father had sent Gwendolyn, his own grandchild, away after she was born, as if she were rubbish.

Men, even ones who should care for you, weren't to be trusted.

"She'll be fine."

When they stopped for the day, Liam tended the horses with Gwennie perched on his shoulders. He'd bend down to pick up something, pretending to drop her and making her giggle, while Evelyn's heart sped with worry. But he always had a hand securing her, always protecting.

It was damp and chilly when night fell. When Evelyn steered Gwennie to the other side of the fire and settled in to sleep, Liam got up and came to lie next to her. Before she could protest, Liam threw his plaid around them.

"Put her between us so we can provide heat for her," he ordered.

"She's fine."

"Did you promise before God to obey me or not?"

She couldn't see his face in the darkness, but she heard the strength in his voice as he continued.

"While I'm not going to be the type of husband to take advantage of your oath, I will in this. I'll not have my wife and child fall sick from a chill when I can do something for it. Now put her between us so we can keep her warm together."

She did as he said and relaxed when his warm arm reached across her. He was like a second fire, and she let his warmth sink in.

"We'll be home tomorrow," he said quietly.

She didn't remember much of the landscape when she departed Dunardry the last time, so she hadn't noticed they were so close to the holding.

"When I first saw Gwendolyn, I realized it wasn't that you wanted to marry me as much as you needed a way to escape from your home so you could be with her. I don't blame ye, and I'd never hold it against you. Mothers should never be kept from their children."

He shook his head. "But I must ask before we meet up with my clan tomorrow, do you want to be my wife, Evelyn? I'd rather allow you refuge with my clan and say we never wed than be shamed in front of my men and laird when they see how much you despise me. I wouldn't want anyone to think I forced ye."

He let out a shaky breath while her mind whirled with the opportunity he offered. She'd be free to live among the MacKinlays. Just her and her daughter as she'd planned.

"You don't need to answer right now. Sleep on it and let me know your answer in the morning. I don't wish to sway your decision, but know that I *did* want you for my wife. So much that I faced your father three times to ask for your hand, and I'm willing even now to give you and Gwennie whatever I have to see to your happiness. I know what happened to you with the McCurdys, and while I have to confess to wanting you in that way, I'd never force myself on you. Ever."

Tears rolled silently from her eyes. It was evident she'd

been so wrong and had treated him horribly. And, while she still wanted to live alone, she also wanted Liam's name to protect her. She couldn't be cast out if she was the wife of the war chief.

But she wouldn't lie and pretend their marriage would ever be anything but in name only. After what had happened while she was held captive, she'd never welcome a man's touch again. And Liam was a man. A large striking man. He would come to expect things from her she simply couldn't give.

"I don't need to wait until morning. I'll remain your wife, Liam, but I can never be a real wife to you, so perhaps I should ask you if you wish to change your mind. I wouldn't blame you. This isn't what you planned for when we wed." She shuddered as more tears escaped and his hand rubbed her arm. There seemed no limit to his compassion. No matter how badly she'd wronged him, he still offered comfort she didn't deserve. "I'm sorry."

"Shh… you don't need to be sorry, lass. I've already waited years for ye. I'll wait as long as you need."

His hand cradled her face and his thumb brushed away her tears.

"We'll be fine, Ev. So long as we face things together."

She smiled at his shortened name for her. It was a casual thing husbands and wives did. And she was this man's wife despite her wish to be free of men. She wished she'd met him before she'd been broken by the men who'd captured her. They may have been happy together. She might have even been happy. He was a fine-looking man despite her not being interested in him in that way. It wasn't fair that he ended up with her, but she wasn't strong enough to send him away for his own good.

Motherhood had made her desperate. She knew she was capable of doing anything to ensure the safety of her child. It was embedded in her bones.

His fingers brushed her hair. He touched her as a person might a horse they thought might bolt. She didn't know how long he continued to touch her like that, but she managed to relax. She hadn't known how scared she'd been all this time. She tensed once again when she realized she'd let her guard down.

Gwennie twitched and muttered something in her sleep Evelyn didn't recognize. She wondered what the girl dreamed of. It was one of the many things Evelyn didn't know about her daughter. She'd given birth to her, but in many ways Evelyn was as much a stranger to the little girl as Liam.

"What do you think she dreams of when she murmurs in her sleep like that?" he asked quietly.

"Probably rabbits floating out to the sea and making friends with a seal."

His chuckle was low and soft and so soothing to her frayed nerves she almost started crying again. She reached up and placed her hand on top of his, stealing this small comfort for just a short time.

Her eyelids grew heavy. She opened them again to see Liam was closer than he had been. Her heart started pounding, and she froze as still as one of Gwennie's wooden rabbits.

"May I kiss you, wife?" he asked so quietly she wasn't certain she'd heard him correctly.

Kiss her?

Without calling the memories, they rushed in. The foul breath of the men who'd captured her as they forced their lips to hers. The grotesque way they pushed their tongues in her mouth. The crack of a hand across her face when she'd bit them.

She recoiled from the man lying next to her, no longer seeing Liam, but a mottled memory of the men who had taken her. She no longer remembered their distinct features;

instead her mind had mashed them into one disgusting fiend.

"Stay away," she warned as she gasped for air. She didn't know if he said anything in response. All she could hear was the sound of her blood rushing in her veins as she picked up Gwendolyn and carried her away from the fire.

They may be cold tonight, but they'd be safe.

Chapter Eight

Liam lay in the darkness, silently admonishing himself for his carelessness. He'd told Evelyn he'd wait for her to be ready for as long as she'd needed, and then had gone and straightaway pushed for a kiss. Not only had he frightened her, but he'd taken a step back in earning her trust.

When she'd put her hand on his, he'd wanted to strengthen the connection between them, but he'd moved too fast. His wife had been harmed by men in the past, and he didn't want her to think he was like them. But what else could she think now? He'd allowed his desires to take over.

Keeping his distance, he found her and Gwendolyn huddled together by a tree.

"Please. Take her back to the fire and sleep there. I'll stay here and leave you your space. I promise." Hearing the words out loud only made him angrier with himself. What did his promises mean now?

Either because she trusted him or because she feared she and Gwennie would freeze in the night she took him up on the offer and went to settle the little girl next to the fire. He was certain it was the latter.

Liam sat next to the tree and gave his head a good knock against the rough bark for good measure. He'd made a grave error and would need to choose his next steps carefully.

As was normal, he woke before her. Keeping his distance from the opposite side of the fire, he watched the morning light change upon her face. The way her hair seemed to change color as the sun touched it. From darker gold to bright red. The freckles that reached out across her nose and cheeks.

He knew soon enough her darker lashes would flutter and her eyes would open. He'd be tempted to fall into eyes so dark it'd be impossible to distinguish the center from the rest.

He glanced down at the child at her side. So different from her mother when their eyes were closed. Gwendolyn's hair was dark brown with only a hint of her mother's fiery threads mixed throughout. Her skin was clear and pale without a freckle. Her nose, lips, cheeks, and chin were all given to her by a man who'd been vicious and dishonorable. Yet Gwennie was perfect in her innocence, and would be taught to be kind, by Evelyn and himself. She'd never need to know how she came to be or who sired her.

He placed a kiss on his fingertips and pressed it lightly to her head and snugged the cloak closer around them. Letting out a breath of contentment, he looked back to Evelyn to see her eyes on him.

"I worried you might hate her for who her father is," she whispered, her voice barely moving the cool morning air.

He smiled at her and said vehemently, "*I* am her father."

The dark eyes staring at him glistened and she swallowed. "Thank you."

"It was easy enough for me," he whispered. "She's impossible not to cherish. I'd be the biggest hypocrite to not accept a child not my own when I was accepted by a clan that's not mine by blood."

Evelyn blinked and looked away, her silent warning that he was getting too close and she was uncomfortable. Despite the distance between them, he was learning her ways.

He stepped back. "She'll be expecting breakfast and a new bunny for her collection this morning, so I must get moving. Stay for a bit and rest. I imagine in the past you didn't get much time to hold her like this."

Tucking the blankets around them, he pulled away to tend to things. He quietly placed more wood on the fire hoping the blaze would warm them and allow them to rest a little while longer. The morning was cool, but the sun was coming and would warm them soon enough.

Once his catch from the stream was roasting, he began working his knife over the wood. Evelyn came to sit near him, though he noticed she wasn't close enough for him to touch her, not that he'd try again until he was certain he was welcome to.

"Do you think this resembles a seal?" He held up the crude rendition.

"I canna say. I've never seen one."

"No? I'll have to take you and Gwennie to Baehaven someday. The beasties come up on the rocks there to lie about in the sun. They've no legs, their backs slope down to wide fins. They rather lumber about on land, but in the water they float and swim effortlessly." He laughed at himself for what he was about to share but went on.

"When I first saw them, I felt pity for them, unsuited for the land as they are. But then I felt a fool seeing them in the water, and I realized I was similar."

"How so?"

He frowned. "I told you how I was found by the old laird wandering on his lands, half-starved and filthy. All alone, only a little older than Gwennie is now. He took me in, gave me a place. I know he and the mistress did their best to give me a home, but like the seals on land, I never took to it. I didn't know how to go about being part of their family."

He smiled widely when he looked at his wife and back to the carving. "Now, having my own family to care for, I feel like I might be good at it." He looked to her. "I might be very good at swimming."

Evelyn looked at him in a way that drew him closer. He knew well enough she wouldn't welcome his kiss, but it almost seemed like she wanted... something. He needed only to lean closer, but before he could risk making another mistake, movement stole his attention. He thought Gwennie had woken. But it wasn't Gwennie.

Three men had stepped into their camp. The intruders smiled in a way that sent ice down his spine. They weren't friends, and they were moving closer to the sleeping girl. Liam moved to protect his family; the small wooden seal snapped under his boot.

...

In the end, Evelyn had been utterly useless. She'd stood there as stiff and unmoving as one of Gwennie's wooden bunnies.

The men who'd entered their camp carried the faces of her attackers. In reality, they may have looked completely different, but Evelyn couldn't see past memories and the fear that had taken control of her body.

They spoke, words slurring together. Their intent to take the horses. The larger one looked her over with a gleam she was familiar with from her time in captivity. His leer suggested they might want to take her as well. The man took a step forward, his hand resting casually on the pommel of his stained and rusty sword.

Liam moved on the men like a wolf descending on its prey. His long body leaped over Gwennie to place himself between her and the threat. He was but one man against three larger. A battle cry tore from his throat, and his sword flashed bright in the sun.

A new memory came to her of the night she'd been blessed with her freedom. The night Cameron MacKinlay unleashed his wrath on the five men who'd touched his wife, Marian. The same men who had touched Evelyn.

Like that night, the fight was over quickly.

Evelyn was startled back to reality by her daughter's cries. Gwennie was somehow safe in her arms, placed there by Liam who stood blocking the bodies of the men who would have done them harm.

He was speaking to her. His words came from far away, echoing in her mind that was still frozen.

"Ev? Evelyn?" He pulled her up to stand on shaking legs and moved her away from him. "Sit here, don't move." He left them and went down over the bank of the stream as she sank to the ground in a shaking puddle.

It'd been the same when she'd been with her captors. She'd retreated into herself where it was still safe and blocked out everything around her, except she couldn't do that now. She had someone else who needed her.

She came back to herself in a rush. "Gwennie?" She pulled the girl away to check her over and gasped at the sight of blood on her gown. Pushing up the sleeves to look closer, she found nothing marred her daughter's skin. When the sleeves fell back into place, she noticed the stains formed two large handprints, and matched the stains on her own sleeves where Liam had moved them to safety.

Was he hurt?

Jumping to her feet, she pulled Gwennie into her arms and rushed to the stream to see him naked and scrubbing the blood from his skin. The red washed away from his pale hair and didn't return. It wasn't his blood. He was safe.

She turned away to give him his privacy. When he returned to them, his clothes and hair were wet, but clean from blood.

He reached for her and she flinched.

"I know you must be afraid of what you saw me do. But I beg ye to let me hold you for just a moment so I can feel you both alive in my arms. Please don't let your fear fester and ruin what little trust I've managed to earn."

She understood but was unable to invite him to them. He moved slower and, when Gwennie turned to face him, he offered a smile, the same easy smile that was her memory of Liam all these years. He was safe. He was kind.

He'd killed three men in a raging assault and washed their blood from his body without a thought, but she also knew he wouldn't hurt her. He wanted a real marriage in the physical sense, and she knew she could never offer that, but even still, she knew he wouldn't hurt her or Gwennie.

She stayed in place as he took the final steps to embrace them both in his shaking arms. "You're safe. I'll not ever let anyone hurt ye. Never. Do you understand? I'd die to protect you both."

They were the pretty words of a warrior. A man trained to act first without emotion when called on to protect his clan, but she believed him.

She let him take Gwennie into his arms and kiss her head. "You dropped your bunnies, but I'll get them for you straightaway. Just as soon as my hands stop shaking." He squeezed Evelyn's hand. "I think Mama's hands are more settled than mine. Will ye do me a favor?" he whispered to Gwennie loud enough for Evelyn to hear. "Give your mama kisses until she smiles? Don't stop."

He handed Gwennie back and her daughter set about kissing her repeatedly until she was indeed smiling despite herself. Her forehead and cheeks, even her eyes and chin,

Gwennie continued her assault until they were both laughing.

Liam strode away and collected the scattered bunnies Gwennie had dropped. He picked up the pieces of the seal and tossed them into the fire. When he returned to them, he brushed her cheek with now-steady hands.

"We're all right. I'll bring the horses and our things. I don't want you too close to them. I'm afraid there's no saving our meal, so we'll have to make do until we reach home. I'm sorry."

He'd saved her and her daughter, and perfectly handled the chaos afterward and he was apologizing because their meal had been burned.

She reached out with the arm not holding her child and squeezed his hand in thanks.

"No apologies are needed. Thank you for your bravery."

He smiled widely and nodded. "Let's go home."

Chapter Nine

Liam felt a stirring of anticipation and pride as he led his family over the next rise. Seeing the castle perched on the hill opposite them, he experienced the warm appreciation of home.

"Do ye see that castle over there, Gwennie?" He pointed. She nodded.

"That will be your new home."

"Mama too?"

"Aye, Mama's home too. 'Tis called Dunardry. And there are many children your age to play with and a few dogs as well."

"Bunnies." She held up one of the wooden rabbits. She seemed to favor the one he'd made her first, and he liked that he knew some small thing about her. He'd known her only two weeks and already they were forming a bond. Or so he hoped.

"I'm sure there are a few rabbits about." He'd not tell the girl they were likely to have a few of them for their supper.

He smiled at a nervous Evelyn. "Don't worry, wife. There

shall be plenty of friends for ye as well."

She offered a strained smile. "They may send us away when they hear the tale of how I came to be here."

"I plan to tell them ye begged me to take you with me and I felt sorry for you."

That got a smile out of her, even if it was a small one. His wife wasn't free with her smiles, which made them all the more valuable when he happened to earn one.

"Let me take care of things with the laird. It'll be fine, I'm sure. And if it isn't, we'll be on our way to find a place that'll have us. But I tell ye this, we'll be together. Always."

She didn't respond to his declaration, not even a nod. Whether she didn't believe in his abilities to take care of them or if she worried about being put out, he wasn't sure. He decided not to ask.

Everyone was waiting in the bailey when they came through the gates; he'd seen the messenger dispatched by the guard when they'd crossed over into MacKinlay lands.

All eyes were on Evelyn as she offered a warm smile to the gathered MacKinlays. No one noticed Gwennie until he dismounted and pulled her into his arms. The chatter stopped abruptly.

He grinned proudly when Evelyn came to stand next to him. "Everyone, I'd like to introduce you to my wife Evelyn MacKinlay, and my daughter, Gwendolyn."

At the stares, Gwennie hid her face in his neck and squeezed him so tight he feared she'd cut off his breath.

There were a few blinks of surprise until Lady Kenna came forward and hugged him first before hugging Evelyn. She held out her arms and Gwennie went to her. Kenna kissed the top of her head. "Welcome to Dunardry. I hope you'll find your home here." She tickled Gwennie, earning a giggle. "We've so many lads, it's nice to have another lass."

Mari came closer and brushed a hand over the girl's hair.

"You seem the same age as my Lizzy. I'm sure you'll be great friends."

Gwennie held out one of her wooden rabbits at the word friend.

"Let's find some treats for this little one in the kitchen," Mari said, taking her from Kenna. If Evelyn had worried their daughter wouldn't be accepted, it was a waste of her time. The mistress and her sister loved children no matter where they happened to come from.

Their husbands could be a different story when Liam got to telling them the full story.

Kenna wrapped an arm around Evelyn. "And while my sister sees to your daughter, I'll show you to Liam's chamber. We'll let the men discuss things and see them for the evening meal." Kenna linked her arm through Evelyn's. "You look so much better than last we saw you. I've thought of ye often over the years. It's so nice to have you here with us."

Evelyn looked back at him, worry clear in her eyes. Liam swallowed, hoping the memories of this place wouldn't be too much for his wife.

Large hands slapped him on the back, nearly knocking him over. "Congratulations," Cameron said.

Lach smiled before pulling Liam into a hearty embrace as well. "I have to admit, I was a bit worried the old bugger wouldna agree this time. I'm glad you convinced him."

He hated to have to disappoint the man, but he'd never lie, especially not over something as serious as this.

"About that…" He paused, allowing one more moment of happiness to settle upon him. If he was forced out, it'd be better to leave after the meal when they were fed and rested, but he'd not take advantage. "I'm afraid I didn't earn his approval yet again."

As expected, Lach looked at him with his brows raised. "Yet ye stand before me a married man."

"Aye." He'd not put the blame on Evelyn's shoulders, but he wanted it to be clear he hadn't coerced the woman into becoming his wife. "I was in the stables preparing to leave." He shook his head. "Nay. I was kicking about in anger over bloody Hugh Stewart's rejection. Evelyn found me there and suggested we marry anyway."

"Ye eloped with the Stewart laird's daughter?" Lachlan shouted.

Cam just chuckled. "At least he didn't do so accidentally."

"And I did marry the lass ye intended me to marry," Liam put in unhelpfully.

"I gave ye permission to *ask* for her hand. I didn't give you approval to take her off her lands without her father knowing. Do you realize what you've done?"

He nodded once. "I do. And I'm prepared to leave with my family if we're no longer welcome here, but I couldn't leave her. It was a selfish thing, I know, but once she said she wanted to be my wife I couldn't do anything else. And I'll not apologize for it, because I'm not sorry."

"Your apology will do us no good now anyway." Lach huffed and shook his head. "You're not the first man to think with his heart." He paused. "Or worse parts."

"Trust that I'm already being punished." He frowned. "For the marriage hasn't been a blissful one so far. I realized right away she wed me only to escape her father, who wouldn't allow her to be with her daughter. I'm but a means to her true desire to be a mother to Gwennie. In fact, I fear it may never be a true marriage."

"That seems to be how most of us start out. Don't despair over it," Cam said. "Things have a way of changing."

Liam wasn't so sure of that. It'd been weeks and he'd not so much as kissed his bride.

"I thought it'd be easier." He'd spent hours imagining how things would be between them when they married, but so far the reality was nothing like he thought it would be.

Lachlan laughed harshly. "Whatever gave you the notion it would be easy? Did you not stand by and watch while Cam and Bryce made a hash over their marriages?"

"I did. But I also knew they didn't want to marry, while for me it was the only thing I truly desired."

"Things don't always work out the way we desire them, Liam. Sometimes, if we're very lucky, they work out even better." Cam gave him a nod before turning to Lach. Cam's voice was teasing when he spoke. "Do we displease the Stewart laird by allowing the outlaw to stay?"

It was a fact Liam had never done one thing against his laird—either of them—in all his days of residing with the MacKinlays. Not since he was a small lad. He'd never risked being cast out.

He thought he'd lose his stomach on his boots for having to stand before Lachlan now knowing he'd earned whatever punishment the man commanded.

"I'll think on the best way to handle the situation, but this is your home. You and your family will remain here." Lach patted him on the shoulder. "Come. We have a wedding to celebrate."

Liam didn't feel much like celebrating the end of his dreams with a woman who barely tolerated him, but he followed the men toward the hall.

Chapter Ten

Kenna led Evelyn into a bedchamber that was fair-sized with a large bed, a trunk, a washstand, and another stand by the bed with a few books piled upon it.

"This is Liam's room. You should've seen his face last year when I told him it was his. He'd never had a place for himself before. I'm not ashamed to tell you I cried to see him so excited." She shook her head.

Liam had mentioned getting a room as if it were a major event. She understood better now. She'd taken for granted her rooms at Scalloway Castle where she was raised. Where her father well knew by now she'd fled with Liam. What would he do? She knew he'd be angry, but angry enough to send for her? To start a war between their clans?

She didn't think he'd mind the loss of her so much. He'd complained on more than one occasion of how much trouble she was. But he didn't like to be disobeyed.

Kenna waved to the space on the other side of the bed. "There's a small bed in the solar I can have brought over. It will fit in that corner nicely for Gwennie."

"Say thank you to the mistress," Evelyn prompted her daughter.

"Thank you," Gwennie said holding out one of her rabbits as a gift.

"Oh my." Kenna took it with a smile. "You keep this one. I have a bunch of them myself." To Evelyn she whispered, "He's still not mastered anything other than rabbits, I see." With a laugh she patted Evelyn's shoulder. "He has many other fine qualities. A heart of gold, that one."

Evelyn couldn't argue. So far, Liam did seem to have a heart of gold, and she feared she'd made a number of dents in it during their short time together. She glanced at the bed and tried to swallow down her panic.

They'd be sleeping there together. What if he would expect his rights as a husband? She didn't know how she might bear it.

At the doorway, Kenna paused. "I'll leave you to get settled and rest a bit before the celebration begins. Please let me know if you need anything. I want you to be happy here."

"Thank you, my lady." Evelyn managed to hide her growing panic enough to smile at the laird's wife.

"And I want you to call me Kenna. We will be good friends." The woman left, closing the door behind her.

Gwennie was already playing with her bunnies on the floor. It calmed Evelyn to watch her. To see her daughter happy and safe and know that they'd be together was worth any difficulties that might come next.

She'd find a way to get through them. Even lying with her husband. She'd do it if it meant staying here.

A few minutes later, there was a knock at the door. A lad delivered their bags from the horses. Not even a quarter hour later there was another knock and a different lad came in with a stout bed made to hold two children Gwennie's size.

Evelyn remembered from her time here that Kenna had

twin boys a little older than Gwennie.

"Look, love. You have your own bed," she said and was rewarded by a large smile. It seemed Liam wasn't the only one excited with the room.

"For me?" The little girl wasted no time removing her shoes and climbing into her bed.

"Do you want to take a nap?" Her question was met with a quick shake of the head. "Of course not." Evelyn wouldn't push the issue. "Why don't you lie down with your bunnies for a bit while I unpack our things in our new home?"

Gwennie nodded in agreement, collecting her bundle of bunnies from the floor and lining them up on her mattress.

"We can stay here?" she asked.

Evelyn bit her lip. Tears burned in her throat at the innocent question. How many times had Gwennie asked her to stay when she'd had to leave to return to the castle? Each time a piece of Evelyn's heart was torn away.

She was careful with her answer so it wasn't a lie. She kissed her daughter's head and smiled. "We get to stay together now."

She didn't expect Gwennie to understand the weight of that promise, but she nodded and continued to move her bunnies around. Evelyn had made sure not to say where they'd be staying. For tonight, they'd be here. But tomorrow…

Evelyn had unpacked only a clean gown for dinner before looking over to see Gwennie had fallen asleep.

Evelyn opened Liam's trunk to put her bags out of the way. There was nothing in the trunk but a shirt and a few pair of stockings. She glanced around the room, seeing the pegs on the wall, and thought maybe Liam hung his things there. Still, it meant he didn't have much clothing.

A good wife would see that he had a few extra shirts. She thought of it as she dressed. Perhaps once she had the chance to get fabric and thread. It was the least she could do to show her gratitude. She'd wanted to be his wife in name only, but tonight they'd sleep in the same room. She looked at the bed and hoped a few shirts to show her gratitude would be enough.

. . .

Liam stepped into his room and smiled when he saw Ev bent over the trunk. It wasn't just the fine view she offered in that position but the fact she was here in his chamber that made his heart race.

She placed her index finger over her lips and pointed to the corner. With his height he needed only to stretch slightly to look over Evelyn's head to see Gwennie sleeping soundly in a small bed with a bunch of bunnies surrounding her.

He recognized the bed as being the one he'd helped Cam build for the twins when they'd gotten too large for their cradle. He'd be sure to thank everyone for it.

"Did you have enough space for your things?" he whispered, though he knew the lass could sleep through almost anything. She'd slept in his arms while they rode.

"Aye. But I don't think there's room in the trunk for your things now."

"I don't need much. I'm set with a spare shirt and extra stockings. I wash down at the loch and see to my clothes then."

She nodded and stood to the side so he could pass by her. He frowned and looked about the room. The day he'd been given his own chamber had been one of the happiest, save the last weeks. But it seemed small and dreary now.

"I wish I had more to offer you than this one room. I know you're accustomed to having a place of honor." Her room at Scalloway was probably exquisite. She probably had a suite of rooms with a fancy bed and carved furniture.

She was quick to shake her head. "No apologies are necessary. It's a fine room. The window looks out over the loch. I imagine it's a beautiful sight in the mornings when the sun comes up."

"Aye, it is." He nodded.

"The most important thing is we can be together."

He knew she spoke of herself and Gwennie, but he didn't allow her words to bother him. "I hope you and Gwennie will be happy here. I want this to be a home for all of us."

She nodded once and looked away. He wanted to touch her and convince her that they'd have a good life together, but he'd learned from his past mistake and kept his hands by his side.

He let out a breath. "And now, whether we want it or no, there's a celebration beginning in our honor. I'm not one to enjoy being forced to the front of everyone's attentions but, since I wouldn't be facing it alone, I should be able to manage."

Another nod. She seemed distracted. This time he was certain she was looking at the bed, and he thought he understood why. Did she think he was going to throw her down and take her before the meal with a child sleeping a few feet away? As he had before, he tried not to take offense.

He wished she knew him better, but in truth they were barely more than strangers. It was odd that he'd thought himself in love with her all these years. He'd made her out to be someone in his mind. But, so far, it hadn't gone as planned.

Her past experiences with men hadn't been pleasant. Between the beasts that took her and her bugger of a father, she'd need time to see Liam didn't plan to treat her roughly or take advantage.

Rather than bring it up now, he pointed to Gwennie. "I don't want to have to wake her."

"We must, otherwise she'll be awake all night asking you

to tell her stories about the bunnies."

Liam smiled, thinking that didn't sound so bad.

Gwennie was a bit grumpy when Ev woke her, but the girl allowed him to carry her out of the room, her head tucked under his chin. With his free hand he reached for Ev's hand, but when she stiffened, he let it go and led them down the corridor toward the great hall.

"I get to introduce my family to the rest of the clan. I don't think I've ever been so honored."

They were greeted and patted as he led them to the front table where the laird and lady waited with Cam and Mari. He helped Evelyn into the seat next to Kenna and took the seat next to her, setting Gwennie on his knee. Cameron was next to him and Mari was at the end. She leaned out to wave to Evelyn.

Liam wouldn't be able to thank these women enough for making his wife feel welcome.

The laird stood and tapped a glass to get everyone's attention. "Tonight, we welcome Evelyn and Gwendolyn into the MacKinlay clan and into our hearts as family."

Liam smiled at his wife and kissed Gwennie's hair. He knew he probably looked a fool beaming with happiness as he was. But that was how it was when a dream he'd had since he'd been a child was finally fulfilled.

He was part of a family.

Chapter Eleven

Liam couldn't stop smiling as his clansmen drank to his happiness and wished his family well. The laird could decide to make them leave in the morning for the safety of the clan, but for that night Lachlan stood before their people in welcome.

Liam hoped it was a good sign. He'd spent the afternoon thinking of ways he may win over his wife and have a true marriage. He hoped tonight she'd allow him to kiss her goodnight. It seemed a small thing, but it would be a huge step toward bringing them closer.

Gwennie was asleep when he carried her up to their room. The festivities had wound down, and it had been a long day with big changes for everyone.

After settling Gwennie in the little bed in the corner he removed his weapons and kilt, hanging them on the pegs as usual.

"It was nice of your clan to go to such effort to welcome Gwennie and me," Ev said while sitting on the edge of the bed. Her fingers twisted and released the fabric of her gown.

Liam found he was as nervous as she. He didn't want to make another mistake and move too quickly.

He pointed to his kilt. "I generally make use of these pegs. Unless it bothers you to see my things hanging about."

"No. It's your room, do what you wish."

He let out a breath and came to sit next to her. When he placed his hand on hers, she flinched and pulled away.

"I'm sure it's common for new couples to have a bit of adjusting when they come to live together. It's probably more so in our case, since this isn't what you wanted."

"Liam—"

"It's fine, Ev. I know why you did it, and as I've said, I don't blame you for it. But we're married now, and we'll have to find our way together. I don't want to spend the rest of our days doing something that bothers you because you don't feel comfortable to speak up. Let's promise to be honest with each other. I think it'll make things easier, and perhaps save me from irritating you to the point you pull my dirk across my throat while I sleep."

He laughed but she didn't. She still looked unsure. His dark humor hadn't dislodged the creases on her forehead. He puffed out a breath. "Tell me true, do my things bother ye hanging on the pegs?"

She shook her head. "They don't."

He grinned. "Very well. I vow I will tell you the truth, always."

She nodded as he washed. He turned back to her, still wearing his shirt, which covered him to his thighs.

"Do you need help with your gown?" During their travels, she'd slept in her gown, but now she could be more comfortable in the privacy of their room.

"I can do it myself," she said and slid off the bed to move into a dark corner of the room. When she returned, she placed her gown on the trunk and slipped into bed in just her shift.

"Do you wish for me to sleep on the floor?" he asked. When she opened her mouth, he held up his hand. "The truth."

Her lips pressed together for a moment before she answered. "You don't need to sleep on the floor. If you'd planned to press me on my duties, you'd have done so before now. And if you changed your mind, it wouldn't much matter if I gave you permission to lie next to me or across the room."

While he wished her decision was founded on trust rather than common sense, he gave a nod and climbed into bed next to her. After extinguishing the light, he shifted until he was comfortable. Her arm warmed his where they brushed briefly.

In the darkness, he listened to her breathing as he readied himself for his next question. He wanted to ask permission to kiss her. This morning she hadn't been ready, but maybe now it'd be different.

...

In the end, he didn't press the matter. They'd have the rest of their lives for kisses. One more night wouldn't matter.

When she shifted in her sleep, her arm rested next to his. He focused on that contact until he dozed off. At some point in the night, one of them—or perhaps both—had moved closer together. He'd woken with her back tucked against his chest. His arm draped over her waist and her perfect bottom was pressed tight to his hardness.

He didn't dare move and distress her. Unfortunately, his cock did its own business and lurched out against her. When she gasped, he realized she was awake as well. So much for figuring out how he might extricate himself from their tangle without distressing her.

"I'm sorry. I truly didn't intend to take liberties." His voice was rough with sleep but clear with remorse.

"Liam, I—" Whatever she might have said was interrupted when Gwennie popped up at Ev's side of the bed, her hands full of wooden rabbits. Once the pile of bunnies was in the bed, Gwennie struggled to crawl up herself. Liam reached across his wife and grasped the girl's nightgown to help her up.

She sat cross-legged and held out the first bunny to him expectantly. Not giving up his spot, he told a story of a bunny who woke up in her own bed for the first time in her new home and was excited and a little scared.

As always, Gwennie thought it should end with the trip down the river to meet up with a seal, and Liam gave in.

Normally, he wasn't in bed this late. Being war chief meant early drills and checking in with the border guards. He donned his kilt and ruffled Gwennie's hair before heading for the door.

"I'll see you at the midday meal," he said and left them when Ev said nothing in return.

This wasn't at all how he'd imagined their life together in his adolescent fantasies, but he wouldn't give up.

After a hard morning of drills, Liam looked forward to seeing Ev and Gwennie in the hall, but they weren't there. He didn't think anything of it, since Kenna and her children were absent as well.

No doubt they'd all gone to visit Mari at her home on the other side of the village.

At the end of the day, however, he felt uneasy when he saw Kenna and Mari alone in the hall. Perhaps Ev was waiting in their room. But the only thing waiting in his room was emptiness and a note.

Liam,

Please forgive the cowardice of leaving only a letter, but I didn't know how to tell you I couldn't stay.

You've been nothing but kind since you arrived at Scalloway and I will forever be grateful for what you did for Gwendolyn and me. I'm sorry I can't be the wife you wanted.

Ev

He crumbled the paper and tossed it into a corner of his room before washing for dinner. Pain quickly turned to anger.

His wife had left him with nothing more than a few words scratched onto a piece of parchment. She'd used him to get away from her father, and now that she was free, she no longer needed him.

He'd been cast aside and was alone again.

Chapter Twelve

Evelyn thought she might be ill the next morning when Gwennie stood by the door crying.

"Bunny?" That single word communicated what she was truly asking. Where was Liam?

Evelyn had managed to distract her child last night with the excitement of their new cottage and stories by their hearth until she fell asleep. But the mornings had been a time for Gwennie and Liam. Each new day had brought the arrival of an addition to the carved bunny family without fail.

She briefly wondered if he'd carved another wooden rabbit that morning even knowing she and Gwennie were gone.

Evelyn was a coward. There was no arguing that. She'd waited until Kenna had left the castle with her brood to visit Mari before bundling up Gwennie and their few belongings and heading to the village. After getting a less than fair price for her mother's necklace, she had enough to let a tiny cottage with a single room for them. It was only slightly bigger than Liam's chambers at the castle, but the bed was narrow. Only just big enough for her and Gwennie to sleep. Perfect.

Evelyn had thought she'd manage sleeping next to him. And even allow him his husbandly rights at some point, but after waking yesterday morning entwined with him, she knew she needed to leave.

The worst part was that it hadn't been fear that made her tense when she'd woken and felt the hard evidence of his lust pressed against her. It had been her answering interest in the warmth of him.

She'd wanted nothing to do with men for over three years, but her deeply buried instincts had surfaced in response to his touch. She couldn't allow her body to lead her to pain. And she knew well that only pain came from coupling with a man.

She knew some women enjoyed the act, but she wasn't made for it. Despite the pleasurable tingling he'd evoked the morning before. She'd felt more than just physical pleasure, she'd felt safe, cherished, and wanted, things she hadn't felt in a very long time.

She refused to be lured into such things again. She knew how her own once-doting father had turned on her. His own blood. What loyalties could she expect from Liam, a man who barely knew her?

As soon as she disappointed him—and she was certain to do so—she'd be despised. This was better. Or it would be as soon as she consoled her crying child.

"Was I bad?" Gwennie asked and Evelyn felt a sharp jagged pain in her chest.

"No. Of course you weren't bad." She brushed away her daughter's tears, but more came. "We were not sent away, love. I wanted us to have our own home. Together, like I promised."

The lass looked up at her through lashes spiked with tears and held out one of her carved animals. "Bunny."

"I will make you a bunny, and it will be the best one of the lot." She'd make sure of it.

Thinking *best* surely equated with *big*, Evelyn selected a good-size log from the hearth and set about fashioning a rabbit from it. The sun had set and a pile of tools had collected around her, but when she was done she held out her offering.

"Broke." Gwennie helpfully pointed at the large piece of ear that had snapped off during the process.

"Yes, well, he's a warrior rabbit. Big and strong and he's seen his share of battle."

Appeased by the explanation, Gwennie reached out to take the newest addition but struggled to hold it. When it fell, the other ear snapped off at the skull and Gwennie pointed. "Broke."

Tears gathered in Evelyn's eyes. It had been only a day and already she'd failed her child.

"Mama will fix it," Evelyn said. "Mama will fix everything." If only she knew how.

...

"You're all sorry excuses for warriors!" Liam shouted at his men the second morning after his wife had left him. "The steel for your swords would be better used for wheels to carry us all away from Dunardry during an attack, for you lot will never save anyone." He kicked the dirt as the men murmured to one another.

"Perhaps I should go ahead and change my name to MacDonald or Stewart, since we're sure to be overtaken soon enough."

He'd never yelled at his men, and it was clear they were confused by his outrage. Rather than try to make sense of it, he threw his practice sword down and stormed off. "I'm done with all of ye."

He headed for the gate but didn't get far.

"Ho there!" the laird called.

Liam stopped but didn't turn to face the man. He couldn't bear the shame of looking him in the eye.

"What's amiss? I've never seen you run drills like that. Cam and Bryce acted as such only when having trouble with their women. Are ye well?"

When Lach came around to stand in front of Liam, he had no choice but to raise his head and face his laird. "Aye," he answered, then shook his head. "Nay. Evelyn left and took Gwennie."

"She's gone back to the Stewarts?"

Liam threw his hands up in frustration. "I don't ken where she went. I doubt she'd go back to her father."

"Did she take a horse?"

Liam glanced toward the stable. He hadn't thought of that. "I didna ask."

"Let's find out."

Together they spoke to the groom and learned Evelyn hadn't taken a horse.

"Then she'd be on foot with a little one, which means she couldn't have gone far. We can inquire in the village," Lach said, looking proud of himself.

"To what end? She clearly doesna want to be my wife. She wanted only my name and a home where she could be with Gwennie."

"Not everything we wish is easy. And most things are sweeter for the effort put in to get them."

"And some things will never be ours, and it's better to stop throwing yourself against a wall with no hope of breaking through. You'll only injure yourself." With that, he stormed off to the village.

He'd promised never to force Evelyn to do anything, and he'd hold by his word. But he would find her and have his say.

He needed to ask only two people in the village to find the cottage where Evelyn was staying. It looked to be the smallest one in the village. He knocked twice and before anyone would have had time to answer he knocked again.

She opened the door and stepped back so he could come inside. Immediately Gwennie ran to him. "Bunny. Bunny!"

Without hesitation, he reached into his sporran and pulled out the rabbit he'd made for her. He kneeled down and placed it in her free hand, the other one clutching her favorite.

"Bunny broke," she said pointing to a clump of wood on the floor. The other carved rabbits were gathered around it. "Mama bunny."

Somehow knowing Evelyn had attempted to take this one thing he had with Gwennie made him even angrier at the woman.

"Can you stay here with the bunnies while your mama and I step outside to talk? We'll be right outside the door if you need us."

The lass nodded and skipped off to play alone.

When Liam stood, he realized how much he towered over his wife. Or perhaps it was that she seemed to be huddled in on herself instead of standing tall like she usually did. "Outside," he ordered and was surprised when she simply followed him through the door.

"I don't understand," he started. "I asked you before we arrived if you wished to remain my wife and ye said you would. I gave you the choice and you chose me only to run off the first chance you got. My clan celebrated us just two nights ago and now I'm the gossip of the castle with how my wife left me. There's talk that I beat you and the lass. Me! I'd never hurt a soul unless forced to protect my clan, but they think..." He walked in a small circle to release his pent-up anger. "And I could deal with that. What I can't fathom is what I did to make you leave, and without the respect of conversation first."

The anger he'd been carrying for the last day deflated like the loss of winds in a sail. He was hurt and embarrassed, but mostly he missed her and Gwennie. It hadn't been an easy relationship, but they had been his, and now...

・・・

"I'm sorry." Even hearing the words, Evelyn knew they weren't enough. She'd done a dishonorable thing by sneaking away without talking to Liam first. She understood his anger—short-lived that it was. "I thought I could do it, but I can't."

"You can't do what?"

"Lie with you. As your wife."

His eyes went wide. "I told you I'd never force myself on ye if you were unwilling, Ev. Why would you doubt my word?"

She hadn't doubted his word. She knew he wouldn't act if she was unwilling, and that was her fear. That she'd be willing. The feelings he'd aroused scared her.

So far, she'd tricked him into marrying her to escape her father. Hidden the fact she had a child until he was well and thoroughly trapped and left him without a reason and through it all he remained peaceful. If she'd been testing him, he would have surely proven he'd not harm her or her daughter. He was all kindness and devotion, things any woman would want in a husband. Things any woman—herself included—could grow to love in a man. But loving and wanting Liam hadn't been part of her plan. She'd left rather than give in to the possibility of those things. How could she explain?

"I know you wouldn't push me into anything, but that wouldna mean you wouldn't desire those things."

He tilted his head. "Of course, I desire ye, Ev. I have thought of little else than lying with you since I met you. But I'm not an animal who canna control his urges."

"Though you'd grow to resent me for denying your rights. And you would continue to tempt me to relent."

"Is it wrong of me to want to hope for a chance to have you as my wife in every way? I know I tried to kiss you when it was too soon, but I can wait. In time—"

"That's where you'd be wrong, Liam. It will never be the right time for that. I don't want it. I'll *never* want it."

"You do not wish for more children? To grow old with someone by your side? To protect you with their very life?"

She swallowed down her first answer, because in truth everything he said sounded wonderful. More children to laugh with and love. A partner she could always count on. But men were fickle beasts. What they wanted was more important than anything. And what they felt was best for someone wasn't always the case.

She gathered her strength so she could look him in the eye and with a steady voice she said, "No. I don't." Before she could break down, she turned and rushed back into the cottage, shutting out her husband, and whatever they may have been, from her heart.

...

Weeks had gone by and Liam had fallen back into his old life before he'd gone to Scalloway Castle and requested an audience with the laird. He could almost pretend he'd only dreamed of marrying Evelyn. After all, he'd dreamed of it for many years.

Unfortunately, his men didn't allow it. While they were doing drills or defending against a raid, Liam was in command and they respected him as war chief. But in the hall over their meals the men were just friends.

"Has your horse left ye yet, Liam?" one of them asked, causing the group to bark in laughter.

"Have your laughs now. You'll pay for it tomorrow during drills." That caused them to hold their tongues. For a while at least.

The nights were the worst. Remembering what it had been like to have her in his bed. The warmth of her hand on his arm. It had just been that one night, but somehow, he felt her absence as if she'd been with him all his days.

"The laird wishes to see you." A messenger waited next to him for acknowledgment of his request.

"Of course." He nodded to the lad, recalling his days of chasing down men to deliver the laird's summons.

He knocked on the doorframe of the laird's study before entering. "You asked to see me?"

"Aye. The Stewart laird has sent a message to me as well as Evelyn. I thought it best if you delivered it to her."

He held out a letter with the Stewart coat of arms pressed into the seal.

"Does he plan to attack us?" Liam asked.

"Not yet. His missive contained only a demand of his daughter's return untouched." Lachlan lifted a brow. They both understood what that meant. He didn't wish to receive her back in the same condition she'd returned the last time—with child.

"We expected he'd bluster a bit," Liam said.

"I don't know how a father could be so cruel." Lachlan shook his head.

"He thinks it's Evelyn's fault what happened. If she'd obeyed him and stayed in the castle she never would have been captured and assaulted."

"She was just a lass. She couldn't have known what would come of her simple rebellion."

"He doesna see it that way. And he surely doesn't approve of me for her husband."

"He's an arse."

Liam smiled in agreement. "I'll see that she gets the letter." Though he'd have to wait until he was ready to visit without begging her to give him a chance. Today would not be the day.

"Do you think she might want to return? I can't imagine she enjoys living in a small cottage alone. Kenna said she and Mari visited the day before yesterday and Evelyn seemed tired."

"I think the only thing she allowed herself to want was to be a mother to her daughter, and she has that now."

"It wouldn't hurt for you to show up at their home with more than a few wooden rabbits," Lach said.

"What else would I take?"

After an impatient sigh, Lach answered. "Take them some food. Bread, meat pies, but also some treats. Tarts and such. Collect some flowers along the way, and for the love of Christ make sure to change to your best shirt."

"Why would I need my best shirt to deliver a letter?"

"You're not just delivering a letter. You're trying to woo a woman."

Liam had never needed to woo a woman before. He'd had plenty enough offers from the serving maids. While he hadn't taken advantage of every offer, there'd been a few. And they'd been happy to take him in his second-best shirt.

But Lachlan was a happily married man, so Liam would follow his instructions and hope they earned the same results the laird enjoyed. It surely wouldn't hurt to try to win her over.

· · ·

Gwendolyn flinched when the yelling started up again. So far, Evelyn was content with their tiny cottage in the village. Making their meals herself was a bit of a challenge, but she'd managed. She and Gwennie were building an unbreakable bond, just as she'd wanted. Everything might have been perfect if not for the fact she still missed Liam and that the man in the cottage across from hers spent the better part of the day in a drunken rage.

Evelyn had seen a young wife and a small boy—perhaps a few years older than Gwennie—doing chores outside the home. Gwennie had offered one of her rabbits to the boy, who thanked her quietly.

Evelyn attempted to converse with the other woman, but it was clear her lip was too swollen to make talking easy. She knew what that felt like.

Every time the man started yelling, Evelyn wished she were brave enough to confront the man and make him stop hurting the poor woman, but while she'd walked over to the house twice, she hadn't had the courage to knock. Both times, she froze as the roaring voice coming from inside called up a memory from her past.

Being the prisoner of five men had meant one of them telling her to do something that one of the others didn't like and punished her for. They fought among themselves often enough, but she was the one who took the worst of it.

She was about to retreat yet again when the door flew open and the little boy rushed out, knocking into her.

"Help," he said with tears running down his dirty face.

The man was still yelling inside. Evelyn turned to see a few other women standing about, none willing to risk entering the house. She would have to do this herself. She would have to save someone like someone had once saved her.

Steering the lad to her home, she reached for the dagger she kept on the mantel out of reach and went back outside after instructing both children to stay inside.

A boy no older than ten had come forward but had stopped outside the home.

"Run to the castle as fast as you can. Tell the guard at the gate that Evelyn MacKinlay needs her husband to come immediately. Can you do that?"

The boy nodded and ran off like a shot.

With a steady breath and a tight grip on her knife, she went inside.

...

Liam was in the bailey punishing his men for their remarks the night before when a boy came running up to the open gate.

"Please help! Evelyn MacKinlay..." He paused to catch a breath as Liam ran to him, ready to shake the next words from his mouth if he didn't continue. "She needs her husband immediately."

"I'm her husband. Take me to her. Now." He gave a nod to two of his men to follow along as well and off they ran.

The boy was young and the trip from the village to the castle was not a short one. He was slowing down and soon Liam was running ahead, dragging the poor lad behind him. But he wouldn't have needed the boy's guidance as he knew to go toward her cottage.

Once there, it was easy to know why he'd been called. He saw Gwennie standing in the open door of their cottage. A boy a bit older hugging her as if he was keeping her from going to the other cottage where all the shouting was coming from.

It took a moment for his sight to adjust to the dim light in the room. When it did, he couldn't believe what he was seeing before him.

A dark-haired woman sobbed in the corner while Evelyn stood in front of her, dagger held out against a man larger than Liam.

Evelyn looked like a warrior defending the other woman against a giant. Had he not noticed the way her hand shook as she held her weapon clenched in whitened fingers, he would have thought she battled large men every day.

"Stay away from her. You're in your cups and you've hurt her."

"Get away from me wife, ye foul bitch. 'Tis not your place," the man said, lurching toward Evelyn. It was time Liam stopped this.

"Ho there!" Liam stepped up, halting the man from striking Evelyn. It wasn't until Liam was closer that he noticed the blood at Ev's mouth. The man had already hit her.

Rage lit his soul, and it was all he could do to stop himself from drawing his sword and ending the man where he stood.

The man stumbled, and Liam grasped his arm to hold him away from the women.

Nodding to the men who had come with him, he gave the order. "Bind this man and take him to the gaol until Lachlan can determine what should happen with him. Send a cart for this woman and take her to the keep so Lady Kenna can tend to her."

The men nodded their agreement and Liam went to Evelyn. It took a bit of effort, but he was able to pry the dagger from her fingers. "You're fine. The danger is gone now. You did well, Ev. I'm proud of ye for protecting the woman from her lout of a husband."

It wasn't until the woman was hauled away that Evelyn collapsed in a fit of tears.

"He was hitting her."

"I know. Shh. You're fine. Everyone is fine."

To his great surprise she allowed him to move closer

and wrap his arms around her. He held her longer than was probably necessary, but he didn't want to miss the opportunity to comfort her while he had the chance.

Eventually, her tears stopped and she managed to take a few deep breaths. "I must get back to Gwennie."

"Aye. I'll help you to her."

Together, they walked to the smaller cottage and found Gwennie clutching the other lad.

"This is Sheamus. You met his father and mother," Ev said.

"I should take him up to the castle so he can stay with his mother while she heals."

Evelyn nodded and slumped in the chair, staring at nothing.

He didn't want to leave her again.

He glanced down at his shirt, the one he wore when running drills. The one that was now stained with a few spots of blood. Definitely not his best shirt. He'd not stopped for flowers and had not brought any treats from the kitchens.

So much for wooing the woman. He thought it to be dishonest to leave and come back later with her father's letter so instead he knelt next to her and held out the missive. When she stared blankly at him, he questioned if it was wise to give her more upsetting news on top of what she'd already been through, but it was too late. She'd taken it.

"Mayhap it would be better to read it—very well, now is good also."

He read over her shoulder.

Daughter,

Your mother would be horrified to see what a deceitful child she bore. To run off with the worthless MacKinlay rather than stay and do your duty to your clan.

I'm sure ye thought this would be the end of it, but I assure ye, I don't give up so easily. You have brought shame to your people and your laird.

You'll return to Scalloway at once. If you do not return, I'll be forced to involve the MacKinlay laird. I leave the choice in your hands. Do not be foolish.

It wasn't signed Father or Papa. Only his cold initials written in a flourish at the bottom.

"I'm sorry. I should have waited to give it to you," he said when a tear streaked down her cheek.

"It's of no matter," she said crumpling the letter and throwing it in the unlit hearth. "It is only what I expected of him. He's angry. We knew he would be. He'll get over it soon enough."

"You're not leaving?"

"Do you wish me to leave?"

"To be honest, I don't see that it matters to me. It's not like I would notice if you were here or not." With that, he left the cottage and escorted Sheamus to the castle.

Liam had let his hurt and anger tinge his words. Rather than woo her, he'd no doubt done the opposite.

. . .

When Liam was gone, Evelyn picked up Gwennie and held her as a few more tears fell. She shouldn't be so upset. She had exactly what she'd wanted—a home for her and her daughter where her father couldn't use her as a pawn to forge his alliances. He was angry, but she'd known that. Then why was she still crying? She didn't want to think too deeply on it for she worried if she did, she might not like the answer.

Liam.

He'd come to her aid immediately and helped her out of a

bad situation, and this hadn't been the first time. He'd helped her out of many bad situations.

When he'd held her and rubbed her back, it'd been nice. Better than nice. But she knew if it went unchecked it would grow into something more, something she didn't want.

"Mama sad," Gwennie announced and placed her chubby hand on Evelyn's cheek.

"Yes, love. Mama is sad."

"Bunny?"

Before she could answer, a wooden rabbit was shoved in her face, making her laugh.

The next morning, after they'd eaten, Evelyn took Gwennie's hand and they headed toward the castle. Evelyn wanted to check in on Sheamus and his mother. She would also visit with Kenna and Mari if they were about. Gwennie would enjoy playing with the other children as well.

But when her heartbeat quickened as she passed through the gate, she knew the truth of why she'd come. She'd wanted to see Liam. And see him she did. He was in the bailey working with his men. Sweat had made the ends of his blond hair curl up in an oddly appealing way. He nodded in their direction but didn't come over to speak to her.

She couldn't blame him for the distance between them. It was entirely her fault. Maybe she hadn't needed to keep him so far away. She wasn't able to be a real wife, but if they could be friends…

She shook the thought away sadly. He was a man. Her husband by right.

Being friends would never be enough.

Chapter Thirteen

Liam had made it all the way to the castle gates and then turned around and went back. After two hard thumps on the door, it opened to a teary-eyed Evelyn. He wanted nothing more than to pull her into his arms and comfort her, but he knew well she wouldn't welcome his touch.

"I spoke hastily earlier. I do wish to know if you plan to leave. And if you do, I'd request we handle the annulment here so that I might move forward. That I might find a wife who truly wants me. It was wrong of me to try to make you fit into the life I'd dreamed up for us. I see that now. But it doesn't change the fact that I do want a family someday, so I pray you will release me if you choose to leave."

"Of course, Liam. I know I've been selfish throughout everything. I wanted out of my father's reach and I saw you as an opportunity."

He couldn't help but wince at her words. What a fool he'd been to think everything would finally fit into place and allow him happiness. He'd long wondered what he might have done at such a young age to earn such punishment.

He'd been given a clan who accepted him, but he was unable to accept their love.

He'd been given the wife he'd dreamed of for years, but he was unable to win her heart.

Always so close to what he wanted, but never quite reaching it.

He nodded. "Please send word of your decision."

This time when he left the village, he wasn't angry or hurt, he was simply numb. He stayed that way until the next evening when he stepped into the hall and made for the head table where he held a place of honor next to the laird.

But as he greeted the clansmen, he caught a glimpse of fiery gold. Evelyn and Gwennie were seated at a table near the front of the hall. Wee Sheamus sat next to Gwennie.

Changing his course, he went to their table, preparing to hear her choice.

"Good evening, wife."

"Bunny," Gwennie said with a smile and reached for him. He picked her up and pretended to drop her as was their game. As usual, he earned a shriek of laughter that made the clan laugh as well.

He pulled three rabbits from his sporran and held them out. "Which one do ye think we should give to Sheamus?"

"Dis one." She held it out to the boy, who smiled tentatively and took it. "Thank you," they both said when Evelyn cleared her throat.

"Would you care to sit with us?"

He hesitated a moment, wanting to put off the news that she planned to leave Dunardry. He took his seat on the other side where the children were busy playing with their rabbits.

"I wanted you to know I've decided to stay."

He nodded. He'd expected to feel relief with this answer, but oddly he didn't. Things hadn't changed between them. He was no closer to having what he'd wanted with her decision.

In fact, further from it. If she'd annulled the marriage and left him, he would have been free to start over.

Now he would be trapped in this hell for the rest of his life. Having a family, but unable to reach them. He'd drifted for a moment and then noticed Evelyn was speaking.

"Unless you wish me to go. My father threatened the clan if I didn't return. If you think it too great a risk, I'll return." She swallowed and looked up at him. "If you wish me to go because I'm not the wife you expected, I'd understand."

He let out a breath and shook his head. "The laird would never turn you out of the clan. He's said as much to me. You are a MacKinlay now and as worthy of protection as anyone else."

"And you?"

"I took a vow to stay with you through sickness and health and good times and bad. I do not break a vow." Even if it meant never having what he truly wanted.

"Might we take our evening meals together each day?"

He blinked in surprise. His wife had offered him an invitation to be with her and Gwennie each day. He looked up at the dais where Lachlan sat next to Kenna, and their boys took up the places by their sides chatting excitedly about their day.

"Yes," Liam said, grasping at this chance to be with Evelyn and their daughter. "I'd like that very much."

...

Evelyn hadn't known she was going to suggest they dine together each night until she opened her mouth and the words came out. But by the next week they'd fallen into a pleasant arrangement.

Evelyn had sent off a response to her father telling him she planned to stay with her husband. She found she looked forward to each evening meal when Liam met her and Gwennie at the same table to dine and talk about their day. Liam always had a new rabbit for Gwendolyn.

After dinner, he'd escort them back to their cottage and tuck Gwennie in with a story of a leaf that carried a small bunny to the sea where they'd meet the seals. Anytime he attempted to deviate from the story to make it more exciting, he was strictly corrected.

Occasionally, he would help with a household chore like bringing in wood so she'd have it to cook in the morning or carrying in water. Then Liam would leave with a simple, "Good night to you both. I look forward to seeing you in the hall tomorrow."

The following week, Sheamus and his mother returned to the cottage across the way and he and Gwennie were good friends, often playing with the growing army of rabbits in the yard next to their cottage.

Hearing the rumble of thunder in the distance, Evelyn stepped out to bring the children inside. When they weren't in the side yard, Evelyn walked across the lane to Sheamus and Madra's home.

Sheamus opened the door with a smile. Since his father hadn't returned, the boy had more smiles to spare these days. "I came to bring Gwennie home before the storm." But as Evelyn glanced around the cottage not much bigger than hers, she didn't see her daughter.

"She's not here," Madra said turning to the boy. "Where is she, Sheamus?"

"Gwennie went with the tinker. He said he had a giant bunny to show her." The boy's smile faded to a pout. "I wasn't allowed to go along."

Evelyn's vision grew distorted at the edges. She remembered losing consciousness and knew the peace it brought, but she couldn't allow it this time.

She needed to find her daughter.

• • •

Liam tossed another spade of dirt onto the growing hill and wiped the sweat from his brow. He and a few of his men had come to Cam's to help him with one of his new buildings. The man was always designing a structure. This would be a small house for the dowager duchess who came to visit often.

With the sun high in the sky, Liam ordered the men to take a break, and they headed to the wagon that had arrived with their meals.

In the quiet as the men ate, Liam heard the clanking of another wagon. The tinker had left the village and was heading away from them.

"Doesn't the tinker go to Baehaven when he leaves us?" Liam asked Cam.

"Aye. Old Duncan probably forgot where he was heading."

"Did he forget his wife as well? She doesn't appear to be with him."

"I hope she hasn't taken ill," Cam agreed. They both knew the pair were always together on visits to Dunardry.

"I was thinking of getting a trinket for Ev. I'll head him off and set him on his way west."

"Very well. I'll see to the men once they're fed."

Liam mounted his horse and took off for the rumbling wagon. When he caught up with the man, he was surprised to see his grim expression rather than the normal smile on his face. It was clear something was wrong, and from the absence of his wife, Liam worried if he was now alone.

It was one of the parts of marriage Liam hated to think of. Hopefully, he and Ev had many years of health before them. He felt the two of them had come to an understanding in the weeks since they started taking their meals together. He hoped one day they might build on that.

"Ho there," Liam called when the man didn't stop. "Are ye well, Duncan?"

The man shook his head and broke into tears. "Nay, I'm not well at all. I've done a terrible thing."

"What is it? Has something happened to Joan?"

The man finally stopped the wagon and nodded. "Aye. She's been taken from me."

"Was it an illness?" Liam asked, his heart going out to the man.

"No. She lives. Or at least she did when last I saw her. Two men hold her."

Liam shifted in his saddle and he dismounted to come closer. "Someone has taken Joan?"

The man nodded.

"Did they say why? What do they want with her? Do they want money?" Liam didn't have much, but he'd help if he could.

The man's face crumbled again. "I shouldna done it, even for Joan. She'd hate me for it."

"Hate you for what?"

"The men told me I must go into the village and find a little dark-haired girl named Gwendolyn and bring her to them if I wanted to see my wife alive again."

Liam couldn't breathe.

Duncan shook his head. "I carried out the deed as they told me, but when I met them at the edge of the forest, they took the child and left without returning my wife to me."

"Where? Where did they take Gwennie?"

The man pointed back toward the village. "Other side of the village. By the woods. They had their own gig with two horses. The others rode separate."

"How many men?"

"Six, maybe seven?"

Before the man had the full sentence out, Liam had turned and nudged his horse to get back to his men. He couldn't take on that many men himself, and he'd not risk Gwennie by making a mistake.

"Mount up and follow me. They've taken my daughter." Cameron joined the group as they galloped around the village, heading for the tree line.

When they entered the darkness of the forest, Liam stopped and called for silence. They needed to listen so they could tell where the kidnappers were. But all they could hear was the blowing of air from the horses.

"They must have crossed the wood to the fields."

Liam agreed with Cameron, and they maneuvered through the trees and brush to the meadow on the other side. Unfortunately, the hills obscured their view in all directions.

"We'll need to split up. Four men in each group. There are six or seven of them so be ready."

The men divided up quickly and dispersed. Cam, Colin, and a young lad they called Wolf stayed with Liam and headed in the direction of Scalloway Castle.

On the second rise, Liam spotted the group. Joan was on the seat next to one of the men with her hands bound, but he didn't see Gwennie, though she was small enough to fit in the back of the gig.

With a battle cry that came from the depths of his soul, he launched his horse into action and descended like hell's own fury upon the men who had taken his daughter.

In the end, Liam hadn't needed much help to dispatch the men. His rage had given him the lightning-fast reflexes that came only when faced with the fear of losing a loved one. No amount of training could match the protective instincts of a man fighting for his child.

When the men all lay dead around them, and Cam was

helping release Joan from her bonds, Liam moved on shaking legs to the back of the gig. He'd never prayed so hard in his life as he begged God to let him find Gwennie unharmed.

He flipped open the tarp and there was Gwennie bound and gagged with tears on her dirt-smudged cheeks. Liam wiped the blood from his dirk so he could cut her free. She reached for him right away despite the blood splattered on his clothes and face. He held her tight, hating the way her little body trembled in fear.

"See that Joan gets back to Duncan," Liam ordered the men as he bundled Gwennie on his horse with him to ride back to the village. He needed to keep his distance from the tinker to stop himself from doing something violent to the man. Gwennie was safe, that was what mattered.

He squeezed her close. "Are you well, lass?"

She began to cry. "My bunnies. Broke."

Liam smiled and kissed the top of her head. "Don't worry, love. I'll make new ones straightaway."

She looked up at him and smiled. She was no worse for her ordeal if a promise of crudely carved rabbits could so easily put a smile on her face.

...

Evelyn was in the solar with Mari and Kenna when a messenger came rushing in to let them know Gwennie was safe and on her way back to the castle with Liam.

After finding out her daughter had been taken, Evelyn had run to the castle for help. She'd been told by the guard on the wall that they'd spotted Liam leading Cameron and a group of men into the forest.

She'd wanted to get her own horse to follow after, but Kenna and Mari told her to let the men take care of retrieving Gwennie. They'd ordered the maids to bring food as if they'd done this sort of thing before and knew how to prepare for what was to come.

It felt like hours before Liam stepped into the room, carrying the little girl. Evelyn hurried and pulled Gwennie into her arms. After she'd held her tight and gotten over the initial panic, she pulled away and frowned.

"Are you hurt?"

"A little bumped up, but nothing that won't heal," Liam answered. Of course, he would have already checked her over.

Gwennie whimpered and Evelyn looked down to see marks on her daughter's wrists. Evelyn well knew what had caused marks like these. Ropes.

"Someone bound your wrists?" Evelyn asked, her voice broke.

"Y-yes."

"Who? Who did this?" Evelyn's demand startled Gwennie into tears.

"It was the tinker, though he was forced into it by a group of men. They took his wife and demanded he bring Gwennie to them or they would kill her," Liam said before turning to address the laird.

Evelyn worried what the men had done to her daughter in the time Gwennie had been gone. She choked on her own tears and held her daughter close. "Did they touch her?"

"I've never known Duncan to be a cruel man. I'm sure he wouldn't have hurt her," Mari said, always the peacekeeper. But Evelyn would have none of it.

"He tied her up. What kind of man does such a thing to a little girl? And to turn her over to…" She didn't finish that thought.

Kenna was by her side. She took Gwennie and brushed away her tears. "It will be fine," the woman said.

"You're frightening her," Mari whispered as she pulled

Evelyn aside. "Let Kenna see to her. If she's been hurt, Kenna will help."

Evelyn knew it was best, but it was hard not to cling to Gwennie.

"Take a breath," Mari said while rubbing circles on her back. The maid came over with some water. "I know how memories can color things and make them more than they are. Gwennie was not gone very long. Let's not assume the worst just yet."

Evelyn nodded and took a sip of water, never taking her gaze from Kenna and Gwennie.

"She'll be fine," Liam said near her shoulder. "The men did not have time to do anything. Besides, they wouldn't have harmed her. That wasn't the reason they took her."

"Men who snatch up little girls do so for the vilest of reasons," Evelyn said.

"She wasn't taken at random. They wanted her specifically."

A chill ran over Evelyn as she turned to face Liam. "Stewarts?"

He nodded.

"My father sent them to kidnap my daughter with the intent of forcing me to return home," she said. "I hadn't realized he would go this far. I thought he'd make his threats and rant at me for my disloyalty to spare his pride, but this..." She shook her head, not understanding how her father, who had once been her greatest ally, had become her biggest fear.

A moment later, Kenna set her daughter down and Gwennie ran over to Lizzy and started playing as if nothing had happened. Evelyn sagged in relief. Surely, she wouldn't be so quick to get back to playing if she'd been damaged in any way.

She turned to thank Liam for saving Gwennie, but she paused when she noticed his grim expression.

She noticed other things as well. He was wet. His blond hair still dripped water on the floor, though the storm had passed and there wasn't a cloud in the clear blue sky. He looked at Evelyn and pressed his lips together as if struggling to keep from breaking down.

"I killed them all, Ev. Every one of your father's men. I couldn't stop myself. All I knew was they were trying to take Gwennie and I reacted without thinking. Your father is sure to be even angrier. I don't think he will resort to empty threats now. I'm sorry."

She held out her arms to embrace him. "Thank ye, Liam. I would have done the same thing if I'd been there. Let it be a message to my father that I will not give up my daughter without a fight."

"My fierce warrior princess," he said with a fleeting smile. When his lips turned into a firm line again, she worried she wouldn't bear more bad news. "I will ask something of you, but know that you don't truly have a choice, for I'm already set on it."

Her shoulders stiffened at his authoritative tone. "Ask."

"You and Gwennie will move back to the castle. I have already sent one of my men to gather your things. I'm your husband and I have yet to make any demands as such. I will have my family close so I can protect them, Ev."

She nodded immediately, easily agreeing to his terms. She would've made the request herself if he hadn't. It was clear she couldn't protect her daughter alone. She needed a fortress around her.

She needed Liam.

...

Liam was happy to have Evelyn and Gwendolyn back in the castle and his room. As he settled Gwennie in the small bed in the corner, he turned to tell Ev that he'd sleep in the hall with his men, but she surprised him by rising up on her tiptoes to place a kiss on his cheek.

"I can never repay you for what you did for us today. I would've lost her had you not responded so quickly." She glanced away and then smiled. Or tried to. Her expression was a brittle, shaky thing meant to make him think she was well, when clearly she wasn't.

She reached for the laces of her gown and began to loosen them. At the sight of the creamy flesh, he was momentarily distracted, but then he noticed the way her hands shook, and when he looked to her face, he saw her eyes were pinched closed. Definitely not the look of a woman who willingly wanted to give herself to a man.

He placed his hands over hers. "Ev, stop. This is not right."

Her eyes opened and along with the relief he saw on her face, he also noticed her confusion.

"I'm your wife. I thought you would want my body."

He let out a humorless laugh. "I'll not lie to ye, Ev. I do want your body. And at times I'm all but consumed by the thought of it. But when I imagine us joining, it is with both of us smiling and happy to share ourselves with the other. Not like this. Not in repayment for something I did as my duty to Gwennie as her father. You owe me nothing."

He took her hands away from her bosom and held them by her sides for a moment before letting her go.

"I'll sleep in the hall." He turned to go, but she stopped him.

"Please stay here with us," she asked.

He realized she must still be frightened from the events of the day. It made sense she would want to keep him close so he could watch over them.

"Very well." With a nod, he took his bedroll from the

items on the pegs and stretched it out in front of the door. "You and Gwennie are safe here. No one will get past me, I swear it."

He wished her a goodnight as he would come to do for weeks to come. He thought she'd get over her fear and bid him to sleep in another room. But almost a month later, he was still spending the night with them in his room.

It meant he was sleeping on the floor. But their shared evening meals had extended to include all their meals, as well as the time around those meals. In fact, the only time they weren't together was when he was with his men for drills.

To anyone else, they might've seemed like a normal family, but behind closed doors he was still giving her plenty of space.

He knew Evelyn cared only for her child and had no room in her heart for anyone else. Once she was certain Gwennie was no longer in danger, she wouldn't need him anymore. He was merely a temporary sentry.

He'd do best to protect his heart from expecting anything more.

Chapter Fourteen

Evelyn felt like a butterfly stuck inside its own chrysalis. Yes, she was safe inside, but with each day, she felt more compelled to break free and fly.

She knew her strange feeling had everything to do with sharing a room with Liam over the last month. He'd been nothing but the proper gentleman, seeing to her and Gwennie's needs, never asking for anything in return, even though she was sure he had needs as well.

She'd seen how he ached in the mornings when he woke, and the way his thin blanket tented over his erection. Yet, he never complained or pushed for anything from her.

The night she'd offered herself, he'd turned her away, and that had been the last time anything of that nature had been addressed. It was exactly what she should want out of this situation. However, she felt a strange frustration that wouldn't go away. She wanted his lips on hers as much as she didn't, and was shocked to acknowledge such a thing. She didn't trust men. She didn't enjoy sexual relations with them.

But a kiss. A kiss from Liam rather intrigued her.

"Are we to expect a blond babe anytime soon?" Kenna asked while they were in the solar after breakfast. She and Gwennie had made a habit of joining the group each day so Gwennie could play with the other children. Evelyn didn't mind chatting with the sisters. Kenna and Mari had become good friends, but she didn't like being asked personal questions like this one.

"Kenna, you know better than to ask something so impertinent."

Kenna rolled her eyes at her older sister and turned back to Evelyn, obviously still waiting for a reply.

"No. We are not expecting."

Kenna frowned. "I'm sorry. Perhaps next month."

Would the woman continue to ask each month? Evelyn looked closely at her and determined she probably would. Best to deal with it straightaway.

"There will be no children."

"Surely, it's too soon to know that for sure."

"I know it for sure." Evelyn could feel the heat spreading from her cheeks to her neck.

Kenna opened her mouth, but Mari interrupted. "It is not our business, and we will not ask prying questions. Please know if you ever have any questions, we'd welcome them and do our best to help. It's not easy starting a relationship with a man. And I'm sure it's even more difficult for someone who's gone through what you have. You and Liam need only do what's best for you and Liam."

Kenna let out a sigh. "My sister is right. Forgive me for meddling."

Evelyn was relieved when the conversation turned to sewing new dresses for Lizzy and Gwennie. But later, without warning, Evelyn said, "I've not kissed Liam."

Both women seemed surprised. Whether because of what she said or that she'd blurted it out after Mari had suggested a rose fabric for Gwennie's dress, Evelyn wasn't certain.

Kenna cleared her throat. "Do ye mean you've not kissed him down there?"

"Down there?" she asked not sure what the woman meant.

"Kenna!" Mari turned as red as Evelyn felt. "Ignore her. I take it to mean you've not been intimate at all. Not even a kiss."

"Yes. You see, I didn't think I'd ever welcome such a thing, but now I find myself curious."

"Curious is good," Kenna said with a wide smile.

"I think it's too late, though. Liam hasn't tried to kiss me at all since I've been back at the castle. I've considered asking him to kiss me, but what if I find I don't like it? How do I go back to the way things are now if that proves to be the case?"

"I can't imagine you'd not like it. Kissing is divine," Kenna said.

Mari gave her sister a soft slap in the arm. "I imagine you're afraid the kiss could turn into something...else. Something you're not curious about."

"You're correct."

"Just grab him by the ears and kiss him. Then leave the room."

Mari reached out and put her hand over Evelyn's. "You must speak to him. Tell him exactly what you want and do not want. Mark me, men do appreciate a bit of guidance in such matters."

Kenna smiled. "Very well, yes. You should speak to him. But if that doesn't work, then you might want to try my way."

...

Liam cleaned up in his room and went down to the hall for the evening meal. When he didn't see Evelyn and Gwennie sitting at their usual table, he felt a squeeze of panic.

"Bunny!" Gwennie shouted from the head table.

Relief flooded his body when he saw the little girl sitting at the table between the twins. He searched the high table for his wife and didn't see her. Mari smiled and waved him closer.

"Evelyn is in the solar waiting for you. You'll take your meal there this evening."

Liam glanced at the little girl he was responsible for.

"We'll see to Gwendolyn. Don't keep her waiting."

Hurrying up the stairs, Liam paused before knocking on the door to the solar.

"Come in."

Inside, he found Evelyn sitting at a table piled with bread and meat. He sat in the seat opposite her and looked around in confusion.

"What is this about?"

"I wanted to speak to you about something of a private nature, and Kenna and Mari thought it better if we discussed it here alone."

The panic had returned, making him tense. She was done with him. He'd been expecting this. He'd kept his heart shielded so this wouldn't be such a surprise, but perhaps he hadn't done a good job of it, for he already felt the stirrings of pain. He was going to lose them.

"Shall we eat first?" she suggested.

Eat? He didn't think he'd manage a bit of food past the lump in his throat. He shook his head.

"Nay. Please just say what you wanted to say so we can have it out with."

She twisted her fingers before reaching for her glass of wine. He'd never seen her drink wine before. Was she nervous?

"Very well." She cleared her throat. "Would you be

receptive to kissing?"

For all the king's gold, he couldn't have kept his mouth from falling open.

"Kissing? Aye. I would be receptive." His heart pounded with excitement. His wife wanted to kiss him. Unless… "You do mean between the two of us?"

"Yes."

He nodded slowly so not to make any quick movements that might scare off the skittish woman. "I'd be quite receptive to kissing, if you're sure it's something you want."

She frowned. "That's why this is so difficult." She rubbed at her temples until he took her hand and held it loosely.

"Tell me."

"I find myself… curious as to what it would be like to kiss you. However, if we do and I don't like it, I'll feel as if I've deceived you."

He shook his head. "You think I will get carried away and not stop at kissing?"

She winced but nodded. "That is part of my concern, yes. But, also, what if I dislike kissing you? Will you feel cheated if I don't wish to do it ever again?"

"It wouldn't be different from how things are now between us."

"True. You'd be willing to try?"

He nodded eagerly. "Yes. I welcome the opportunity to kiss you, even if it's just this one time."

"Very well. How should we go about it?" She moved to stand but he held out his hand to stay her.

"Not yet. If this is my one chance, I need to make sure it exceeds your expectations. Please allow me until the end of our meal."

She nodded and he watched her relax as they went on with their meal. They talked about their day, and Liam made sure to touch her when the opportunity arose. Just a brush of his fingers against hers as he passed her the bread. The warmth of his leg against hers under the table.

When they'd finished eating, he reached over and leisurely took her hand, rubbing his thumb softly over her knuckles until she relaxed again.

"You expected me to launch across the table as soon as you swallowed the last morsel on your plate?" he teased.

Her lips pulled up in a rueful smile and she nodded.

"Kissing is best when it's not just about two people pressing their lips together."

She tilted her head. "I thought that was exactly what kissing was."

"No. Well, yes. But I think more than the actual kiss, it's the anticipation that makes a truly great kiss."

"And have you kissed many women?"

"You have set a fine trap for me, wife, but I'll do my best not to fall into it." He winked at her so she knew he was jesting. "I've kissed women, but whether it was many or just a few, none of them will compare with you."

He studied her dark eyes as they warmed over. He stood and moved around the table. Still holding her hand, he helped her to her feet and was encouraged when she swayed toward him.

When he placed his other hand lightly on her cheek, she closed her eyes. He waited another breath before leaning down and touching his lips to hers.

...

Liam's kiss was like nothing she'd ever experienced before. He didn't rush or push or tug at her. He seemed perfectly content to allow the soft connection to grow on its own.

And grow it did. As he sipped small kisses from her lips, the tiny flame of interest she'd felt earlier erupted into an inferno of need. When his tongue touched the seam of her lips, it was the most natural thing to open to him and allow him in. His eternal gentleness fractured, and his hand slipped from hers to rest on her lower back and pulled her in.

But even that gesture was more an invitation than a demand as his tongue caressed her own. She moaned, surprised such a sound came from her. His answering groan of appreciation melted over her like warm honey.

She wanted more. She kissed him deeper as her arms slid around his neck, trapping him to her. The rest of her body pressed against his and she felt the proof of his excitement against her stomach.

Surely that should have frightened her, but she was caught in a haze of desire and couldn't think clearly. Liam apparently could, for his tongue retreated from her mouth and the kiss turned softer until it ended after just a few more touches of their lips. He reached up to take one of her hands and placed another kiss on her palm before resting his forehead to hers. She watched as he opened his eyes and grinned his angel smile.

His light blue eyes seemed to blaze with happiness.

"Well?" he asked, though she didn't know what he meant. "That was as good as kissing gets. Would you care to do it again?"

"Yes," she said, unbothered by how desperate her voice had become. She moved to connect their lips again, but he pulled back. "What's wrong?"

"I don't want to risk that either of us gets caught up in kissing to the point that we proceed too quickly. We'll stop for now."

Stop? She never wanted to stop. But when he stepped away, awareness seeped back in. She'd very nearly begged him to take her. The place between her legs—the place she never wanted any man to touch ever again—had grown damp with desire, and her breasts ached for his attention.

She pulled in a quick breath in surprise. How had she become so overwhelmed? It had been only a kiss.

"If you'll excuse me, I'm going for a swim in the loch before returning to our bedchamber."

"But it'll be freezing at night."

"Yes. I'm counting on that."

She didn't understand, nor did she need to. He left her in the solar alone and she slumped into her chair as her world shifted.

As they'd raced out of Scalloway Castle after they'd wed, Evelyn thought only of how she might get out of the marriage so she wouldn't need to be a real wife to a man.

It was amazing how differently she felt about Liam now. He wasn't just a man; he was her husband. He'd accepted Gwennie. Even more, he knew about Evelyn's past and where Gwennie came from and it didn't mean a bit of difference to him. She could tell in the way he smiled at them that they were the most important people in his life.

And she'd seen how shaken he'd been after killing those men to save Gwennie. Despite being the war chief, he wasn't a violent man. But he'd done violence for Evelyn's daughter.

She hadn't truly understood what it meant for Liam to bring them home to Dunardry, but it was clear now. Her husband had never had a family, and now he'd claimed them as his own.

A crease of worry pulled her forehead as she brushed Gwennie's hair before bed. She didn't want Liam disappointed. He'd wanted her all this time. He'd asked her father for her hand three times.

The worry was chased away by a thread of anger. She wouldn't be put up as a saint and then feel guilty because she couldn't live up to his expectations. She'd spent the last few years disappointing her father and feeling guilty for it.

She'd not feel guilty anymore.

Gwennie had fallen asleep while Evelyn watched the latch of the door, waiting for Liam to return. What would happen? Would he lie next to her? Would he kiss her again? Touch her?

After the haze from their kiss had lifted, she worried what Liam would want from her. She'd nearly worked herself up into a fit by the time Liam stepped quietly into the room and removed his weapons. In the darkness, she pretended to be asleep, but watched him in the moonlight coming through the window. He hung his sword belt and kilt on the pegs and tugged off his boots before taking his regular spot on the floor.

She relaxed again.

"I know you're still awake. You're breathing like a deer being chased by a wolf." His voice was low and quiet, with a hint of laughter. "Thank ye for the kiss, wife. Know I'll be receptive to kissing you whenever ye wish it."

She smiled in the darkness and dreamed of when she might have the courage to ask again.

After dressing herself and Gwennie the next morning, they went to the hall to get their meal. Liam had been gone when they'd awakened and wasn't in the hall. Kenna and Mari were waiting for her.

"How did it go?" Kenna blurted as soon as Evelyn took her seat.

"Kenna, don't overwhelm the woman with questions the moment she takes a seat," Mari chastised before smiling at Evelyn. "I hope it was most pleasurable."

"It was. I must admit, I'm surprised I liked it so much with Liam when I hated the very idea of it before."

"That sounds like a fine start."

The smile slipped from Evelyn's lips at Kenna's words. "While I very much enjoyed the kiss, I'm not certain I'll ever manage the other things."

Mari patted Evelyn's hand. "Good for you. You don't need to make a decision on that right now. There's plenty of time. Just allow yourself to enjoy what you have at this moment."

Evelyn nodded. Liam said he would welcome kissing her when she asked. And hadn't said anything about more. Perhaps that would be enough.

After the morning meal, the women settled in the solar for a bit to talk while the children played. It was wonderful to see how well Gwennie fit in. She was close in age to the other children. She even allowed the others to play with her bunnies and shared the stories Liam had told her while adding her own embellishments.

When the children slowed down in the afternoon, the little ones climbed on their mothers' laps to be swayed to sleep while the others settled in the beds. Evelyn was surprised to see her daughter get in next to Lizzy without a fuss. Soon enough, the solar was quiet. The babies were put in their cradles and Kenna went to the hall to request the nurse.

"Let's go to the kitchens," Kenna said once the older nurse was seated by the window to stand watch over the children.

Quietly, they left the room and went downstairs and out of the hall to the kitchen. It was warm and cozy inside with four other women scurrying about. Kenna took her place with them as Mari pulled out chairs for herself and Evelyn.

"I could help," Evelyn offered, though her skills in the kitchen were functional at best. Gwennie had turned up her nose a few times at the meals Evelyn had created while they were living in the village.

Mari pointed at her sister who was elbow-deep in dough. "Don't feel obligated to assist. If they need us, they will ask."

Evelyn relaxed as the wine was passed around.

"Let us officially welcome you, Evelyn, to the kitchens, where the women rule. We're so happy to have you join us," an older woman named Millie said with a cheery smile.

They all held out their cups and she swallowed around the lump in her throat to say, "Thank you, truly. It means so much to be accepted into your circle of friendship."

After the wine was consumed, Evelyn relaxed deeper into the warmth of the drink and the comradery.

Kenna shared a letter she'd received from Dorie. "You wouldn't have met her, for she married Bryce after your visit."

Evelyn nodded, recalling the *visit*.

It was clear they all missed the other woman, their friend. Evelyn couldn't help but worry she'd make a poor replacement. She heard her father's harsh words echo in her mind. He'd made her doubt herself. But she was not worthless, or a disgrace here with these women. She was one of them.

She forced a smile, promising she'd not let her father ruin her new home as he had her other one.

The chatter continued around her, but she didn't feel pressured to participate. The group seemed content to let her observe. It seemed the older women who worked in the kitchens were quite fond of telling naughty tales of their husbands. Kenna and Mari laughed and occasionally shared a small intimacy, but nothing like the blatant stories of the others.

"...and if he thought swatting me on the backside was a way to get me to listen, he was wrong. I'll disobey him at every turn now, just so he can spank me and what it leads to after."

Evelyn's cheeks heated. Surely, the woman didn't seriously enjoy being manhandled by her husband. The thought of such a thing sparked a memory of her time with the McCurdys, and her breath caught.

Mari patted her arm. "Don't worry. No one expects you

to share anything. They're more than happy to do all the talking."

Evelyn nodded, though Mari had misunderstood what had caused Evelyn's distress. Or perhaps she had understood, because she cleared her throat and spoke in her soft, cultured voice that barely sounded like a Scot.

"My first husband was a monster. Because of him, I can't bear the thought of being touched roughly. I prefer Cam's gentleness. It always surprises me how tender a man of his size can be. The way he puts my needs first. Always." She gave a crooked smile. "Unless I demand he let me have my way with him and pleasure him first. Occasionally, I tie his hands above his head so I may torment him." She shook her head. "I'm always the first to give in. The man has the patience of a stone."

Millie snorted and waved a flour-coated hand. "Please. I care only if my man's cock is like a stone."

They all laughed, but Evelyn was intrigued by the thought Mari had planted in her mind. Evelyn having Liam spread out before her. His hands tied to the bed so he could not touch her. How safe she would feel knowing she was in complete control of the encounter.

She'd be able to run her hands over the dips and valleys of his hard chest and stomach. She still couldn't imagine anything more than touching him.

She thought of the kiss they'd shared the night before and how much she looked forward to kissing him again.

Perhaps even tonight.

Chapter Fifteen

Liam was late going to their room that night because one of his men had been injured and he needed to see to him.

Thinking about the possibility of kissing her again had him hurrying once he cleared the stairs. He'd thought of nothing else the whole day. His men had noticed his distraction and teased him about it.

They didn't realize how close their crude jests were to the truth.

When he entered, she was sitting on the bed in just her shift. Her long hair was braided over her shoulder, and his body stirred. Until Gwennie shifted on the little bed and let out a sigh in her sleep. He stepped closer and took a seat on the edge of the bed.

"I'm sorry I missed the meal. I feel it's my place to stay with my men while they're being tended by the healer if they're injured on my watch."

"Of course, a very honorable thing. I saved you cheese and bannocks in case you were hungry."

He couldn't hide his surprise that she'd thought of him.

"Thank ye."

When she smiled, her gaze drifted down and color spilled across her cheeks. What had she been thinking of? And whatever it was, he wanted to try it that minute. Instead of saying that, he offered his best grin and ate his food.

Her eyelashes fluttered and Liam knew his wife was not unaffected by his closeness. It took all his strength to wash up for bed without looking at her. Not that he needed to. He could feel her watching him as he changed into a clean shirt.

When he took the blanket to go sleep on the floor, she finally spoke.

"Liam?"

"Yes?"

"I wondered..."

"Yes?" He tried his best to remain calm, but inside he was silently begging her to ask for another kiss.

Instead, she said, "Nothing. Goodnight."

"Goodnight to you." He nodded and took his place on the blanket, making sure to hide his disappointment when she blew out the light.

He didn't look forward to spending the night frustrated and aching, and not from the hard floor. But he needed to wait for her. And if she never wanted to move beyond that single kiss, he'd best get used to being uncomfortable.

"Liam?" she said in the darkness.

"Yes?" He hoped this time she'd have the courage to say what it was she wanted. He'd give her anything, she had to know that.

"I wondered if it was terribly uncomfortable sleeping on the floor."

"Nay. I've spent my share of nights sleeping rough with rocks poking me," he said. It wasn't until he'd answered that he realized she'd probably thought to invite him to sleep in the bed with her. But he'd basically told her he was fine.

"That is, of course, only a few nights here and there. Not every night as I've been on the floor. I do suffer some stiffness in the mornings."

The stiffness had nothing to do with the floor.

"Perhaps you'd rather sleep in the bed?"

"I would happily take you up on the offer, if you're sure."

"Yes. It seems only fair, since it is your room."

"It's your room as well. But I won't pass up the chance to sleep on a bed when offered."

He got up and slipped under the covers as she moved across to the other side of the bed. He couldn't see her, since the moon hadn't moved high enough yet. But he wondered if she'd squeezed into just a few inches of space opposite him.

"Thank you," he said.

When she said nothing in response, he worried she'd changed her mind. Mayhap she thought it would be a nice gesture, but she didn't want to be this close to him.

"Are you sure this is all right?"

"Yes. I was wondering if we might try another kiss tonight?"

"If you wish it, I'd be more than happy to oblige," he said, trying not to seem so eager he ended up scaring her away.

Her answer came immediately. "I do."

Slowly, he rolled closer and reached out until he felt her hair, and from there he touched her face. With his palm on her cheek, it was an easy thing to move closer and find her lips with his own.

Her mouth was as sweet as it had been the night before when he'd first explored it, and it didn't take him long before he'd gotten swept up in the moment. They were in bed together. Touching, kissing, panting...wanting.

When he rolled over on top of her, he felt her entire body stiffen, and he realized his mistake. Taking her waist, he rolled onto his back bringing her with him so she was above him. In control.

She relaxed a bit, and this time she took over the kiss, pressing her tongue against his in a slower rhythm than he'd used originally.

He could barely catch his breath when he finally pulled away. "We should stop now, before we go too far."

He felt her nod rather than saw it, and she retreated to her side of the bed. Before he fell asleep, he reached across the empty space between them and found her hand. Then he laced his fingers through hers.

He was glad for the darkness because it hid his big smile.

Over the next few nights, they'd kissed each other before going to sleep. And each night the kiss had become deeper—more intimate. He'd not dared to do anything more. He'd vowed not to ruin things between them by pushing for too much.

Their nightly kiss was all she'd given him permission for, though he'd be lying if he said he wasn't hoping they were moving toward more together. He was a man, after all, something his body made a point of proving at the most inconvenient of times.

This night, when he stepped inside, he was happy to see she was still awake. She'd taken down her hair and was brushing it to a high shine. The candle on the stand by the bed cast shadows across her night rail, but he thought he had made out the shape of a pert nipple in the thin fabric as she walked to the bed.

He smiled down at Gwennie before bending to place a kiss on her head and whispering a wish for good dreams. He removed his boots and stockings then unbuckled his weapons belt and the belt that held his kilt. He draped everything on the appropriate pegs and slid into bed in just his shirt. His bare leg brushed up against Ev's and once again his body incorrectly took it as a sign that something was to happen tonight.

"May I—" He didn't even get the question out before his wife lurched toward him. Her lips pressed against his for a moment before she opened to him. He slipped his tongue in the warmth of her mouth.

While he didn't allow his hands to roam, she didn't adhere to the same rules. The fingers of her right hand grasped his shoulder as she tangled the fingers of her left hand in his hair, holding him tightly in place. Not that he had any intention of moving away.

When she slid her leg up the outside of his to rest on his hip and pressed against him, he gasped and pulled away.

"Liam, please. I need you," she whispered.

He blinked and shook his head. He must have some kind of madness brought on by frustration. He was hearing things his wife wouldn't say. Except she said it again. He watched as her lips moved and she reached for him, pulling his lips to hers again. His hand was on her breast and he had no recollection of whether he'd placed it there or if she had.

It didn't really matter, as his hand was filled with her warm breast and he was overwhelmed. It was quite clear what she needed from him, the way she rocked her hips and searched his mouth with her tongue. He needed her just as badly and had for some time. Years, if he was being honest.

Then he heard a mumble from the opposite side of the room. From her much lower bed, Gwennie wouldn't be able to see what was happening in the higher bed. But could she hear them?

He raised his head and saw she was still asleep. But for how long? He didn't want her to be afraid if she was awakened by…sounds. *Christ.*

"Wait. Ev." He held her away from him even as she tried to pull him closer with her legs. "Gwennie," he whispered.

"We'll be very quiet."

But he couldn't risk it. "I canna do this with her in the room. What if she wakes and thinks I'm hurting you?"

"Then be quick."

"When the time is right, I will take my time to make sure you reach your pleasure first. Now is not the right time. I don't want you to regret anything between us."

"Liam, I promise I won't regret anything. I ache for... something. You."

This was not what he'd wanted their first time together to be. A quick and quiet tupping in the dark. He'd wanted her for so long he longed for the chance to explore her body.

He'd seen only parts of the women he was with in the past. No clothes were removed, just pushed aside, hinting at what was under them. He had a room now, and privacy. He wanted to do things right. Which, to him, meant naked.

"Tomorrow. We'll allow her to sleep in the solar with the other children. When we're alone, I can see to you properly."

Her only answer was a frustrated groan as she rolled away from him. Her hair covered her face, but he brushed it away to see her better. He'd planned to say something funny to lighten the situation, but he saw tears glistening on her cheeks and panicked.

"Ev? What is it? What's wrong?" He was certain he'd made a muck of things, but he wasn't certain how exactly.

"Do you not want me because I'm soiled?"

"Soiled?" He looked down at her pristine gown in confusion. She smelled like clean woman and freshly baked bannocks.

"Because I've been ruined."

"Oh." He startled when he realized what she was saying. "Don't ever think that. You're not soiled or ruined. You're perfect. You have no idea how much I want you, but this is your first time."

"I assure you, that's not true." She wouldn't look at him.

He reached over to turn her chin so she could see the truth in his words.

"What I mean is, this is your first time with a man who cares for you and wants you to enjoy it. It's your first time wanting a man in that way. I worry if we go too fast, I could scare you or destroy the happiness that could be between us. I want to wait until we can go at a more comfortable pace."

"I thought you'd be eager to—"

"Oh, aye. I'm very eager." His words came out so fast, she wouldn't be able to doubt him. But just in case she still wondered, he pressed the most eager part of him against her hip to prove his attraction for her. "But I'm even more eager to make sure you never look at me again without thinking of the ways I make you burn." He kissed her neck, making her laugh.

"I am burning. I've spent days in the kitchens listening to the women tell stories of things they do with their husbands, and I'm intrigued. They all seem to enjoy it. I never have before and thought I was different, but I think it must be different with someone you care for."

"I think it must be." His chest felt full at her admission that she cared for him.

"I doubt I'll be able to sleep in this condition." She shook her head. "I didn't realize I'd ever feel like this. To want this. I thought for sure I was—"

"You're a woman. The same as the others." He was quick to cut off whatever she might have said. He thought the word ruined might come up again. He didn't think he hated a word more than that one. "You have needs."

"I'm not completely like the others. Did you know Bettia likes her husband to spank her?"

He blinked. "I didn't and I probably could have continued on not knowing that for the rest of my days." They laughed together, then she turned quiet.

"I wouldn't like that, Liam."

"I wouldn't think so." He understood why she wouldn't. "Is Earl angry when he does it?" He couldn't help but asking.

"No. It's a game. Playful."

"Hmm. I can't say I've ever wanted to spank a woman before." He shook the thought away to focus on his wife and what she needed now. "Come with me. I have an idea." He picked up his plaid and led her out of their chamber and across the hall to an empty room. It was rather small, and he felt her shiver in the cool night air coming from the large hole where the window used to be. "You can see why it isn't used. Don't worry, you won't be chilled for long." He spread his plaid out next to the door so they could still hear if Gwennie called for them.

He kissed her again, building her fires higher once more. When she was gasping and clinging to him, he trailed his hand up the inside of her thigh.

She opened for him with a quiet sigh as he teased and tickled her. When she whimpered, he thought she had waited long enough for satisfaction.

She'd offered him a great gift; it was his time to repay her for her trust by giving her exquisite joy.

...

Evelyn had never felt such turmoil in her body before. She shook with desire and heat, and did her best to remain quiet so not to wake her daughter.

After her time with the McCurdys, she'd thought herself broken and hadn't had a bit of interest in lying with a man. In fact, she'd planned to avoid it for the rest of her life if possible. But here she was, pulling Liam to her, wanting him in a way she didn't know and couldn't explain.

All she knew was she spent her days thinking about the

kisses from the nights before. The women's naughty tales had made her curious, and she began to imagine the things they spoke of but replaced the actual couple with visions of herself with Liam.

That was when the aching had become too much to bear, and she realized she wasn't completely broken, because she did want a man. Or rather, she wanted one man.

When he touched her between her legs, she expected it to feel like an intrusion, but she welcomed his caress. She couldn't even compare her past experiences with this, they were so different. Those weeks with the McCurdys had been a torturous hell, while what Liam was doing to her was intense delight.

He was slow to enter her, using one finger at first and then a second. He built the rhythm, faster and faster. He was taking her somewhere she longed to be. She had no choice but to trust he could get her there.

Then his thumb moved against some place that sparked the fire so hot she burst. Wave after wave of heat escaped as she lost control. She must've cried out for Liam pulled her against him to muffle her surge of pleasure. Even her breathing was so loud worried she might still wake Gwennie from across the hall.

It wasn't until Liam had tucked her against him that Evelyn began to worry.

What if she enjoyed what Liam did too much? Would she become wanton? She'd heard hushed comments from some of the men who had heard what had happened to her from her father. They'd suggested she'd lied about being captured. They said she'd probably run off with a lover and when she'd grown tired of him, she'd come back with tears in her eyes. They'd called her a whore and said she'd wanted what had happened.

She hadn't wanted any part of it. But now with Liam…

she wanted. Could she become consumed with the feelings he conjured in her to the point she didn't care about anything else?

She needed to remember why she'd left Scalloway in the first place—to be with her daughter.

Not so a man could make her break apart into bliss, though she did wonder if she couldn't have both things. From the way Kenna, Mari, and the other women in the kitchen spoke, they managed to care for their little ones and also enjoy time alone with their men. And they enjoyed it enough to speak of it nearly every time they were gathered. Yet they still tended to their children and found the time to do other things.

"What is it, Ev? I swear you're thinking so loud it's keeping me awake."

She couldn't help but laugh. "I'm sorry. This is all so new. Not new exactly, but different. The feelings that go along with being with someone the way we just were. Not that we were together, really in that way, but—"

"I know well what you mean. And lucky I do, for you're going about the explanation horribly."

She pinched his side and laughed when he yelped.

"If it makes you feel better," he whispered. "It is new for me, too. Not being with a woman, though I will admit, I've never been with a woman like this. To see only to her pleasure. As a lad it had been more about me, I'm embarrassed to say. And I will apologize to the maids when I have the opportunity, for I see now how bad I was at it."

"Perhaps it works best when you're with a person you trust."

"I think you have the right of it. Before, it was just physical. It felt nice, but there wasn't anything else. Tonight, I cared only about you."

"When you apologize to the maids, don't mention how

you might not have cared for them."

"I'd guess they didn't care about me, either. I think we got what we wanted. Like a temporary partnership. And then went our own way."

She nodded. "Obviously, there was no pleasure in my past experience with the act. I never thought to want such a thing. But it's not the same at all."

"I think I understand. It's like eating a warm tart straight from the ovens and eating a slimy snail. They're both eating, but one brings joy and the other is disgusting."

She smiled that he understood so clearly what she was trying to say. "Yes. Just so." She blew out a slow breath and let the warmth of the moment comfort her. She'd never felt this way before. The throbbing in her core had settled, but she still felt the happiness of having Liam close.

"I'm sorry." He held her tighter to him. "I'm glad I get to be the warm tart, but I also wish I could take your pain away."

She nodded into the darkness. "You said that very thing when you were escorting me home and I broke down crying. Not the part about the tart, but how you wished you could take the pain away. You held me tight."

"I hope I didn't hurt ye."

"No. Even as tightly as you held me, I worried I still might fall apart into dust. There was a time I wished for it."

"What about now?" he asked, quietly.

"No. I have Gwennie now. And each new memory I make puts those other memories further out of reach. They still intrude from time to time, but not as much as when it was still fresh."

She felt him nod. "Liam, I enjoyed what we did, but Gwennie is the most important thing to me. I can't have her cast aside for a few moments of pleasure."

Liam stroked her hair and kissed her temple. "I can't be

sure because I've never been a parent before, but I believe that is the reason Kenna and Lach, and Cam and Mari run off to their rooms in the middle of the day when the children are napping. You don't have to choose just one thing. You can have everything, Ev."

"Everything," she repeated and thought she might be the luckiest woman in the world.

. . .

It wasn't the first time Liam lay next to his wife with a raging discomfort between his legs. In fact, it had become a nightly experience since their first kiss, but this time he managed to push the discomfort aside to enjoy what had happened between them.

They'd taken another step closer to being truly married.

He woke in much the same fashion as he'd gone to sleep. With a relentless cockstand and nothing to do for it. Had he still been alone, he might have seen to matters himself. But now he had a woman and a child getting ready for the day around the room. He managed to get up and dressed. Perhaps he might delay breakfast for a dip in the cold loch.

After kissing Ev last night—or rather her kissing him— and what happened after, Liam was more than happy to have things moving in that direction, but he grew concerned that he might not do things to her liking and worried he'd not be given another chance if he failed.

The concern had grown through the day until, putting his pride aside, he found himself walking up to Cameron's house that evening, hoping to ask for his assistance—knowing well the payment would be years of jests.

Still, he'd gladly pay if it meant taking care of his wife the way a husband ought. He rapped on the door twice and stepped away.

Mari opened it with a smile. "Liam, I'm so glad you're here. Would you mind helping me in the kitchen?"

"Of course, my lady," he said, earning a scowl.

"It's Mari to you, and you know it well."

He was always being scolded for his formal address, but it didn't make a difference. He still called her and Kenna ladies out of respect, as was their due.

She had him get down a number of things for her. "May I ask, how do these things get up here in the first place, you being too short to place them here?"

"My dear husband doesn't like me to work too hard and puts them beyond my reach to hinder me from doing so."

"Are you increasing?" he assumed. The MacKinlay men became even more protective of their wives when they were carrying.

She laughed. "Yes." Her smile faded. "But don't say anything to anyone. Only Cam knows. It's early. It's the scariest part."

"I'll keep your secret and wish you well." He frowned at the pot in his hand. "Mayhap I should put this back. I surely don't want Cameron to be angry with me when I've come to ask for his help."

"You'll do no such thing. I'll tell him I used sorcery to retrieve them. It wouldn't hurt for him to think I hold some great power." She winked to let Liam know she was teasing him.

"I assume he's not about?"

"No. He took the children to the stream to play and cool off."

"Ah. Very well. I'll return to speak to him another time."

"Are you having trouble with the men?" she asked holding out a meat pie for him and a mug of ale. It appeared he was staying for a bit.

"Nay. It's more of a personal matter. I wished to ask his

advice regarding my wife."

She laughed. "If you need advice regarding a woman, perhaps you should ask a woman."

"True enough, but I have only Cameron." He wiped his mouth and looked at her when she said nothing else.

Her hand rested on her hip. "I am a woman, am I not?"

"Oh! Aye. But I surely can't talk to you about… well, what I came to speak to Cam about."

"Physical relations, you mean?"

"Aye." He squeezed his eyes closed in embarrassment, feeling his ears heat.

"As we just confirmed, I'm increasing for the third time, so I can assure you I'm well familiar with physical relations between a man and his wife."

"Yes. I'm sure you are. It's just I don't think I can speak of them in front of ye." He looked around. "I can wait until Cam returns."

"The other reason Cameron took the children to the stream was in an effort to tire them out so we might have some time alone when he returns. I expect he'll send you on your way when he gets back without any assistance."

"Perhaps tomorrow then."

"Or you could ask what it is you wish to know and let me help. I'll not be scandalized. I'm married to Cameron. Surely, no man in the Highlands has a heartier appetite."

"But you're so small and delicate. He doesn't… isn't…"

"Rough with passion? Oh, I assure you he is at times, but at other times he's gentle and tender. There are many different ways to join with a partner. I can't imagine you don't know your way with a woman. Not with the way the maids in the hall flirt with ye."

Liam worried his ears would burst into flame, though he'd gladly welcome it to be free of this conversation. Unfortunately, there was no way out of it without offending

Cam's wife.

"It's true enough, I'm no virgin. But I think it's different being with one of the maids than to lie with my wife. Evelyn is skittish and has been hurt by men before. She won't welcome a quick romp against the wall behind the kitchen like the maids."

"I daresay the maids probably didn't appreciate it, either," Mari said.

He nodded in agreement. After giving Ev her pleasure the night before, it was clear the maids hadn't been served as well.

"That is true. I did have a few complaints for it being over too fast, but at the time I thought it was a kind thing to spare their back against the stones."

It was obvious Mari wanted to laugh and struggled not to let it out. She was a graceful lady. She cleared her throat and smoothed her skirt.

"Even still, you'll not want to be fast about it. Not that there isn't a time and place to be quick, but for your first time, and with Evelyn's past experiences, you'll not want it to be hurried. It will need to be slow and she'll need to be in control of it."

Liam gave that some thought and couldn't manage it in his mind. "I'm afraid I'm not sure how I'd do that."

"You may recall I was mistreated by my first husband."

Liam was aware she had killed him with a fireplace poker, and he hoped to avoid such a thing with Evelyn.

"Yes, the duke."

"It wasn't the same kind of mistreatment as your wife experienced, but with anything of the sort, it's about control. When it's been taken from you without permission it's a difficult thing to allow anyone to ever take it again."

Liam thought that through and nodded. "I understand."

"You can't truly. You're a big warrior. You have an

opportunity to fight where we do not. If a man forces us to do something, we can do little to stop him."

Liam nodded once more. "You weren't here when I was a lad, but even a few years ago I was nothing more than a wiry boy. I remember well enough what it was like being small."

"But the men you sparred with were friends. You trusted them. You knew they'd never truly harm you. Evelyn has been at the mercy of men without compassion. And while she knows you'll not harm her, the fear rises up when she's put in that position of being powerless."

"How do I give her the power?"

It was Mari's cheeks that flushed this time. She swallowed and looked away. "You should allow her to be on top, to guide the joining and the movements between you."

Liam envisioned it and then winced. "I'm not sure our parts would match up that way."

She looked up toward the ceiling and then to him. "You should lie on your back on the bed. Then she will straddle you. Like a horse but facing you."

"Oh. Oh! I see. That… That could work."

"It does." She looked toward the door. "Quite well."

"And she would like it? It would be…pleasurable for her?"

"Yes."

He needed to go. He was truly grateful for her help, but he wanted to flee as quickly as possible now that he'd gotten the information he needed.

"Liam, you'll want to see that she…" She took a deep breath. "My, this is more difficult than I thought it would be when I offered assistance." She fanned her face and took a sip of her drink before continuing. "You'll want to see that she has… *finished* before you finish."

"Yes, of course." He now knew what it was like to see a woman *finish*, and it would be his goal moving forward. "I should go now. Thank ye." He practically fell over the bench as he stood and turned for the door.

"I'm glad I could help."

Liam all but ran for his horse, but of course Cam chose that time to call his name. Liam turned to see the large man coming closer with Lizzy on his shoulders and had a memory of his father carrying him that way. He'd been frightened to be so high, but happy. His fingers clenched in the man's hair.

He started from the memory and closed his eyes trying to hold onto it, but that was all there was. Just that small thread. He couldn't even be sure the man had been his father. It was just a feeling.

A feeling that no longer mattered.

Chapter Sixteen

"Are you well?" Cam asked and Liam nodded and smiled back, letting the brief warmth of the memory drift away.

Aiden was in Cam's arms, asleep. Liam imagined how it must feel to be cared for like that. He pressed at the dim memories, trying again to remember who he might have belonged to, but it was no use. That fragment had been all, there wasn't enough to grasp onto.

Mari came out and took the children. She glanced at Liam and turned red again. He felt the flames licking at his neck.

When she was gone, Cam crossed his arms. "What was that about?" he asked, his brows creased.

"What was what?" Liam looked away.

"What did you do to my wife?"

"Nothing! I mean, we spoke on some things. Personal things I came to speak to ye about, but she offered and—Christ—I don't think I'll be able to look her in the eye the rest of my days."

Cam still looked angry but relaxed a bit. "What was it

you wanted to know?"

"Mari suggested I let Evelyn control things between us. In our bed."

Cam's eyes went wide in surprise. "You spoke to my wife of bedding?"

"As I said, I wanted to speak to *you* of it, but she insisted she could help. In truth, she did help a great bit. But I wasn't able to ask her the most important part, for I was afraid our embarrassment would be such that the house might burn down around us."

"What was the part you still want to know?" Cam's shoulders relaxed but his arms were still crossed.

"It's fine. I'll figure it out."

"Liam, you must be desperate if you took to relying on Mari for answers. Just have out with it."

"You'll make light of my situation."

"Probably. But do you want to know or not?" Cam grinned at him and smacked his shoulder.

Yes. He did want to know. "It's just, I may not have another opportunity with Ev if I don't do it right the first time. She's skittish and even if she's in control, I'm not sure she would care do it a second time if I do not give her reason to enjoy it. Do you ken what I'm saying?"

"Aye. You want to know how to please her."

"Very much so."

"I'm sure you have your own…ways of doing things."

"I do, but I'm certain they're not good enough. Mari pointed out how women don't like it to be over fast, and I may have been rather hasty."

"Christ almighty, you spoke to my wife of such things?"

"Nay. She spoke to me of them."

"Go slow," Cam barked.

"Aye. I got that part already." He definitely needed to apologize to a number of the maids for his error when he saw them again.

"When you do something, if she makes a good sound about it, do it again." Cam scratched his head and looked away. Were his cheeks turning pink?

Liam wouldn't have expected the big man to be embarrassed by anything. He might have laughed if he wasn't so bloody uncomfortable with the conversation.

"That...that makes a great deal of sense," he said.

"Once you're more comfortable with each other, you can ask her straight out what she likes and doesn't. Listen well when she tells you what pleases her and, by God, make sure ye do it."

"Aye. I will. Thank ye. And please thank Mari for me again." Liam mounted his horse and turned for the castle.

He would make sure tonight would be perfect.

. . .

Evelyn left her chamber with a smile on her face. She'd had a smile most of the day and when she glimpsed Liam in the bailey that afternoon, she felt her blood heat. Perhaps tonight he would allow more between them.

She still had plenty of worry over whether she'd see it through. What if she'd been right and joining with him wouldn't feel as good as his touch had the night before? She'd seen his length briefly when he'd changed his shirt and worried it would be too large.

She considered how such a thing might work as she headed toward the kitchen to help with the evening meal. Surely the women would give her plenty of things to ponder.

Before she made it to the door, she was stopped by one of the maids.

"I've a letter for ye, missus."

"For me? Who sent it?" Evelyn frowned at the parchment

as if it were a snake. Her heart beat fast. Was her father here?

"I'm not sure. I was in the village when a man came by offering a nice bit of clink if the letter was delivered to you. I have to return with a response to get the rest."

Evelyn frowned and flipped the missive over, noticing the Stewart seal was still intact. Her hands trembled as she opened it and began reading.

After his first letter demanding she return to Scalloway, Evelyn didn't know what she expected from this missive. Perhaps understanding. Maybe forgiveness for what she'd done. At the very least, she considered he'd disown her and have a few last grumblings of displeasure before he formally ended the relationship that might have remained between them.

She hadn't thought he'd offer her what she'd wanted in order to carry out the ruse as planned. Originally, he'd wanted her to play the innocent virgin for her intended, when in truth, she'd been forced to lie with five brutes, given birth, and was now married. The very idea was preposterous.

She'd always tried to be a good daughter, but where had that gotten her? She'd made one mistake and he couldn't see to forgive her. Instead, all he cared about was cattle.

Of course, she realized what cattle meant for her clan. Livestock was traded and thieved in the Highlands as currency. And her abandonment had cost her clan a great deal.

Which must have been why he was suggesting a compromise.

Dear daughter,

I realize now my plan to claim you a virgin will not do. If you come home and agree to marry the Morgan heir, I will allow you to keep the child with you. We can claim you a widow. And the child will serve as proof that you're able to bear offspring.

Return to Scalloway immediately and we'll put this insolence behind us. If you do not, I will have no choice but to come and retrieve you myself even if it means war with the MacKinlays.

Don't be a fool. The war chief you married will be forced to choose his clan over you.

Like the first letter, it wasn't signed with an endearment. Just his abrupt initials. She folded the letter and brushed a tear from her eye before it had the chance to fall. She knew what must be done.

She'd hoped for too much. Friends, a safe home, to watch her daughter grow up. To lie with her husband and feel as if the past didn't matter. She'd been a fool to think her father would give up so easily.

She had not yet atoned for whatever sin she was guilty of.

"Will you write back, ma'am?" the maid asked hopefully.

Evelyn offered a shaky smile. "I'll be a minute and I'll return with you to give my message in person."

"Oh, aye. I'll wait for ye here."

Evelyn nodded in agreement and went to say goodbye to Gwennie in case she didn't return.

・・・

"Does this look like a seal?" Liam held up a blob of wood for Angus's inspection when he led his horse into the stable.

"A seal?" the stable master grimaced. "Nay. It looks like a cock with a tail at the end."

"Bugger." Liam tossed it aside as the groom laughed. Liam wished he could see one of the blasted things again so he could get it right. "Gwennie asks me each day to make her a seal. I hate disappointing the lass."

"It's only a bit of wood." Angus shook his head.

It wasn't just a bit of wood. It was a chance to win a smile and a laugh from his new daughter. He let out a breath as he left the stable toward the hall.

He stopped when caught a glimpse of red-gold hair. His wife was leaving the bailey with a maid. She carried a bundle and he wondered what business she had in the village. Especially one that had her hurrying so with dark nearly upon them.

Rather than earn her ire for intruding, he held back and followed his wife from a distance.

His curiosity rose as she passed the shops that stood closer to the castle. Winding through the cottages, he watched. Finally at the far end of the homes she came to an abrupt stop. She paced a few steps and wiped at her cheeks.

He saw a man he'd never met standing at the edge of the woods with two horses. The man flipped a coin to the maid and the girl rushed off, a wide smile on her face.

What was this? Evelyn stepped away from the man, but he didn't respect the space she'd put between them. He grabbed her by the arm and pulled her toward the horses.

Liam heard the slightest whimper from his wife, followed by the rasp of metal as he drew his sword. What happened next he couldn't be certain as his vision had gone to a red haze. When he came back to himself, the man lay dead at his feet and Ev was sobbing in his arms.

"Who is he?" Liam's voice sounded icy in his ears.

"A Stewart."

"Your *father* sent him?" The word came out of Liam's mouth as a curse. The man had no right to such a title for how he treated his only daughter. Could he not leave her to peace? She was happy here. Or could be. It seemed the man didn't want her, but he wouldn't let her go.

"Aye. He-he..." She struggled to speak. "He has threatened war with the MacKinlays if I don't return immediately."

Liam didn't let go of her, worried she'd fall if he didn't hold her up.

"And you were just going to leave? Without so much as a word before you rode out?" He understood the power her father had over her. She'd not liked disappointing the man. She'd allowed him to send Gwennie to the village and forbid Ev from seeing her.

Liam couldn't blame her in that, for he knew well the power of wanting to please someone. He'd have done anything for the old laird and did. He never wanted the man to regret taking him in.

"I thought maybe if I went to him and explained, he'd let me go."

"And if he didn't let you go?"

She frowned. "It's not fair to make you choose between me and your clan. You're the war chief and it's your duty to protect your people. If I become a threat—I thought I could stop him before that happened. Before you were forced to make a decision."

"When I married ye, I promised I'd protect you. Do you remember my words?" he asked.

She nodded. "But I don't want to bring trouble to Dunardry. And I won't take Gwennie away from here. This is her home."

"She'll be cared for and happy because you will be here to see to it. This is your home as well. We'll find a way to settle Hugh Stewart and keep you here where ye belong. Do you trust me to do so?"

She looked up at him with red-rimmed eyes. "Liam..."

"You're my wife. I'll not give you up so easily."

"But the clan—"

"My laird will support us on this. He doesn't take kindly to other lairds taking his people by force."

"I shouldn't have married you. It was a mistake."

Liam felt like she'd run him through with a dagger. He'd known she hadn't wanted to marry him. She'd seen him as a way to get to be with her daughter. But he'd thought things had changed over the last few days. After what they'd shared and had planned to share that night.

But he saw now things hadn't changed at all.

...

It took Evelyn a few hours to calm down enough to write a response to her father. She'd started with begging, then anger, and finally resolve. In the end, it was no more than a few lines.

She still hadn't told Liam that her father had promised her to the Morgan heir. And she hadn't shared the letter the messenger had brought with her father's compromise to include Gwennie in the match. Liam assumed her father was just angry at their defiance. She was a coward.

As she'd said, she should not have married him. It had been a mistake to get him involved. She should have left with Gwennie on her own, long ago and gone somewhere her father wouldn't have found her. But the last time she'd gone away on her own she'd been captured by the McCurdys. She'd been afraid to leave the Stewart lands on her own again. But binding herself to Liam had given her father only more leverage to bend her to his will. Another person to be used against her.

For when the time came—if a war became unavoidable—she'd have no choice but to leave.

For now, Liam and the laird thought her father was a tyrant who didn't want to be defied, and for that they had bound to protect her. But what would they do if they found out another clan was involved? That she had been promised to another? Would they honor the arrangement and send her away? And what would become of Gwennie?

Liam sat across from her to scratch out his own correspondence, though he'd not spoken or allowed her to read it. She worried what trouble he might have instigated in his missive but was too exhausted to push the matter.

For her own letter, Evelyn had no choice but to keep hers simple. She settled on a stern and determined message.

Father,

I am Liam MacKinlay's wife and that I will stay. We are returning your horses, as I'm afraid your man is unable. If you have ever loved me, please leave us in peace.

Evelyn Grace Stewart MacKinlay

She didn't sign it as *daughter* for she was abandoning that privilege along with the duty. It seemed a mockery of what she'd once wanted that now she could only hope he would disown her.

There was no chance now for them to have anything more.

Liam agreed, reluctantly, to keep the situation between them and not tell the laird unless her father refused to give up. He left to have one of his younger warriors dispatched to deliver her message along with the horses.

She knew it would be weeks for her father to receive her missive and weeks longer for him to respond, but she did know a response would come. And she knew it wouldn't be pleasant.

She lay in the darkness waiting for Liam to return.

But he didn't come back to their chamber. Or her bed.

Chapter Seventeen

Liam was certain the matter with the Stewart laird was over this time.

After he'd seen to the slain Stewart's body, Liam had returned to the hall and found Ev struggling over a piece of blank parchment, Liam decided he had something to say as well.

He'd been direct with her father in his letter, stating that he and Ev were married before God and he wouldn't give her up. He also mentioned his disgust for the way the man had treated his only child.

To think he'd once felt inferior to Hugh Stewart as he'd begged the man for his daughter's hand. The laird was a disgrace and not worthy of the title.

If the man had written about missing Evelyn or how he wanted better things for her than a war chief, it might have struck a chord with Liam, but the man's hatefulness served only to make Liam more certain of his protection.

He'd never treat Gwennie that way. Liam understood children of lairds were often married in alliances to gain something, but Ev had been home for years and he'd not made such a match for her.

Liam couldn't help but think that making her live alone without a husband or her daughter was his way of punishing Ev for what happened with the McCurdy bastards. She'd more than paid the price for leaving the castle unprotected; she wasn't at fault for what happened after.

Liam might have written more, but there was the chance, given Liam's poor penmanship, that the man wouldn't be able to read it anyway.

After sending both letters and the horses on their way with one of his guards, he returned to the hall to sleep. He'd thought he'd covered ground with his wife and that she was beginning to welcome him as her husband. He tossed and turned on the floor as thoughts and visions tumbled through his mind, seeing that man grab Evelyn's arm. What would have happened if she'd gone with him to talk to her father?

When the sun had risen high enough, he knew he couldn't allow Gwennie to wake without a rabbit waiting for her. He also needed to speak to Evelyn.

"I'll ask that ye not leave the castle," Liam said quietly when Gwennie had gone to gather her bunnies. He was ready to put the matter behind them, but her safety was still an issue.

"If you think I would try to leave again—"

"No. I know you'll not leave Gwennie," he said, making it clear he understood Gwennie was the main reason she'd stayed.

"I'd not leave either of you," she said, surprising him.

He thought she considered him nothing more than a way to have what she wanted. They'd kissed and he'd given her pleasure, he'd thought she'd grown to care for him. But then she'd said marrying him had been a mistake.

"Last night you said you shouldn't have married me."

Her shoulders slumped. "I meant that I shouldn't have involved you in my troubles. You don't deserve this, Liam. It was a mistake to run away with you and bring my father's wrath to your gate."

He let that settle around him for a moment before he cleared his throat and went on.

"Your father will give up when he realizes he will only lose more men by trying to take you or Gwennie against your will. But until we're certain, I ask you to stay within the walls of the castle for your protection. Your father has already ordered them to kidnap Gwennie, and his man was going to take ye last night. Let's not allow another opportunity."

"Aye. I don't venture far from the castle anyway. In truth, I'm afraid of wandering about alone. As you know, it didn't do well for me the last time."

"I like to think you're safe here on our clan lands, but I know what happened to you here. And I'll not make promises I have no ability to keep."

"I understand."

"Do you?" he asked. "The other women don't listen well when it comes to their protection. They don't like to be ordered about by their husbands, and I can tell you from experience, when they get of the mind to disobey, it's near impossible to guard them. Slippery as eels the lot of them."

She smiled and rested her hand on his shoulder. "I promise to be less of a challenge."

"I canna think of losing ye," he said with more sincerity than he'd wanted to reveal.

"I will be a good wife and stay in the keep as you've asked."

"Thank you." He wanted to suggest they seal their promises with a kiss, but he bit the words down.

He'd be patient and wait for her. It felt as if he'd been waiting for her all his life.

•••

It had been days since that horrid night when the Stewart came bearing her father's message, and Liam had not done more than kiss her before they went to sleep each night. Evelyn might have worried he was no longer interested in her in that way if she hadn't felt the evidence of his interest pressed against her each morning when she woke in his arms.

After spending much of that morning in the kitchen listening to Kenna and the other women speak of their relations with their husbands, Evelyn felt hot and eager to see Liam again. She'd spotted him at the noon meal, but he'd turned and rushed away without saying much.

"Look at them playing," Mari said, her gaze on Lizzy and Gwennie laughing with her collection of rabbits. They'd moved to the solar in the afternoon to work on their sewing. "They get along so well. Would it be all right if Gwennie stayed with us tonight?"

"Oh. I…" She didn't want to offend the woman, but she didn't want her daughter out of her sight for that long. "It's just that it's not been so long that I've had her with me."

"I understand, but she will be safe. And a newly married couple should have some time alone."

Ev swallowed and nodded. At first, she had used Gwennie cowardly as a shield to keep her husband's affections at bay. Liam had been more than patient with her. He'd not once complained and hadn't pressed for more.

She both appreciated and was frustrated by his unyielding patience. She thought it would be better to have done with it. Then it wouldn't be such a huge thing between them.

It wasn't that she was afraid of him, for she knew well in her heart he would never abuse her. What she feared was that she'd be unable to lie with him without thinking of *them*. Liam didn't deserve that. But she didn't know if she would be strong enough to keep the nightmares from ruining what was growing between them.

She was the first to their room that evening. When he arrived, she was already dressed for bed with her hair braided over her shoulder.

He looked to the small bed as he hung his sword on the peg in the wall.

"Where's Gwennie?" he asked, fear clear in his blue eyes.

"Mari invited her to stay the night with Lizzy."

"She did?" He bit his bottom lip. "I see." With his gaze on her he tilted his head. "You allowed it?"

"I did, but to tell the truth, I've been struggling with not having her here. I know she's safe with Mari and Cam, but it worries me when she's not with me."

"Then I will go get her right now. I'll not have you fretting." He took up his weapons belt again, prepared to leave. For her.

"No, wait. Please. One of the reasons I allowed it was I thought it would be good for us to be alone tonight." Her voice wavered and she cleared her throat to cover her nervousness.

"*You* thought it was good? Or was it Mari or Kenna?" He lifted his brow, clearly suspecting the truth.

"It was Mari's suggestion, but she's right. A newly married couple should be alone at times."

He let out a deep breath and hung up his sword again. He came to sit on the bed as if he were heading for the gallows. He didn't appear eager for them to be alone and all that meant for them. He focused on his hands before speaking.

"I promised you I'd never force you into anything. And while I know I haven't pressured you physically, I fear you may be offering this only because it's expected. And maybe you feel that my patience is to be rewarded before I give up on ye. But I don't want you to lie with me because it's expected. Or because a certain amount of time has passed. Not because we've touched and you feel I'm not content with that, and especially not because Mari has told you it is the way things should be between us. When—if—we are to be together, it must be because it's right for us. And not before."

He rested his forehead against hers. "I want you so bad I ache with it, but it's been that way since I first met you. I'm quite used to it by now."

She licked her lips and nodded. "I have recently felt the ache of which you speak."

He smiled, that easy grin that made him look like a naughty boy. "I can ease the ache, as I have before, but leave the rest of it—the bedding—for another time." He kissed her softly. "Can you trust me to stop if you ask it?"

She nodded immediately. She might not trust her own body, but she trusted Liam's completely. He'd not harm her.

She swallowed and set him back so she could look into his eyes. "You'll show me how I might ease your ache as well."

"You needn't—"

"Am I your wife, Liam MacKinlay, or no?"

He grinned and nodded. "Aye. Though sometimes I'm sure I'm dreaming. If I am, I don't ever wish to wake up."

・・・

Liam thought himself a king when he was able to make Evelyn scream out in pleasure. She'd called his name when she reached her peak and he thought hearing it would end him as well.

With her lovely chest heaving, she slumped against him, her eyes closed. He assumed the offer of returning the favor was forgotten for the night. He didn't expect her to put her hands on him in that way. She owed him nothing.

But her eyelids flickered back open, and she stared at him as if she were not yet satisfied. He didn't see how that could be. He'd felt her body clasp his fingers and heard her breath catch. Perhaps she was quick to recover. He'd gladly spend the rest of the night seeing to her needs.

She kissed him and he kissed her back, pulling her on top of him so she could set the pace as Mari had suggested. She kissed his lips for some time before moving to his jaw and his neck. He enjoyed it but gasped when she nipped the skin above his collarbone.

"Vixen," he said with a smile and reached for her to return her mouth to his.

She held back and looked down at him. "Take off your shirt."

"Take off my—but then I would be naked."

She giggled. "Aye. I want to see you."

He looked at her, still in her night rail, though it was pulled up to her thighs and hanging off one shoulder low enough to expose her breast. He'd feasted on that bared nipple as well as the one still covered by fabric. Still, she hadn't been completely naked.

But who was he to withhold anything his wife wished? With a shrug, he sat up and tugged the garment off to toss it to the floor.

She wasn't subtle as she stared straight at his cock and gasped. Perhaps he shouldn't have thrown the shirt so far away. He reached for the blanket to cover himself, but she stopped him.

"No. I'm sorry. I was just surprised. I wasn't expecting it to be so..."

Rather than push when she remained silent, he took her hand and gave her fingers a squeeze. "This is the bastard that's been nudging you awake in the mornings."

She smiled slightly. "It's as if I should say, 'Pleasure to make your acquaintance.'"

Liam laughed. "When it's right, I'll make sure it is indeed

a pleasure."

When she reached out, he grabbed her hand. "You don't need to touch me. This is more than enough for tonight."

She brushed his hair back and smiled at him. "Lie back and let me do what I wish."

He thought perhaps this had been a bad idea. When her fingers stroked over his chest, across his stomach, and into the thatch of hair surrounding his manhood he couldn't help but hiss at the perfect torture of her touch.

Rather than touch him where he throbbed, her fingers glided lower to his thigh. At his knee, he was grateful she switched to his opposite leg and started back up his other side. But this time she lingered and softly, with one finger, touched his most eager flesh.

He nearly wept from the ache. He tensed, trying not to embarrass himself. He shouldn't have allowed his need to get this bad. He feared any attention from her would end him immediately.

He closed his eyes tightly in an attempt to rein in his desire. Wet warmth forced his eyes open.

"Bloody hell," he said as he sat up, pulling her away. "What are ye doing?" His voice, choked as it was, still held a bite of disapproval.

She blinked and her cheeks blazed. That stubborn chin jutted up as she spun away from him and shrugged her gown up, hiding her from him. He hadn't handled that well at all.

"I'm sorry," he was quick to say, as it was the most important thing. He was sorry for his reaction. Not just because he'd hurt her feelings, but also because it had felt incredible and she'd stopped.

He pulled her against him, allowing her to hide her face under his chin.

"I'm sorry," he repeated. "It was a great shock. I've never experienced such a thing. I thought…" He shook his head. "I thought it was done only by whores. I never expected a lady such as yourself would do such a thing."

"I'm not a lady, Liam."

"You were raised as one and I will always think of you in that respect."

"I'm sorry to have lowered myself in your opinion." From the snappish retort he could tell her apology was insincere and for good reason. "Heaven forbid I cast a shadow of impropriety on what you've intended all this time. I'd hate to ruin your expectations of Lady Evelyn Stewart by being myself."

He was an arse. He heaved out a breath and rolled her over so he could look down at her. When she tried to look away, he guided her back. It was important she see him.

"I've worried over this moment for some time. I've been so afraid I'd ruin it by being too eager and moving too quickly. I didn't want to ruin my one chance by not pleasuring you properly. It's weighed on me since I said my vows. And now here I am in disbelief of how horribly I've muddled it."

"I was quite pleased," she said. "I thought only to do the same for you."

"And that's where I went wrong. I thought it would be about you. I didn't think you'd want anything to do with me like that."

"Yes, you were wrong."

"I'm sure it will happen many times as we go on. I guess I'm wondering what happens next. Was that my one chance?"

"You thought things would be perfect between two strangers and if they went wrong that would be the end of it?"

"I hadn't thought to blunder it so badly."

She smiled then and he felt hope rise in his chest. "I'm sorry you didn't like it. The women in the kitchen made it seem like their men enjoyed it."

"Ev, I can hardly breathe when I think of seeing you with

your lips around me. It was the most exquisite pleasure I've felt in my life. I was startled and reacted poorly."

"So, I might try it again sometime?"

"Aye. I'd welcome it."

They lay there in silence for a few minutes. His fingers trailed through her hair. His cock lurched under the sheet, calling attention to itself.

To his surprise, he didn't move to hide it or feel embarrassed. Her words made him realize how much better the true Ev was from the one he'd created in his mind. She wanted him to accept her as herself, which meant he needed to be himself, even when he behaved like a dunderhead.

Perhaps the true Ev might come to like the true Liam. Maybe he didn't need to be perfect. Maybe he didn't have only one chance to earn her affections.

He took a deep breath, feeling the freedom of being himself with this woman. His cock lurched again. This time he cleared his throat. "I would not be opposed to trying again right now," he said, his heart seizing with panic. He bit his lip to keep from taking back the words.

To his relief Ev looked up at him with a crooked smile.

• • •

Evelyn felt empowered as she pleasured her husband, bringing him to a release that was under her control. She never thought physical relations could feel like this with a man.

Her past experiences had left her feeling the opposite. But this was so different, and they hadn't even completed the act.

Liam laughed through his gasps and held her close, kissing her hair and thanking her repeatedly. She felt like a queen being worshipped for pardoning a prisoner and smiled at the silly thought.

She'd done as she wished—she'd touched and explored the parts that made him a man and he'd enjoyed it. And the way he looked at her now was even more adoring than when he'd thought her to be a princess he was unworthy of. She felt closer to him, as if she knew something about him no one else in the world knew.

He certainly knew the secrets of her pleasures, but she knew his as well.

"In all the years you thought of us being man and wife, you never considered this?" she asked as she traced a fingertip around his nipple.

"No. I'm sorry to say my imaginings lack adventure."

"But this was better?" she asked, hating the nervous tremor in her voice. The power she'd felt was already fading back into insecurities.

"So much better. I'd love nothing more than to spend the rest of the night telling you all the ways you enchant me, Ev. But you've thoroughly drained me of my strength, and I fear I'm about to succumb to the sleep of the dead."

He laughed at himself, and she laughed, too.

"Alas, I'll have to make do with the general knowledge I have enchanted you."

"I will make up for it in the morning when I'm rested." He leaned over to kiss her before flopping back on his pillow.

He fulfilled his promise before dawn when the sky outside their window was no more than a pale gray. She woke to the shock of his mouth on her. What was the word he'd used? Enchanted?

Yes. She was indeed enchanted.

When she woke again later, it was full light and Liam was gone. Rather than leave their bed right away to get ready for the day, she took a few moments to settle in to the joy she'd experienced with her husband. She felt safe with what they'd done so far. Her chest tightened with worry when she thought of having a man lie on top of her.

The weight of him crushing the breath from her body, the burning pain…

The old panic returned, and she tried to calm her heart while pushing away the memories of foul breath and cruel laughter.

Tears welled in her eyes as she angrily got dressed. She hated that this nightmare had taken hold and pushed away the security she'd experienced earlier with her husband.

It wasn't fair that every joy was tainted by those men. They were dead, yet they still haunted her life, ruining her happiness. Even now, as she left their room, she couldn't remember the scent of Liam, instead recalling sour ale and sweat. Rather than go down to the hall, she turned and found her way to the battlements.

She huddled in a corner and wailed out her rage, allowing the wind to carry the sound and the pain away.

Chapter Eighteen

Liam was much too happy to spend his morning leading drills. Instead, he sent them off to do work in the village and he spent time in the bailey playing with the horde of children.

The MacKinlay men had created quite the brood over the last years. Four boys from Lachlan and Kenna, and a girl and boy from Cam and Mari. He loved hearing them laugh, especially when Gwennie joined in.

She'd been shy with the bigger lads at first, but she'd found her way, and now she followed them about. Sometimes too closely, which was the case when Douglas turned sharply and ran into the little girl, knocking her over and falling on top of her.

The lass made no sound at first and Liam felt as if his feet were weighed down, keeping him from reaching her fast enough. When he did, it was to get the first blast of her cries as she gripped onto him so tightly he couldn't even see where she was hurt.

"I'm sorry," Douglas said with wide eyes.

"It's fine, lad. I know you didna mean to do it." He mussed

the boy's hair. "Go quick and ask your mother to come help." With a nod, Douglas ran off.

Kenna knew about healing, though Liam didn't think there was much to be done for this injury. Still, if there was anything to help his daughter, Liam would surely try.

"Let's see what we have here. Och, your hands are a bit brushed up, and your dress is torn, but it will be well." He scooped her up to carry her over to the well. Removing a bit of cloth from his sporran, he made it wet to clean the blood from her hands. She let out another wail, but he continued on knowing it had to be done.

Liam picked up his dirk to cut the tattered piece of her dress away, and she cried even louder. He'd sooner pull his dirk and cut out his heart than have to cause her harm.

"Please, no." Her begging nearly did him in.

"It will be over soon enough," he promised, trying to be quick about it.

The next thing he saw were stars as he fell backward. Evelyn stood over him with a large stick screeching at him.

"Don't hurt her!" she screamed.

He blinked, trying to understand why she was so angry at him. Did she think he had hurt Gwennie?

He took in the scene before him. Gwennie sobbing, blood on her palms, and Liam holding onto her with his dirk in his hand. He realized then what it looked like to Evelyn. That he was threatening their daughter with his knife.

Stumbling away, he dropped the cloth. He had been trying to help, but Evelyn obviously thought he had caused her injuries. He would have thought she knew him better than that, but of course, she would have jumped to this conclusion given what she'd seen.

Still, it hurt him to think she didn't give him the benefit of the doubt. He'd made strides to earn her trust, but she had jumped to the wrong conclusion. Rather than make things worse, he left through the gates and kept walking.

• • •

Gwennie was crying so hard, Evelyn put her down to look her over. She saw the blood on her daughter's dress and began to shake uncontrollably. "I'm so sorry."

Kenna rushed up with a distressed Douglas. "I'm sorry. I didn't mean to fall on her," the little boy said. "Will she be all right, Mama? She's crying so."

"She'll be fine, Douglas," Kenna said. "You know how a scrape can burn for a bit. I'll put something on it straightaway."

It wasn't until Kenna pulled up Gwennie's dress that Evelyn saw her bloodied knee. "Oh, God," she gasped. Douglas's words repeated in her mind. Gwennie had fallen.

"Calm yourself," Kenna whispered. "If you act like it's nothing, they'll go along with it most times. They follow our lead."

Evelyn slumped to the ground, covering her face with her hands.

"What is it? Are you one to swoon when ye see blood?" Kenna asked patiently.

Ev shook her head. "I stepped into the bailey to see Gwennie crying, and Liam was… There was blood, and he was holding his dirk. I thought…I… All I could think of was Sheamus and the day his father was hurting him."

Kenna looked at her, confused. Of course, she wouldn't understand, because she knew Liam well enough to know it was beyond reason for him to hurt a child in any way.

It took Kenna a few moments to comprehend. "Liam? Never."

It was then that Mari came up, carrying Aiden and holding Lizzy's hand. Gwennie was instantly healed of her earlier injury and asked to go play with her friend once more.

"What's wrong with Liam?" Mari asked over her shoulder. "I just passed him and he looked miserable. Are you and Gwennie well?"

Evelyn covered her face with her hand. "I've made a terrible mistake. I need to go see him. Would you watch—?"

"Of course. She'll be fine with us," Kenna said before Evelyn had the chance to even ask. With her daughter taken care of, Evelyn hurried to catch up to Liam.

His long legs had carried him quickly away, but Evelyn caught a glimpse of him at the edge of the forest and hurried in his direction.

She was out of breath as she continued to follow him along the loch to the stream. Finally, he stopped. He hadn't seen her when he screamed into the air, "What have I done? When will I have paid enough for whatever sin I committed?"

Evelyn stopped in her tracks when he pulled his sword and slashed through some nearby branches before striking a tree. The blade stuck fast, and he slumped to the ground, his back against the bark.

She delayed for only a moment before going to him. When he spotted her, he shook his head. "You thought I would hurt a child? Please, just leave me alone."

Part of her wanted to do just that, but she'd done him a horrible wrong and needed to make it right, if there was a way to do such a thing. She had to try.

"I must apologize. I made a dreadful mistake."

He shook his head. "It was I who made the mistake. I thought myself in love with you from the moment I met you. I was a foolish boy at the time. Then last night, I thought I knew better what it was like. Not just the way we brought each other pleasure but talking with you. Getting to know the real you."

He tried to free the blade and kicked at the sword when it wouldn't relent.

"I realize now I couldn't have loved you, because I don't know you. And you can't love me because you surely don't know me if you think I could do such a thing..."

He waved toward the castle.

"I wanted a family of my own so badly I didn't stop to think we are really just strangers. But you have to know, I'd never... Ev, I swear it."

She didn't want him to think she doubted him for a minute longer than necessary. As he'd said, she might not know him, but she knew he wasn't capable of hurting a child. Especially one he thought of as his own. How could she even apologize for thinking it? She had to try.

"Liam." Her voice cracked with tears. "I must beg you to forgive me. Of course, I know in my heart you'd never hurt Gwennie." She shook her head. "I would have known better if I'd waited a moment to think. I just reacted."

He nodded. "It seems being a parent is as difficult as being a husband. When I dreamed of this, it was much easier." He laughed, a sad sound that tugged at her.

"Do you remember last night when you said you were sure to make blunders. I'll make them too. We both will, but I think it might be easier if we allow ourselves the freedom to do so while knowing the other person will still be there."

"You believe that I'd never hurt Gwennie?"

"Of course I do. Do you believe I know you would never hurt her?"

He nodded, but he didn't offer the smile that assured her everything was well with them.

She walked up, grabbed his shoulders, and stood on her tiptoes to kiss him. He didn't respond at first, but she refused to give up. She needed them to get back to even footing. They'd come so far; she was ready for more.

She clenched her fingers in his silky hair and pulled his mouth closer so she could slip her tongue in his mouth.

When he finally kissed her back, it wasn't as gentle as his past kisses. A hint of frustration and hurt still lurked in the way his tongue did battle with hers.

Without overthinking, she let her hands drop to his shoulders, down his chest to his belt. With trembling fingers, she worked his weapons belt loose and then the belt securing his plaid.

He gasped when it fell to his feet. "What are you—?"

She cut him off with another kiss as she reached for her gown to loosen it.

"We agreed we'd be there for each other no matter what, yes?"

"Yes, but surely you don't want me now. Not like this." He looked around the clearing.

"Let's be there for each other, Liam. In every way." She placed his palm on her breast and he pulled it away. He dropped his head, resting his forehead against hers.

"I'm not strong, Ev. I want you too much, but you should go before we do something you'll regret. I can't bear to have you hate me. You don't need to give yourself to me to prove anything to me. Your accusations hurt, but I'll be fine. We're fine."

She shook her head. "You were wrong when you said I didn't know you. I do know what kind of man you are. You deserve better than someone who's already been used. But I want you. I've wanted you at night when you lie next to me. I wanted you last night. I'm afraid I might not be able to tolerate it. I don't want to disappoint you, but please let us try."

"Anything you give freely would never be a disappointment."

"Then take me, Liam, for no other reason than we belong together like this." She kissed him again and he eagerly responded. His one hand rested on her hip while the other went to the small of her back, pulling her closer to him.

Evelyn made a small sound of enjoyment which seemed to light something in her husband. She had won him over, and joy rose in her heart.

He backed away to tug off his boots. Unfolding his plaid, he laid it out at their bare feet.

She shimmied her gown off to stand before him in just her shift. The sun was glowing behind her, no doubt outlining her body through the thin fabric, but she didn't attempt to hide from his gaze. Even when her nipples hardened and her legs trembled.

He pulled his shirt over his head and stood in front of her naked. He was beautiful. She caught herself before using that word, thinking he might not like it. Instead, she said, "I'm pleased just to look at you."

Here in the light of day he was even more magnificent than he'd been in their room.

He smiled, the Liam she married with the dimple and easy way about him. "I hope you might be even more pleased to touch me."

She laughed and nodded. "Indeed." She reached out to touch his bare chest and allowed her fingertips to slide over his smooth skin. Over the ridges of his stomach to pause in the soft patch of darker blond hair that surrounded his cock.

"I've never looked on a naked man before you," she shared. He tilted his head to the side as if he wanted to ask but didn't speak. She was glad she didn't have to explain that the men who'd harmed her never did more than tug up their kilts. Not that she would have looked at them with appreciation anyway.

Liam took her hand and kissed her palm. "You're tense,

and I fear your mind has gone off and left me here."

She offered a strained smile and a small nod. "I'm sorry."

"I expected it wouldn't be easy for us at first. The act is sure to conjure memories that I'd rather not be between us. But I'll not blame you for it."

"I trust you. I don't want to be afraid any longer. Please don't give up on me."

He brushed the back of his hand over her cheek. "Never. Now that I know there's something between us to hold on to, we'll make this something for just us. Keep your eyes on mine so you know it's me who holds you."

She nodded in agreement. As long as it was Liam, she could continue. She wanted to continue. Her lower body fluttered in a delicious feeling.

He reached for her shift and lifted it over her head. She fought the urge to cover herself but gave up, knowing it wasn't necessary. Not with Liam. Not like this. He'd seen much of her already. Now he could see everything, and she didn't mind.

He smiled as he looked her up and down. "I've never looked on a naked woman before," he confessed, his cheeks turning pink.

She didn't need to know the reason he hadn't. She knew he wasn't a virgin.

"So beautiful," he said as he went to his knees before her. From his position he was not as intimidating. Even when he guided her closer and pressed kisses to her breasts and then moved lower.

She nearly collapsed when his mouth touched her upper thigh. He took advantage of her swaying to bring her down beside him. He caressed her until she opened for him, never pushing or demanding. He kissed her intimately as she watched. This was Liam. This was good.

No, it was magnificent, especially when he used his

mouth and fingers on her. She cried out his name, unsure if she would be able to hold on.

When he told her to let go, she gave in and allowed the incredible feeling to rise up and wash over her. She thought she might melt away, but he gathered her to him. Keeping her close, he kissed her temple and then her lips. He tasted different than he had before, and she realized it was herself she tasted on his lips.

"Was it good?" he asked, watching her as she attempted to blink him into focus. Everything seemed so hazy and wonderful.

"Beyond good."

He smiled and she allowed him the smug tilt of his lips. He'd earned the right.

She wouldn't have thought it possible that she would feel unfulfilled so quickly after the satisfaction he'd given her, but after a few breathtaking kisses, she wanted more. She told him so and he nodded.

Instead of coming over her, he rolled on his back, and she straddled his hips. His manhood came to settle between her thighs, brushing her heat.

"I'm not sure—"

"I've not done it this way before, either, but let's try it. I can look on you and you can control our joining when you feel you're ready."

She felt tears sting her eyes again, though they were happy tears. This man, large and powerful as he was, had the softest, kindest heart to think of a way to accommodate her needs.

"I'm a very fortunate wife," she said and earned another adorable blush from her husband. He glanced away but she placed a hand on his cheek and turned him back to her. "Keep your eyes on mine so you know who holds you," she repeated his earlier words.

He offered a grin and pulled her down for a kiss. The movement changed their position so he was poised perfectly to enter her. She expected him to thrust up, but he didn't. He stayed where he was and allowed her to slide down his length. She expected pain, but there was none. Her body—now slick with need—welcomed him in the most enjoyable way.

A moan of pleasure escaped her lips.

His eyes squeezed shut for just a moment as he moaned, too. Then they opened and he gazed at her patiently, the normal icy blue of his eyes now darker and warmer. His fingers lightly stroked her ribs and down her hips.

Once she was fully settled on him, she used her legs to rise and lower, much like riding a horse. Though the way he filled her was exquisite. She found herself moving more quickly.

Liam stilled her movements and watched her. "I don't want it to end."

She nodded. She didn't want it to end, either.

Chapter Nineteen

Liam stared up at his naked wife, with sunshine streaming through her gold-red hair. She looked like a goddess on the hunt for something only he could give her.

He'd never realized it could be like this. He'd thought he'd not be capable of going slow. In the past, the urge had overpowered him, and he'd given in to it without a thought. But being with Evelyn was a different experience entirely.

It was all about her. He wanted to give her pleasure. He wanted to see her break apart at his touch even more than he wanted to find his own release.

His own need was certainly there. Her warmth called to him to go deeper and take, but he didn't allow it to overpower him. He settled against the coolness of the earth seeping through his plaid and focused on the way her fiery skin felt under his calloused fingertips. He listened to the sounds she made, accompanied by the birds singing high above them. He twined their fingers together when her breathing became ragged.

She was close again, and this time he wanted to join her

when she reached her peak of pleasure. He didn't slow her this time, instead moving his hips slightly to greet hers with each thrust.

Like the other times, it was his name she called out, her voice echoing in the trees around them until they were nothing more than a buzz as he poured his seed into her.

She collapsed on him in a pile of warm woman and soft skin, and he had just enough strength to reach up and wrap her in his arms.

The sun had moved quite a distance in the time they lay there. She'd shifted to his side while he had dozed to some place beyond this world where peace surrounded him. He'd never known such joy.

He tilted his head to look at his wife. When their gazes met, she smiled at him. This was how he thought it'd be between them, the way he'd imagined. Her hair was tumbled from its usually neat twist, and a rock jabbed him in the hip.

This was real and all the more powerful because of the minor discomforts.

He reached out and touched the corners of her lips where they pulled up. He'd known his wife was beautiful, but when she smiled after being loved, she glowed.

"Are you well?" he asked, wanting to make sure she felt as content as he. She nodded, though her dark gaze glanced away, and the smile fell a bit under his fingertips. Some of the glow faded.

"What is it?" he asked, hating whatever had cast a shadow over this moment.

"Nothing is wrong, truly. I just..." She shook her head slightly. "I know it does no good to wish, but still, I wish I'd been a maiden. You deserved a chaste wife, not one who—"

He pressed his fingers to the center of her lips to stop her words.

"I don't want them here with us. Don't let them take this

from us. You are mine. Whatever happened before is gone."

She nodded. "This is so different. It's easy enough to keep the thoughts away. I thought only that it might have been better for you."

He laughed then and fell back to his plaid. "*Better?* Nothing could have been better than this."

He rolled to his side, ignoring the stone, and kissed her. He meant it to be reassuring, but feeling her nipples harden against his bare chest had him deepening the kiss until her fingers were tangled in his hair.

Both on their sides, he hitched her knee up to his hip and pushed closer.

She gasped, her eyes opening. He smiled. "I'm glad you're not a virgin, for it means I don't have to worry about taking you again." He pressed against her heat and waited for her reaction.

Her face didn't give him a sign either way if she wanted this or didn't. But then she angled closer, taking him in.

His breath left in a rush, and he grasped her hip to join them more securely. Her warmth surrounded him and, while he should have been able to make it last longer the second time, he already felt his body urging him toward release.

"You're perfect, Evelyn," he whispered so she'd know he wanted for nothing when it came to her.

A tear rolled down her cheek. He might have worried over it except she was still smiling at him. He thought perhaps she was just overcome by the moment. He kissed the moisture away as they found their way to the edge of passion. Together, as it should be.

• • •

It was late when Evelyn entered the hall behind Liam. He held up his hand and peeked around the door before motioning her to be quiet.

"Just a few warriors sleeping on the benches. Let's go."

She nodded and squeezed his large hand in her smaller one. She didn't want them to be seen sneaking back into the keep at this hour, especially with her hair a mess and their clothing rumpled, but they'd been so hungry after their afternoon of napping and making love. She would not be able to sleep the rest of the night over the growls of her stomach. Or his.

It may have been such a noise that alerted a few of the men as they walked between the tables.

"I imagine we'll have a late start on drills tomorrow, lads," one of the men said with a hearty laugh.

"Congratulations, chief," another said. "She looks well loved."

Evelyn's cheeks heated and she was glad for the dim light as Liam ignored them and proceeded toward the kitchen.

Inside, he went about searching, making it clear this wasn't the first time he'd done so when no one was around. Lifting a linen, he made a happy sound and held out a meat pie.

It was the best thing she'd ever eaten. Or perhaps it seemed so because it was seasoned with her hunger. He handed over a mug of ale and she drank deeply before handing it back to continue her attack on the pastry. She noticed Liam was finishing his second one and reaching for a third. She couldn't help but laugh.

"What's so funny?" he said with a big smile. "This is your fault. Ye made me ravenous with all the loving ye demanded from me."

She knew he was teasing her but couldn't help feign insult. "And why would you be weary from today's activities when it was I who did the work?"

"Minx," he growled and leaned down to kiss her with a

few crumbs on his lips. "I could almost have you work me over again, but I fear I'll not be able to carry myself to bed when you're done with me."

"Best then to wait until we're in our room," she teased. "We wouldn't want the maids to find us in the morning."

He nipped her lip gently with his teeth. "Then let's be on our way."

Grabbing two more meat pies and a jug of ale, he followed her out of the kitchen. She didn't even mind the comments as they made their way through the hall again. All that mattered was getting upstairs with Liam. They paused at the solar, which served as a nursery at night, and she smiled when she spotted Gwennie sleeping next to wee Cameron.

"She's safe for the night," Liam whispered next to her. "But you're not." With that he swept her off her feet and carried her off to their room. She managed to hold in her laughter until they were behind the thick door to their chamber.

Even then her giggles were cut off by his lips on hers. "I can't get enough of you, Ev. Tomorrow I'll see you armed with a sharp stick to keep me away."

"I have no wish to keep you away, so it'd be a waste of your time searching for a stick when your time could be used in better ways."

She couldn't believe how easy it was to tease him, the wanton words encouraged by a wide grin from her husband.

"If you change your mind, you'll let me know." It wasn't a question, but she heard the concern in his voice. He'd thought her fragile for what had happened to her. And for a long time, she thought it, too.

But being with Liam in this way made her feel powerful. She'd faced down her demons. She'd known the men who'd hurt her were long dead, but their memory had haunted her for so long. She'd never thought to have this with a man. Any time she considered such a thing those old ghosts would come back to steal away her joy.

She was finally free. As Liam touched her, she thought perhaps they were vanquished once and for all.

When morning came a few hours later, Evelyn rose to get Gwennie. When they returned to their chamber, Liam had woken and was securing his kilt. As was their normal routine, Gwennie ran to him, holding up her bunnies so he could make them bounce on her shoulders and head while telling some outlandish story. The adventures these wooden rabbits had to tell boggled Evelyn's mind. Liam was quite the creative storyteller.

But this morning, Liam didn't scoop Gwennie into his arms and tickle her until she giggled. He didn't hold her upside down, stealing Evelyn's breath. In fact, he didn't really even look at the little girl who hopped around at his legs.

"I must be off. Mama will tell you the story this morning," he said, his brows pulled together. Evelyn didn't think he was angry, but he wasn't his usual cheerful self. He placed a kiss on his fingers and touched them to Gwennie's head before going to the door.

That was not their normal farewell. Generally, he gave Gwennie a big smacking kiss on the cheek and then made her laugh by tickling her with his morning growth of whiskers.

Evelyn saw the disappointment in Gwennie's eyes as she watched Liam leave.

"I'll see you both at the noon meal." And he was gone.

After getting Gwennie ready for the day, they went down to break their fast. Mari and Kenna waved Evelyn over with big smiles.

"You were not back in the castle before it was time to put Gwendolyn to bed," Mari said, though, being a lady, she wouldn't come straight out and ask.

Her younger sister had no such issues. "He's put a flush

in your cheeks. Did you have a pleasant time?" Kenna waited expectantly while Mari rolled her eyes.

"You must be careful, sister. You'll scare off another of our dear friends."

Kenna gave Mari a light smack on the shoulder. "It wasn't me."

They all laughed. Ev knew they spoke of Dorie MacKinlay, who was raised with the McCurdy clan though she wasn't one. Her husband was made laird and they ruled Baehaven. The sisters missed their friend and mentioned her often.

"We had a fine day," Evelyn answered, thinking that would be the end of the questions. She'd been wrong about that. Kenna teased details out of Evelyn she'd had no intention of sharing.

Despite his promise, Evelyn didn't see Liam at the noon meal, but she didn't think it was him staying away as much as that all the men had been summoned to Cameron and Mari's place to help. Their home was nearly completed, which was good, since they would need the room at the rate their family was growing.

Evelyn let her hand brush over her stomach wondering if she and Liam would have an addition to their family as well. How different it would be to be increasing with Liam's child. As much as she loved Gwennie now, she'd had no love for the babe she'd carried.

She often had nightmares that the child was a monster trying to crawl out of her womb on its own with large claws and sharp teeth. Of course, her daughter was born a dark-haired angel and Evelyn had no choice but to allow her into her heart.

Could she have another child with white-blond hair and startling blue eyes to love in mere months? A smile grew on her lips at the thought.

It took Evelyn a few days to admit something was seriously wrong with her husband. The first day Liam had run out without playing with Gwennie could be excused as him being in a hurry to have his breakfast before starting drills with his men.

That night, she'd easily brushed it off as exhaustion, since he'd worked the whole day.

The next morning, he rushed off again with no more than a brush of a kiss on Gwennie's forehead. And the next morning it was the same. Later that afternoon Evelyn found him in the bailey with the children gathered around, begging him to play with them. Instead of chasing them as he normally would have, he ducked away and hurried off to the stables.

"I'm afraid Liam doesn't care for my daughter as much as he let on," she practically blurted when she returned to the solar with the ladies. Both women stared at her as if she'd sprouted a second head.

"Liam loves all children. He'd never stop caring for her," Mari said.

Kenna replied as well. "It's clear he sees the lass as his own. Why would you think such a thing?"

Evelyn knew it was silly to think he no longer cared for Gwennie.

"Maybe he's afraid you think he would hurt her," Kenna said. "After your reaction the other day, he might want to make sure you don't think such a thing of him again."

Evelyn rubbed her forehead. "That must be it. He's not touched her since I overreacted that day. But he knows I don't think such a thing." She remembered the sight of her daughter watching Liam walk away from her that morning. "What have I done?"

"I'm sure he'll come around," Mari said, but there was no proof to back up her assumption.

"What if I've ruined things between them forever?

Gwennie loves him and I know he loves her too. I've hurt him deeply."

"Mothers are protective," Kenna said. "No one blames you for it."

"I knew better. I reacted before thinking it through. What am I going to do?"

Kenna's brows pulled together for a moment before her eyes went wide and she held up her index finger. "I have an idea."

"You should know my sister's ideas usually end in disaster," Mari said.

"Not *every* time," Kenna defended.

After seeing the pain on Liam and Gwennie's faces, Evelyn felt the situation was already a disaster. She at least needed to try to fix it.

Chapter Twenty

After bathing in the loch and letting the sun dry him, Liam went to the hall for the evening meal. He was looking forward to seeing his family. The thought welled in his chest for a moment before the sadness of the situation crept in.

He'd not be able to hold Gwennie or play with her. He wouldn't risk his wife worrying he was too rough or dangerous to play with her daughter. He'd never given it a thought before, but now when he was near the lass, he was careful not to do anything that could be confused. And the little girl didn't need him anyway. She had her mother. Liam would see Gwennie was provided for. That was the extent of his duties, though it went against his way not to play with a child.

He loved bairns. The way they needed little encouragement to laugh and squeal.

He looked around the hall and gasped when his gaze fell on his wife with her arm tied in a sling. He practically leaped over the tables between them to get to her. "What's happened?"

She glanced away. "I'm fine. I tripped on the stairs. Kenna said it's broken and that I'm not to lift anything for a few weeks."

"Should you be in bed, resting?" he asked, trying to care for his wife as a husband should.

Things happened to wives. He knew well enough the pain Bryce had felt for losing his first wife and child. Liam wouldn't have been able to bear it.

"I'm not in much pain. It's just...well, I'll need help. I can't lift Gwennie."

"Of course," he said quickly as he reached down for the little girl. She reached up to him, a bright smile on her face and he backed away. "Oh. Uh..." He looked around the room for the nurse or anyone else. "Mayhap..."

"Up," Gwennie demanded, still holding her arms toward him. He lifted her and smiled when she settled in with her head on his shoulder. She was heavy with sleepiness and would be out in no time.

He pressed a kiss to her hair. How much he'd missed her these last days. She held up the wooden rabbit fisted in her small hand, and he kissed the bunny as well, as was the way they did things.

"She's had a busy day trying to keep up with the lads," Ev said.

Liam laughed. "It won't be long before the lads are chasing her. They'll have to get through me first," he said protectively.

"I do not doubt it."

He held the sleeping girl as they ate their meal, then carried her to the solar where Andrew was already sleeping with a nurse on duty.

Evelyn had said Gwennie would be fine in their room, but he didn't want to risk Gwennie climbing into their bed and causing further injury. The nurse would see to her for the evening.

The woman moved to take Gwennie, but Liam shook his head and carried her to the small bed she used when she stayed here with the other children. He tucked her in and took the rabbit to set it on the small table between the beds. "Sweet dreams, love."

When he turned, he saw Ev watching from the doorway with a smile.

"She's exhausted."

"Perhaps we could go to bed early as well," she suggested.

"Of course. Your arm must pain you." He frowned as he led her to their room. He helped her with her gown and settled her in their bed. "Perhaps I should stay in the hall so not to bump it while you sleep."

"I'm sure that's not necessary." She patted the mattress next to her in invitation, but he held firm.

"I don't want to cause you more damage."

"But it doesn't hurt at all. In fact, I'm certain it's not really broken. I'll probably be fine by tomorrow."

"Kenna is a healer. She's not often wrong when it comes to these things. I'd prefer you be careful. Broken bones are a serious matter."

Liam sat on the edge of the bed and bent to kiss her. It was meant to be a soft, sweet kiss, but like most times when their lips met, it spiraled into something more heated. When he pulled away from her, he frowned again at her arm.

He'd not be able to make love to her like this. With another quick kiss, he moved to the door. "Rest well. I'll check on you in the morning first thing."

As he settled in on a bench in the hall, and the men had quieted from giving him grief for being kicked out of his bed, Liam stared up at the high ceiling above him. He remembered all the years he'd lay in this room sending wishes and dreams up to the stones above him.

Tonight, he didn't have to dream of his family to come claim him, for he knew where they were. He didn't need to wish for love, for he felt it growing in his heart for his wife and daughter.

No. Tonight he prayed that his wife would heal quickly. And even hoped that for once in her life, Kenna MacKinlay was wrong.

. . .

"You were wrong," Evelyn accused Kenna the next morning when she found the woman in the solar.

"How so?"

"This is a disaster," Evelyn tugged off the splint supporting her fake injury.

Mari leaned forward. "May I just mention, I warned you of such possibilities."

"Hush," Kenna waved Mari's words away. "It was the perfect plan. I saw him holding and playing with Gwennie while you ate your dinner. It worked splendidly."

"He cut up my food and fed me," Evelyn said, flatly.

"He was attentive. That's not such a bad thing for a husband to be."

"Except my husband is so worried he'll make my injury worse he won't sleep with me or touch me."

"Oh." Kenna winced. "I hadn't anticipated that."

In truth, Evelyn was angrier with herself than with Kenna. The woman had tried only to help. Evelyn shouldn't have attempted to mislead Liam.

"I should have just spoken to him directly." Evelyn let her head fall into her hands. She hadn't realized what a coward she was until she'd started navigating a marriage.

"Aye. A direct approach is usually the most successful," Kenna agreed. "I'm sorry I didn't suggest it."

Evelyn shook her head. "In truth, it might be better this way. Liam wants a family to love. It's a simple enough wish, and he deserves to see it fulfilled more than any person I've ever known."

"It seems an easy thing," Mari said. "Which means there must be something complex keeping it from happening."

Evelyn nodded. "I promised my daughter I'd always be there for her, and then my father forced me to break my vow by sending her to stay with someone in the village so no one in our clan would know she was my child."

Kenna gasped and set a kind hand on Evelyn's shoulder. "I can't imagine such a thing."

"When I had the chance to run away with Liam and take her, I renewed my promise that Gwennie would be my priority. I never wanted her to feel I didn't love her." She took a breath. "But already I've left her with others so I could be with Liam. Last night when he didn't come to our bed, I realized how much I'd been distracted by him. I can't be distracted. I'm a mother."

Kenna sat up straighter and she and Mari exchanged a look of surprise. "Do you think us bad mothers because we leave our children in the nursery at times to be with our husbands?"

"Of course not. I've seen you both with your children and know how much you love them."

Mari nodded. "We do love them very much. They are our hearts and souls. But our husbands are as well. One day, sooner than we think, and with the Lord's blessings, our children will grow and move on with their own lives and we will have but our husbands for comfort. Having a close bond with our children is important, but not more or less so than the bond we have with our men."

Kenna nodded in agreement. "Mari and I understand your fears. Our father was obsessed with our stepmother's happiness over that of our own. But I've come to realize my heart is capable of loving everyone within its grasp. My children don't suffer because I'm smitten with my husband."

"You can have it all," Mari said with a sly smile. "And I hope that you do."

Evelyn looked over at her daughter playing with the other children and knew she was in no danger of ignoring Gwennie. She knew equally well Liam would not dismiss his responsibilities to their daughter.

She needed to make things right with her husband if there was any chance of *having it all*.

"Might I leave my daughter with you again so I can take care of matters with my husband?" she asked.

Kenna smiled. "We wives are always happy to help one another. How do ye think there came to be so many children to look after in the first place?"

Chapter Twenty-One

When Liam didn't see Evelyn in the hall for the evening meal, he worried nearly to the point of panic. Kenna was quick to tell him his wife was fine and wanted to see him in their chamber.

Thinking she may be resting, he took their food with him. She'd seemed distraught the night before when he'd fed her in the hall in front of everyone. Perhaps she didn't like the attention. Liam hadn't minded. It was what was done. Families cared for one another. Or at least that's what he'd seen. He was excited to put the rule into practice with his own family and care for them.

He tapped on the door before entering. To his surprise, Ev was sitting on the edge of the bed. The splint was gone, and her eyes held worry.

He set the tray down and came to sit next to her. "Kenna said you should wear the splint for a few weeks, so your arm heals properly."

Ev frowned as tears glistened in her eyes. She must be in so much pain.

"Do you need willow bark tea?" he asked. "It tastes like the devil's piss, but it helps with the pain. I'll get you some." He stood and went for the door, but she stopped him. Grasping his hand firmly with the arm that was broken.

Perhaps Kenna had been wrong, and it wasn't as bad as she'd thought.

"I'm so sorry, Liam. I lied. I didn't fall. I didn't injure my arm at all."

He stared at her in surprise. He'd known women to act the damsel to get attention, but he didn't think it of Evelyn.

"Why would you do this?" he asked as he sat next to her again. She must have a good reason. His wife wasn't given to unnecessary drama.

She released her grasp to focus on folding and unfolding a section of her dress. The silence went on for a few more breaths before she finally looked up at him briefly.

"I ruined things with you and Gwennie with my ridiculous accusation. You're so good with her, and I made you wary of loving her and being a father to her. I regretted it immediately. And instead of talking with you about it like I should have, I concocted a story to force you into holding Gwennie again. I did it in the hope you would go back to caring for her the way you had before I spoiled things."

"I see." He thought over the situation. "I thought you'd be more comfortable if I kept my distance from her, then you could be certain I wasn't a danger to her. Perhaps I should have spoken to you of my thoughts as well."

"I know you're not a danger to her or any other child. I know it with all my heart. I should have encouraged your relationship, for it's a rare blessing to have a man like you. One who would treat my daughter as if she were his own blood."

He laughed. "I would be the worst kind of hypocrite to not accept her when I don't know whose blood runs in my body. When I married you, Gwennie became my daughter."

"Some might think your responsibility ends with protecting and seeing her basic needs met."

"Perhaps. But I see her as the oldest of my children. And I hope to bless her with many younger siblings." He smiled at her startled expression. "That is yet another thing we should have discussed."

He leaned close and kissed her, his fingers lacing with hers as he tugged her against him. They fell back on the bed laughing and kissing.

"I must tell you something else," she said, and he pulled back to look in her face.

"What's that?"

"I might have continued with the farce of the broken arm if not for the fact you refused to bed me." She laughed again, but he didn't.

Liam's blood heated. His wife *wanted* him. And not just when he kissed her and worked her into lust. Something he was happy to do anyway. But she'd wanted him in her bed.

"You should be rewarded for your honesty," he said with a wicked smile as he reached for the hem of her skirt.

"You may want to rethink that, husband. For I may make up stories relentlessly only so I might confess and earn such glorious rewards."

He loved seeing her playful and smiling. "I wouldn't mind overmuch." He unbuckled the belt holding his kilt. "Now. Let us see about adding to our family."

...

Over the next few weeks, Evelyn settled nicely into her new life.

Her husband was kind and generous. Her daughter was happy. They had a wonderful home and she had friends. It was easy to hope they could continue into old age in this way, but Evelyn knew a threat remained.

While she hadn't heard back, she knew her father wasn't one to give up so easily. Had it been only his anger at her defiance, he might have gotten over it. But she was to be payment for enough cattle to keep her people for many years. He would not let her go so easily.

"What are you thinking of?" Liam asked as he took his seat on the plaid he'd stretched out by the stream.

He'd brought her and Gwennie to one of his favorite places. Gwennie had spent most of the afternoon searching the stream for a rabbit on a leaf but was now sleeping next to Evelyn.

"Nothing." She brushed it off, not wanting to put a voice to her fears.

"You're safe here," he said, not needing her to tell him what had her worried. She didn't know how he did it.

Liam still didn't know she'd been promised to the Morgan heir. She should tell him now, so he and Lachlan could decide what was to be done. But she couldn't make herself do it.

"Liam..." She opened her mouth to tell him the truth, but the words wouldn't come out. If she had only a short time in this life, she wanted to stay for as long as she was able. Still, she needed to warn him.

"What if my father doesn't give up? What if he comes for me again? Because he likely will."

He sat up and touched her chin. "I'll take care of you."

She couldn't help but smile at his sincerity.

"I'm sure you would, but if he sent an army?"

He shook his head. "I doubt it would come to that. To me, you're priceless, but to your bastard of a father, I don't think he'll waste many men to have ye back."

"What if he's so lost to his anger, he does the unexpected?"

He let out a breath and took her hand. "Ev, when we were

in the stable and you were on your knees before me, begging me to take you— Ow, woman."

"That tale grows more ridiculous every time you tell it."

"Aye." He winced as he rubbed his arm where she'd smacked him. "That's how men tell stories. No one wants to hear the telling the same way over and over, you must... liven it up a bit each time."

"Liven it up? I believe you mean exaggerate beyond recollection."

"Yes. Just that." He laughed.

"Why don't you ever say what really happened?" she whispered against his lips. "That as soon as I suggested we marry you grabbed me up and dragged me off to the first clergyman you could find."

He laughed and kissed her, a soft lingering kiss that had her leaning closer so it wouldn't end. But he pulled away and looked into her eyes, his earlier joking gone.

"I was not a complete fool when we agreed to marry, Ev. Yes, my heart was ahead of my mind on the matter, but I did have time to think as we raced toward the clergyman." His lips pulled up a bit, but his face went back to seriousness. "I knew your father would be displeased that I took ye. And if he didn't come after me to tie a rope around my neck, he'd certainly curse me the rest of his days." He shook his head. "But I wanted only you as my wife. I decided I was willing to endure the curses, and as long as I had you at my side it didn't matter much where we lived. If it were to become unsafe here, we'll ride to Baehaven and if he follows us there, we'll get on a ship to England. I'll find work and we'll make a home there."

She gasped. "But this is your home." It was Gwennie's and her home now as well.

"My home is with you. Besides," he sat up and smiled again, "if your father was able to make out my scribbling enough to read my letter, he'll see how unwilling I am to part with you and be scared off any plans to attack."

She smiled and allowed him to soothe her. While the idea of running didn't set well, it was at least a plan that wouldn't endanger the rest of the clan.

And perhaps he was right. Maybe his words had been enough to make her father give up.

Chapter Twenty-Two

Liam followed Lach and Cam to the study as he planned out what he would say. He now regretted not having told them of the earlier attempt to get Evelyn to return to the Stewarts. The man Liam had buried in the woods.

"My wife is concerned her father may not stand down. We should discuss what will happen if he decides to attack," Liam said as soon as the door closed behind him.

"We sent six of his men to the devil already. I would say he knows we're not likely to give her up without a battle," Lach said as he took his seat. Cam flopped down in the other seat as Liam stood at attention.

"Seven, my lord," he corrected.

"For Christ's sake, sit the hell down and stop calling me *my lord*."

Liam did as he was ordered. "Seven," he repeated and shifted slightly.

"Seven?" Cam said. "I thought there were only six who attempted to take Gwennie."

"Yes. That's correct."

"So, six soldiers dead." Cam tilted his head in confusion.

"Yes. Six attempted to take Gwennie. And another one a few weeks ago who came on his own and tried to take Evelyn."

"One a few weeks ago?" Lach repeated. "And what happened to him?"

"Buried. I sent his horse back with a letter."

"A letter to the Stewart laird from *you*?" Lach's voice had become louder.

"Aye." Liam considered making an excuse. In the end he knew it wouldn't matter. It was best to get on with it. "When he touched my wife, I reacted. There was no help for the man then. He was dead. I dealt with him. I should have reported it to you straightaway."

"Ye know well what you *should* have done, which makes it even worse you didn't do it."

Liam didn't respond. There was nothing to say. He deserved the laird's disapproval.

"And what did your letter say?" he asked.

Cam shifted to smile at him. "Not that the man would be able to read it with his scribbles."

"I told him to leave my wife alone. We were married before God and she wasn't going to return to him."

"And you thought that would take care of it?"

"Yes."

"After you killed another one of their men."

Liam swallowed. If a clan would have killed a MacKinlay a mere letter wouldn't have satisfied Lachlan. However, a MacKinlay would never attempt to steal a woman from her husband in the first place.

Liam might have asked what they would have done if a man had tried to take Kenna or Mari from their lands against her will, but he knew it was different. Liam wasn't blood, his wife would not be afforded the same protections as the laird's wife and her sister.

It was the reason he thought to take care of the matter himself. Though as he sat there now, he realized it didn't matter that he wasn't MacKinlay by blood, he'd acted on their behalf as war chief.

"Are my family and I to be cast out?" Liam asked. He would need to find a place for them. Surely he could find work in London. He didn't have many skills but fighting, but he'd do whatever needed to provide for his wife and child.

"No one's being cast out." Lach raised his hand. "I'll take care of things. I'll write to Hugh myself."

"And what will you say," Cam asked.

"I'll tell him that Liam and Evelyn were married before God and that she won't be returning to him."

"That's what Liam already said."

"Aye." Lach grinned. "But I get to sign the letter as Laird of Clan MacKinlay. It means he will deal with me if he presses the matter further."

"Thank you, laird."

"It's an easy thing to do. Something I would have done a few weeks ago if you'd come to me."

Liam nodded. "How am I to be punished?"

Lach and Cam exchanged a glance. "You're not going to be punished, Liam. You didn't do anything Cam or I wouldn't have done if our wives were in danger. It's the way of husbands." He waved his fingers as if it was a simple truth. Perhaps it was.

"Thank you."

"If you run into trouble in the future, I hope you'll come to me."

"Yes. I will." It was an easy thing to promise. Liam could only hope this was the end of it.

•••

Liam was with the laird so long he'd missed dinner. When he finally arrived in the hall, he grabbed up a bit of food and motioned to Evelyn to join him.

She was quick to follow behind him as they went to their chamber. When he reached for Gwennie with his free hand, she took the food so he could take her daughter.

"I brought you something." He dug in his sporran and pulled out the small spinning toy he'd purchased from Duncan. The man had offered to give it to him for free, still feeling bad about his part in what happened with Gwennie and feeling obliged for Liam's help in getting Joan back.

Liam wouldn't have it. He didn't like to owe people if it could be helped.

He set her in her bed with the toy and turned to Evelyn. Liam rubbed his chin and sat heavily on the edge of the bed. She came to stand in front of him.

"What's happened?" She was almost afraid to ask. But curiosity forced her to ask.

"I told Lachlan and Cam about the man who came to take you."

"Why?"

"It's better they know so we could devise a plan as to how to handle things."

"And what was decided?"

"Lachlan has sent Hugh his own letter letting him know his only option is to back down or declare war on us. I don't think he'll do such a thing."

"My father will not like an ultimatum."

He smiled and kissed her. "Maybe not, but I think waging war with a clan with which one holds an alliance is a lot of effort for one fair maiden."

"One who wasn't fair or a maiden." Evelyn walked in a small circle. Now was the time to tell him the rest of it. But Liam was right. Trying to get her back to marry the Morgan was one thing. War with the MacKinlays was yet another, and she was sure her father would stand down now that the laird himself had made it clear what would happen if he tried again.

"He's not in a position to take us and he knows that. He's also not in a position to lose our friendship. He'll concede. He has no other choice."

Evelyn hoped that was true. She relaxed and wrapped her arms around Liam. He rested his head on her stomach. "It's over," she said, willing it to be true.

• • •

While Evelyn remained hopeful her father had given up on her, she knew Liam had been right to speak to the laird and devise a plan. She, too, needed to come up with a plan.

If it came to it, she would not allow the clan to go to war for her. She was Hugh Stewart's daughter and by rights she had a duty to marry whom he chose. She'd known it well enough when she escaped with Liam but could think only of being with Gwennie.

Now that they'd settled here, she knew her daughter would be loved and cared for by this clan, even if she wasn't there to do it herself. She never thought she'd consider such a thing months ago when she'd been married. But now she was counting on Liam's sense of responsibility if Evelyn needed to leave.

"I thought maybe you would want to reward me for my bravery today in speaking to the laird. He could have had me flogged for my insolence."

Evelyn doubted the laird would have done such a thing, but asked, "What did you have in mind?"

"Perhaps a kiss?"

She moved closer, lips pressed against his, and he opened

when her tongue touched his bottom lip. She was becoming bolder in their relations. She now felt comfortable enough to take what she wanted and enjoy their joining.

It would be something she would miss if she had to leave Dunardry. She couldn't imagine having to marry and lie with another man. A stranger. She would store away each memory she made with Liam so she had something to hold on to if it came to that.

The kiss quickly flamed into groping and panting without any encouragement from him. It was only when she ripped his shirt that he must have felt her desperation mixed with her eagerness to get him naked.

"Shh, lass," he said in a low voice. "This won't be the last time we make love," he said before he kissed her.

But she couldn't be sure that was true. If her father came tomorrow, she'd leave with him to spare her new family.

Unable to control her sobbing, Liam quickly gave up on making love to her and instead pulled her close and held her. She settled against his body, wondering if she'd be able to give them up when the time came.

Evelyn stiffened as she entered the solar the next week to see Kenna reading a missive. Surely any word from her father would have been given to the laird directly, not to his wife. But it was clear Kenna was distressed.

"What's the matter?"

"My sister. She's not coming up to the castle today. She's not feeling well. Let's go to see her. I want to check in and see if she needs anything. If nothing else, we can bring Lizzy and Aiden back to the castle so she might get some rest."

"Of course," Evelyn said, and settled Gwennie with the nurse before following Kenna out of the hall into the bailey.

It was still difficult to let Gwennie out of her sight, but she wanted to believe the danger was gone.

It wasn't until they approached the gate that Evelyn remembered her promise to Liam.

"Wait. I can't leave." She frowned up at the blue sky filled with fluffy clouds.

"What? Why not?" Kenna tilted her head. "Did your husband say you must stay here?"

"He did, and I promised I'd obey his order. In truth, after what's happened, I do not much like wandering about with just you for protection, not that I don't find you fierce." Evelyn added that last part when it was clear she'd insulted the laird's wife.

"Very well. We'll get one of the warriors to guard us. I will say, usually I make plans to avoid their watch rather than request it. They may fall over in shock."

They laughed as they approached the warriors. Liam was leading them through their drills, and she took a moment to appreciate the sight of him with a sword in his hand and the morning sun glinting in his white hair. He was lovely, like an avenging angel.

Except when he gave her that naughty boy grin as he was doing just then.

"Get yourselves a drink," he ordered his men and came over to her. He bowed to them both. "What an honor to have such lovely ladies witness our efforts this fine day."

Kenna shook her head, unaffected by his charms. Evelyn, however, was very affected. She'd nearly forgotten why they'd stopped.

"We're in need of an escort. We want to go to Mari and Cam's house, and you asked me not to leave the castle without protection."

"And she obeyed," Kenna put in, though Evelyn thought that was clear enough.

"Thank you for that. I will see you there myself. Shall we go?"

"I don't mean to pull ye from your duty."

"If my men aren't able to come back and run through the drills themselves until I return, I have little faith in them being able to carry out any of my more challenging orders." He winked. "Besides, I'll not give one of my men such an honor, not when I might enjoy it myself."

He came to stand between them and offered each of them an arm. He was smiling easily enough until they left the castle walls, then he stepped forward and drew his weapon. Every bit the protective warrior from his head to his toes. He took the duty very seriously.

When they reached Cam and Mari's home he knocked. Cam opened the door looking worn and ragged.

"What is it?" Kenna barged in. "Her note said she wasn't well."

"Aye. She's not well. She's not been able to keep her morning meal down."

Despite the large man's grim appearance, his mouth tugged up on one side and Kenna gasped in surprise.

"Truly?"

"Aye."

"Congratulations," Liam said offering the man a hearty shake. Evelyn saw the men exchange a knowing glance. It was then Evelyn understood what was causing Mari's illness. She was with child.

A quick stab of jealousy twisted in Evelyn's stomach for a moment before it relaxed. She might even now be carrying Liam's child. It was too early to know, but there was no reason why it couldn't have happened already. And what if she was when her father came? Her worry seemed to double with that thought.

She followed Kenna upstairs to find the dowager duchess

caring for Mari with a cool cloth.

"I'm so happy for ye," Kenna exclaimed, taking the rag and wringing it out.

"I don't remember being this sick with Lizzy or Aiden," Mari said, looking a bit green.

The dowager shook her head. "I remember it well. When you arrived at the town house you were ill for weeks. I thought you'd brought the plague upon us for how you groaned."

"Thank you, Mother." Mari didn't look all that thankful for the reminder. And Evelyn knew well enough the dowager was not her mother, but the mother of Mari's former husband. The man Mari had killed.

"What can I do?" Kenna asked.

"You can keep that beast of a husband away from her after this one is born," the dowager snapped.

Kenna and Mari laughed.

"I'm certain this isn't all Cam's fault," Kenna said.

"I'm just glad to be in the opposite wing so I'm not scandalized with what goes on from their side."

"Should we take the children up to the castle with us?" Evelyn asked.

"No. Cam will stay and see to them. Lizzy came in this morning to rub my back while I was sick. It was the sweetest thing."

"When I was sick with Andrew the twins asked only if they could have my bannocks."

They chatted for a little while, trying to keep Mari distracted until she felt well enough to eat something and hold it down.

When Evelyn and Kenna were ready to leave, Cam and Liam were talking in low tones. Cam offered Evelyn a smile and hugged her. "I'm sorry you must be escorted. Your home should be safe. I'm glad to see you obliged Liam, so he doesn't have to worry."

Evelyn glanced at Liam, who held her gaze.

Of anyone, Cameron was the last person who should feel bad. If it hadn't been for him, Evelyn may never have been freed from the McCurdys. He'd been the one to dispatch them and save her. And he'd helped Liam fight off the Stewarts as well.

Her face grew hot when she remembered the way he'd seen her the first time. She'd not been covered properly. Her dress had been in tatters. She hadn't been able to look the man in the eyes since she'd returned.

"Do not think of it, Ev. You've nothing to be ashamed of." Liam was quick to come to her side and put an arm around her. He always seemed to know what she was thinking and how to reassure her.

Cam shook his head. "I don't think less of ye for what I saw that night. I don't remember anything but seeing Mari in their grasp and the bodies. Everything else is but a blur. I don't think I've ever been so terrified in my life. And I'm glad I was able to free you from them."

He kissed her on the top of the head and turned her back over to Liam.

"Thank you, Cameron." She shook her head and tried to laugh away the tears. "I can never thank you enough for what you did that night, as well as the day the Stewarts tried to take Gwennie." She turned to Liam. "You're both my heroes."

And because of that, she'd make sure they didn't come to harm because of her.

"But me more than him, yes?" Cam nudged her arm with his elbow.

The two men cast jests at each other while she managed a laugh. She was glad enough to get over her embarrassment with Cam.

"Are you ready to return to the castle?" she asked her husband.

"Very well." He turned toward the stairs expectantly.

"Kenna wishes to stay a bit longer with her sister."

"Aye. Then I'll see you home and send someone back for her."

They left and she stopped to face him. "Thank you for what you did. I'd not been able to look Cam in the face since he saved me. I didn't want that night to be between us, but I didn't know how to address it."

"I meant what I said. You should never feel a speck of guilt about the situation. You didn't do anything wrong. They took ye from your lands and hurt ye. To the devil with them."

"My father blames me. He says if I hadn't run off, I never would have been taken."

"Ev, please don't ask me to list all the ways Hugh Stewart is a bloody poor excuse for a man. It's not that far of a walk to the castle, I'd not finish before we get there."

She laughed, which she guessed was exactly what he had intended.

"Perhaps if I spent more time seeing the MacKinlay lands, they wouldn't be as daunting," she suggested, then leaned closer. "Maybe if we visited a secluded spot."

"Secluded?" His eyes went wide, and his lips pulled up in that grin. "Oh, aye. I know just the spot."

Chapter Twenty-Three

Liam stopped to turn back to her as he led her to the secluded spot she'd requested. He'd brought her and Gwennie there for an afternoon together.

"I knew you'd pick this place," she said.

He squeezed her hand. "This is the place I come and think of things, but now it will be known for the place I bring my wife to make love to her in the afternoon."

As was his way, Liam let her be in control of their joining. To both their enjoyment.

Soon they were smiling up at the trees catching their breath.

"You've scared off the birds and animals with your shouting," Liam said with a smug grin on his face.

"I blame you for making me shout."

He kissed her and handed over her shoes as they dressed. "Should I apologize?"

"No. I know you wouldn't mean it."

"You know me too well."

It was true, she'd come to know him well. She knew he

was kind. She'd remembered that trait from the time he'd escorted her home years ago, but she knew it to her bones now. But now she realized other things about her husband. He was brave, as war chiefs were required to be. He didn't give up. He'd asked for permission to marry her even after being turned down before. Which also proved he was honorable.

At least when a woman didn't show up in the stable as he was doing the honorable thing by leaving and sway him into running away with her and marrying in secret.

"I've been nothing but trouble," she said out loud without realizing it.

"You've been a fair amount of trouble, but it's been worth it." His smile told her he was teasing.

"I'm serious, Liam. You should have turned me down in the stables and left me there."

Liam looked surprised. "It wasn't possible. I fancied myself in love with you and had been pining over you for years. Even if you'd been standing there with Gwennie and ten other children I would have agreed to take you as my wife. I would have regretted it the rest of my life if I'd turned away from you."

She frowned and he lifted her chin.

"We may face a bit of trouble with your father, but I still don't have any regrets for marrying you. Having you as my wife is the best thing that has ever happened to me."

"How can you still think that after I pushed you away?"

That smile had returned. "It's just the way I feel, and you'll not change my mind."

She laughed at his answer as he led her back to the castle. He stayed with her when she went to the solar and Gwennie came running. Liam scooped her up.

"There's my lass," he said. "Did you have fun today?" Their coloring couldn't be more opposite. Gwennie's hair and eyes were dark where Liam's were light. But if not for that, anyone would think he had sired her the way he treated her as his own.

Gwennie nodded in answer.

"I can't imagine it could have been very much fun without Davey," he said.

"Who's Davey?"

He pulled a wooden rabbit out from behind his back and held it up. "Why, he's a pirate rabbit. See his patch and his wooden leg?"

Sure enough, the carving had a normal bunny leg on one side and a peg leg on the other. Gwennie laughed as Liam made the rabbit talk in a thick pirate brogue. He was wonderful with children. She couldn't have picked a better father for her daughter. Or the other children they might have.

She placed a palm against her stomach, hoping for something she'd once feared.

. . .

"Why are ye smiling," Colin asked with a frown as he stepped away during a drill.

"I'm sorry. Try it again," Liam urged the lad. But he felt the smile return when the other warrior drew his sword. He had happy news to share with his family that night and couldn't wait to tell them.

"You're doing it again."

"I'm sorry, Colin. It's not you. I'm just happy." There was no denying it. His wife had become insatiable over the last few weeks and, while he knew there was more to marriage than the physical parts, he was beyond pleased with those physical parts.

"Let's stop now. Get your meal and we'll pick up later," Liam gave the command to his men after the morning drills were completed.

Lach gave a nod of approval and then waved him over. "Come with us."

Liam was happy to follow along with Lach and Cam as the men went up to the solar. He could tell he wasn't alone in wanting to see his family.

Little children squealed in delight and ran about as Lach entered first. He snatched up Lizzy, making the girl shriek with laughter. "There are so many children about, I can't tell which are mine," he declared, holding her sideways. "Are you mine?"

"No!" she laughed and pointed to Cam. "*He's* my papa."

"Ah!" He pitched her into Cam's waiting arms, causing more laughter. As Gwennie was usually joined at Lizzy's hip, she was the next to fall prey as Lach hoisted her up in his arms letting her dangle haphazardly. "What of you? Are you mine?"

"No!" she said as Lizzy had. Then she pointed at Liam. "*He's* my papa!" she announced loudly.

"Argh!" Lach tossed her to Liam. It was all part of the theatrics, and Lach went on, grabbing up Andrew who declared he was indeed the laird's.

But the shouts in the room dulled as Liam stared down at the little girl in surprise. "Are you mine?" he asked, less boisterous than Lach had.

"Yes!" she shouted and laughed.

"Aye. You are." He pressed a kiss to her head and looked over where Ev watched. She came over to hug them. "She called me Papa," he whispered to her.

"I heard." She looked up at him. "If you'd rather she didn't…"

"Nay. I was wondering if one day I might have the courage to ask. But it's even better when it's spoken freely. It means something more." He cleared his throat, which had grown tight. "It's a great honor."

It was hard to release Gwennie and Ev to go back to his men after the noon meal, but he managed, knowing his men needed to be in fighting form in case the Stewarts came for revenge.

Liam didn't like to think any of his men could be harmed because of his actions, but he'd taken down the men who tried to take his family. He had only protected what was his, but he doubted Hugh Stewart would see it that way.

...

Liam's grin was wider than normal when he came into their chamber later that night. He had to be the happiest person Evelyn had ever known despite the way his early life had been so hard for him.

He seemed grateful for every small pleasure life brought him. His joy and excitement were contagious, and she often felt guilty when she recalled how cold she'd been to him when they first married.

She never expected to come to care for him and was even more surprised to find how much she enjoyed lying with him, his touch and joining together in pleasure. It was thoughts of the joining that generally caused Liam to smile like this.

"What has ye so happy?" she asked as she glanced over at Gwennie, who was already asleep.

Liam bent to kiss Evelyn. "I've a beautiful wife who allows me to touch her and a lovely daughter to dote on. Why would I ever be anything other than happy?"

He made it sound so simple. And perhaps it was. Liam didn't need a large home or a powerful title. He never worked to position himself above others. He was humble and pleasant even as war chief.

"I've also been given an order by my laird to provide

escort for a delivery of goods to Baehaven Castle." He winked at her even as a bit of her joy dimmed. He would be leaving them.

He went about hanging his things and getting ready for bed as if this were good news. To leave them.

While she'd be content to spend her days with Kenna and Mari and the children as usual. She would miss having Liam in her bed. And their sweet morning routine of kissing until Gwennie disrupted them by climbing into the bed and demanding a story.

"I've asked if I can take ye and Gwennie with me. I want to show her the seals, since I've no luck so far in carving one for her. Have you ever seen the ocean?"

"Nay. I've not." Stewart lands didn't touch the sea and, other than her ill-advised incident, she'd never left her clan lands. She smiled; the joy returned. He was offering them a small adventure.

"If we leave at first light, we can be there late tomorrow night."

"Very well." She nodded as he climbed into bed next to her and blew out the lantern.

"We should get our rest. Tomorrow will be a long day." He placed a single kiss on her lips and settled the covers over her.

She lay there quietly for a few moments, but she found she was too excited to sleep. Her mind was busy thinking of the things she would need to pack in the morning before they left.

She wanted her husband to know how happy she was. She leaned over and kissed him again. When he kissed her just once, she persisted, teasing him with her tongue.

With a groan he gave in easily to whatever weak resistance he'd planned.

"We should sleep." His scold held no bite.

"I will sleep better after ye give me a reason to," she said, rolling away.

He moved on top of her, tugging her nightgown up between them. It was dark and for a moment his grasping reminded her of another time. With...them.

"What is it?" Liam whispered. "Did I hurt ye?"

As quick as it had formed, the memory was gone. Dispersed by Liam's kind words and his gentle voice.

"I'm well." She managed to get the gown off, but Liam hadn't continued. "Why do you stop?" she asked.

"Maybe the darkness and me pushing at you, made you—"

"I want ye, Liam." But he apparently wasn't convinced enough to proceed. She decided to tell him the truth instead of trying to prove the lie. "Yes. For a small moment I remembered the darkness and the weight of a man's body on mine, but it was gone just as quickly. I could never mistake you for them, Liam. Never. The way you touch me and kiss me is nothing like what happened. You are safe and I know it in my bones."

He let out a breath and kissed her softly. Too softly.

"Make love to me Liam. I want ye. I'm not afraid." She found his hair and ran her fingers through it.

"Let it not be said I ever made ye beg me. 'Tis not gentlemanly."

She laughed as he kissed her breast and nipped her skin as he teased her. She didn't know where his lips might land next. Each touch made her whimper with need.

"If you don't want to degrade me to begging, you'd best get on with it, husband, because I can't take much more."

With the naughtiest chuckle she'd ever heard, he entered her. The breath whooshed out of her chest, and she gasped in the scent of him. A smile curved on her lips even though it was too dark for him to see it.

It was for herself and the power she felt as she conquered her fears.

• • •

Gwennie muttered a bit of dissatisfaction as Evelyn handed her up to rest in Liam's lap, but before his horse had taken a step, she'd settled against him and was sleeping again.

Many a time as they'd traveled from the Stewarts, Gwennie had slept just like this, so he knew she wouldn't stir as he and Ev led the group of wagons out of the bailey on their way to Baehaven.

The sun had not yet met the day, but its glow lit their way. It was sure to be a hot day; it was already warm. A light breeze would keep it from being uncomfortable. They'd be in the cover of trees before the sun really started burning.

He didn't expect any trouble, since it was only MacKinlay lands between Dunardry and Baehaven. But an occasional intruder did pass through, so Liam was alert as they moved into less familiar territory.

They'd been riding for only two hours when Gwennie woke fully and blinked. She spun about, looking for her mother and then started crying in earnest.

"What is it, love? Mama is just there." Liam waved at Ev who rode up closer. But Gwennie wasn't to be comforted. Instead, she started crying, "No! No!"

Liam checked her closer to see if perhaps she wasn't truly awake and was having a terror, but she continued crying until he stopped.

"What is it, Gwennie? What's wrong?"

"Don't take me back. I want to stay here with you. Please. I'll be a good lass."

Liam's heart broke. Not just because of Gwennie's confusion, but that she thought his love was contingent on her being good and not a bother. He knew well how hard it was for a child to live that way. He'd tried his best to be good at all times as well.

Not being a MacKinlay, he never wanted them to regret their decision to keep him on as one of them. He'd always gone out of his way to be pleasant. He didn't want the same worries for Gwennie.

He repositioned her so she was looking at him and raised her chin as her lip trembled and tears streaked her rounded cheeks.

"Stop, Gwennie. You're not going back to Scalloway. We're going on an adventure like the bunnies."

She blinked and quieted. He smiled at her and wiped the wetness from her face.

"We're much too heavy to take a leaf to the sea, so we must use horses, you see?"

While she'd stopped crying, she still looked unsure.

"Do you remember each morning after we left our camp how I would tell you a story as we rode?"

She nodded.

"Do you recall the sun was always behind us on this side?" He held up his left hand.

She looked to where he pointed and after some thought she nodded. He could only hope she understood what he was trying to tell her. It was never too early to gain a keen sense of direction.

"The sun is behind us still, so we're heading in the same direction as before. Not back the way we came."

"The seals?" she asked.

"Aye. It will be too dark to see them tonight when we arrive. But tomorrow morning I'll be able to show them to you." He kissed her head. "I promise. Do you trust me?"

She nodded.

"I'll always keep you with me. And you don't always have

to be a good lass for me to love you. Can you understand that?" She was probably too young, but he'd keep telling her all his days until she realized the truth — that she didn't need to be perfect to be loved.

One of the other guards had ridden up to see why they'd stopped.

"We're fine now. Let's go," Liam said, and started out again.

"Did you want me to take her?" Ev offered.

"Nay. We're fine. But I daresay Gwennie could use a bannock from your pack and one for her papa as well."

Ev smiled and gave them three. As they continued on, Gwennie had him tell the story yet again of the bunny that traveled out to the sea and became friends with the seals.

Liam found a shady spot to stop midday. He helped Gwennie down and went to help Ev, who was stiff when he set her on her feet.

"What is it?" he asked, looking around the area. A small waterfall filled a deep basin where the water was clear and calm. It would be a good place for a swim if they didn't have four other men with them.

"I know this place," she said quietly, her arm crossed her stomach in a protective gesture that hurt his soul.

"They're gone, Ev. They can't hurt you ever again." He looked around. "Would you rather we continue on a bit and find a different place to eat?"

The other men had already dug out their meals and sprawled in the shade, but they'd get up if he ordered them to.

She swallowed and shook her head before her shoulders lifted. "No. This is a fine place to stop."

"You don't need to prove your bravery to me. I know how strong you are. If you're uncomfortable here, I will happily move on."

"I won't let them take anything else from me. I'm done

with that." Lifting her chin, she took a blanket from her horse and spread it on the grass away from the other men.

He sat next to her as Gwennie went off to collect flowers. "You don't need to battle these demons alone, Ev. I'm rather large and I carry a sword. I'm happy to defend your weak arm."

"You've already helped me more than you know." She smiled at him. For a moment, he thought she might say something else. The way she was looking at him spoke of deep feelings.

Feelings he felt for her.

He'd thought himself in love with her before he knew her. But now they knew each other well. There was an ease between them, friendship, and comfort, but there was also something more. He felt it growing each day.

Could this be what real love felt like? It wasn't as overwhelming as he'd expected. Instead, it was calming and right, in a way nothing else in his life had ever been.

He wouldn't push for words. Not when he could savor it silently in her smile.

Chapter Twenty-Four

As Liam said, it was late when they arrived at Baehaven Castle. Gwennie was asleep and Evelyn hoped she could join her as soon as possible. It had been a long day of travel.

She let out a breath, irritated with her cowardice. The true reason she wanted to rush off to the nearest room wasn't solely due to exhaustion, but to put off greeting the laird and his lady.

She'd probably met the laird during her brief stay at Dunardry, but she couldn't remember him. According to Liam, he'd not been married then. Kenna and Mari spoke of Dorie often and had both sent letters and gifts to be delivered. If Kenna and Mari liked this woman, she must be nice, but still she worried.

Meeting new people who already knew Liam meant having to explain Gwennie. Evelyn would never allow anyone to shame her daughter. She wasn't to blame for how she came to be.

Evelyn stood close to Liam, knowing he wouldn't stand for anyone hurting Gwennie, especially after he'd expressed such strong feelings about the use of "step" to describe her as his daughter.

A tall woman with black hair came to greet them with a big smile. "Liam! It's been so long. I heard you were wed. This must be your bride."

"Aye. This is Evelyn and you'll have to wait to meet our daughter Gwennie in the morning." He nodded to the girl sleeping in his arms.

Evelyn braced for a question or a look. It'd be better to face it now while Gwennie slept than when she might overhear a cruel word spoken.

But the woman didn't even bat an eye when she placed a hand on Gwennie's head and whispered to Evelyn, "I'm Dorie. I'm so happy to welcome you to our home."

"Thank you. It's wonderful to meet you."

She waved a hand. "We'll meet properly in the morning. Tonight, we'll get you a bite to eat and see you straight to your rooms so you can rest."

In the hall, she summoned a maid and instructed her to gather a tray and bring it to the south wing. Then she led them up the stairs to their room.

"Did you want a pallet made up for the little one?" Dorie asked.

"Nay. She can sleep with us tonight," Liam said before Evelyn had a chance to respond. She wouldn't want Gwennie to wake up alone in a strange room. Liam turned to her. "I wouldn't want her to be frightened when she woke up."

It may have been the exhaustion, but her throat grew tight with emotions. She'd known the worst of what a man was capable of. Perhaps with her punishment paid, she was now worthy to spend the rest of her life with the kindest man there ever was.

"I always knew you'd be a great father," Dorie said while she patted Liam's shoulder. "I saw how you played with the little ones after the battle here. Do ye still carve little rabbits?"

Evelyn laughed. "Nearly every day."

"Have ye not figured out how to carve something else yet?" Bryce asked as he joined them. "Sorry I wasn't there when you arrived. I lost a wager with my dear wife and was tasked with getting our little devil to sleep."

"As you can see, I've already mastered such a skill." Liam waved at Gwennie asleep in the middle of the bed. "She's an angel, though, so she makes it easy."

"You're a lucky man." Bryce said and turned to Evelyn. "Ye look well. Much better than when I saw you last."

"Yes. Much better, indeed," she said. Even seeing the man now, she didn't recall him from her time at Dunardry. She'd been so numb it seemed like a dream.

"Well, it's late. We'll see you in the morning. Don't rush. Take your rest if you can," Dorie said as she and Bryce moved toward the door. With a wave from them, they were gone.

"I'm happy to see them, but I can't say how relieved I am they didn't want to visit any longer tonight. I may have fallen asleep, and you'd have had to carry me to bed," Liam said.

She laughed and held out a slice of cold meat. "I would have left you to sleep in the hall. Like you did when you were a lad."

"I'm afraid I've grown too soft for sleeping on a bench. Not when there's a warm woman and a comfortable bed." He kissed her and let out a breath. "And a wee mite who kicks in her sleep."

Evelyn laughed.

"What do you think she dreams of with so much kicking?" he asked.

"Perhaps she thinks she's a rabbit."

"So you're saying it's my fault?"

"If you'd not traveled all that way and married me in secret, ye'd not be getting kicked. So I guess it is your fault."

He wrapped his arms around her from behind as she braided her hair. She felt desire warm her belly.

She saw his grin in the mirror and knew he was about to say something witty that was going to earn him a thump on the arm.

"If you'd not come out to the stables and begged me to take ye— Ow!" He rubbed his arm. "Damn, woman. You're stronger than you look."

"Always remember that." She quieted her laughter when Gwennie shifted. When she looked back at Liam, he was staring at her, his humor had faded.

"I'll never regret marrying ye," he said.

She hoped he wouldn't change his mind if ever he found out she'd been promised to another.

. . .

The sun was up when Liam woke. He was alone in the bed, but the sound of whispering told him his wife and daughter were still in the room. He opened his eyes and watched Evelyn brushing Gwennie's hair and helping her into a dress.

"Can I wake up Papa now?" Gwennie asked.

Liam was quick to shut his eyes.

"Papa is very tired. He held you the whole way here, even when you were sleeping."

"But I'm hungry."

"Put your shoes on and gather up your bunnies and then we'll wake him."

Liam lay still until he heard Gwennie come closer to the bed. When she placed her hand on his cheek and whispered, "Papa, wake up. I'm hungry."

He snapped at her hand and growled. She squealed and then laughed.

"I'm hungry, too." He pretended he was gobbling up her

hand as he'd seen Cam and Lach do to their children many times. As expected, she held out her hand and forced him to do it twice more before Evelyn saved him so he could get up.

They were greeted warmly by the people in the hall as they made their way to the main table to sit with Bryce and Dorie.

Liam took their son, Dorien, from Bryce and held him up. "He's an armful," he said. "Soon enough he'll be carrying a sword." He took a moment to talk to the lad in the way adults spoke to babes, earning a smile.

"He'll need to learn to walk first. He refuses," Dorie said. "Instead, he crawls wherever he wants to go."

"Children do things when it's right for them," Liam repeated something he'd heard from Kenna before handing over the little boy to his mother.

Liam had planned to take Gwennie to see the seals, but a storm was coming in, so he went with Bryce while Dorie took Ev and Gwennie for a tour of their home.

It wasn't long that he and Bryce were alone. The man gave him a good wallop on the shoulder. "A wife and a daughter."

"Aye." Liam smiled with pride.

"How does it feel?"

"Quite different than I expected, to be honest."

Bryce nodded. "I understand. I didn't think I could love again after Maggie died. But somehow, I was lucky enough to be given Dorie. Some men do not find such women in their lives, and I've managed to find two of the best ones that ever were."

Liam didn't take offense to Bryce's words, and he'd not tell the man that he was wrong because Evelyn was clearly the loveliest. Liam knew well enough they were both lucky bastards to have found such wonderful wives.

"It's not been easy. Getting to know someone who is a stranger never is. I was a fool to think it would be easy as

Cam and Lach enjoyed telling me. But I did think I knew what it was to love someone, and I was wrong about that."

"If you make someone out to be a certain way in your mind, they're bound to disappoint ye. There's no way ye can be what they expect. It's not fair to them. And it's not fair to ye, either. I know you've wanted a family since you were a wee lad, but a real family is not the same as the one you created in your mind."

"Aye. I know. It's much better now. But I'm not sure if Ev will ever really open up and share everything."

"The lass was hurt in a monstrous way."

Liam nodded. "She's been coming to terms with her demons. Even yesterday on the way here, she recognized a place she'd been with them and instead of walking away she stayed. She refuses to let them win. I'm so proud of her. But I think she still blames herself for what happened. If she hadn't left her home she wouldn't have been taken."

"She paid a heavy price."

"Aye. But if she'd never left Scalloway, I never would've met her, and she wouldn't have Gwennie. It's odd to wish for something to never have happened even though it formed a path to something you're glad happened." Liam laughed at himself, expecting Bryce to join in and make fun of him.

Instead, the man nodded seriously.

"Unfortunately, I know well that living on the wrong side of one's future doesn't work well for a happy life." Bryce had spent many years blaming himself for his first wife and child's death. They'd fallen ill and passed when he'd been away. He thought they'd died alone and punished himself for it.

"Dorie loved the idea of me as her husband. She loved the freedom I allowed her. But despite her words, she couldn't really love me until I let her know me. You can love your Evelyn only so much until she gives ye permission."

Liam nodded. There was a time he wouldn't have

understood the difference, but over the last months he knew it well.

"Come. Let's go find our women. I know well where they'll be."

...

Evelyn couldn't hide her surprise as they entered through a door with bars across it. Dorie had said she was taking them to the Children's Ward, but they were clearly descending down into the bowels of the dungeon under the castle.

The steep steps were well lit and dry and opened into a large room. Iron grids broke up the large room, obviously cells. But instead of being cold, dark, and damp, it was warm from the fires in the hearths and full of children's laughter. Rushes on the floor kept the voices from echoing.

"With some of the children being quite small, we needed a secure place to keep everyone. We still have many sweet souls who lost their parents when we took over Baehaven. Some abandoned their children to flee before the battle. Some were widowers killed who left children behind. We made a place for them here until we can find homes for them all."

Evelyn noticed Dorie wipe at her eye.

"I hope it's soon," Evelyn said.

"Aye. Me too. They're happy enough down here for now. But it's not a true home."

Shy at first, Gwennie soon got pulled into a game with the other children. She made quick friends with a small girl with pudgy cheeks and a sweet smile.

In all, there were eight children. Ranging from the little girl with Gwennie, who looked to be a year and a half, to a boy who was probably ten or eleven.

Among the children were a number of cats. One wound

around Evelyn's legs.

"The cats cleared out the mice. We feed them now, since they did such a fine job." She knelt down to pet the black cat at Evelyn's feet. "Didn't you, Sir Midnight?"

The cat purred and stretched before running off to rub against one of the children.

"They seem happy," Evelyn said, seeing the worry on Dorie's face.

"I hope so."

Liam and Bryce joined them then. Her husband smiled at her before getting down with the children to play. Soon, they were all laughing at a story he was telling.

"Bryce says he loves to play with children because he missed his chance to be one," Dorie said.

"Liam?"

"Yes. Bryce told me the way he was abandoned and how, even at a young age, he seemed an adult already."

"Whatever the reason, I'm blessed to have such a wonderful father for my child. I hadn't expected it. I thought he'd give my daughter and me a safe place to live and food for our bellies. But he's given us such kindness. Even when I was not kind to him in return."

"I've never seen Liam angry with anyone. I'm sure he was quick to forgive you. He's wanted ye for so long." Dorie laughed then. "It seems your daughter is much like Liam in her kindness."

Dorie and Evelyn walked closer as Gwennie held out one of her carved rabbits to a little boy. "Do you want one?" she asked, and the boy took it with a wide grin. "Do you want one?" Gwennie moved to the next child.

Soon the bundle of bunnies was down to the final rabbit. Gwennie wrapped her hand around it and looked at Liam. From where Evelyn stood, she could see the black eye, marking this rabbit as the first one he'd given her. It was her favorite and there was still one child who didn't have one. The little girl with the chubby cheeks.

"Rose has taken a liking to your daughter," Dorie said of the small girl who teetered on unstable legs while following Gwennie around.

"She's an angel," Evelyn said. She'd missed so much of Gwennie's younger years. It had taken Evelyn much too long to disregard her father's orders and leave the castle to see her daughter.

"Her da was killed in the battle between my father and brother," Dorie said, then added, "I should say the McCurdy and his son, since I was not related to them by blood." The comment seemed significant to her. "Rose's mother passed just a few weeks ago."

Gwennie was still holding the last rabbit and looking at the little girl. Evelyn could see the struggle of indecision. She also saw the way Liam knelt down next to her and whispered in her ear.

"Just like this one?" Gwennie said.

"Aye," he said.

Gwennie put the rabbit in Rose's dimpled fingers. "This is for you. It's my most favorite one. Take good care of him. My papa will make me another one."

In answer, Rose plopped to her seat and began bouncing the rabbit around as the other children were doing.

He'd helped Gwennie do a kind thing, and promised to make her more rabbits. Evelyn's heart swelled when he looked up at her and winked. He probably didn't realize how he'd helped shape Gwennie to be a giving person with this simple act.

Playing with her was one thing; any man could do that. But teaching her to be kind was the duty of a father. Just then Rose bounced the bunny on Liam's leg, and he scooped her up to play with her, making her giggle.

Dorie laughed. "As Kenna would say, watching her husband with the children makes her want more children."

Evelyn also laughed. "She would've said she wanted to make more children with him right then."

"True. I was attempting to be ladylike."

Evelyn looked at her husband again and felt the urge to make a child with him, right then.

Chapter Twenty-Five

Through the afternoon and evening while Liam did his best to replace Gwennie's bunnies, he couldn't help but notice his wife was looking at him like he was a cool sip of water on a hot day. Her gaze fired his blood and caused his body to respond.

If they'd been back at Dunardry he may have made up a reason to take her to their rooms. But they were guests here at Baehaven, and he hadn't come up with an excuse to get her alone.

To make matters worse, Bryce kept him longer that night than he wished. Liam enjoyed catching up with his friend, but breakfast might've been a better time. Ev and Gwennie had already gone up to their room an hour before him. He feared Ev would be asleep and he'd have to toss about all night with unrest.

But she was awake, and Gwennie was sleeping on a bundle of blankets near the hearth. Far enough away not to see that her mother was not wearing anything when she sat up and allowed the covering to puddle around her hips.

He couldn't get his boots and clothing off fast enough.

"Ye don't know how grateful I am to see you awake and ready. I didn't think I'd make it to morning to be inside of you."

"I've needed you all day. Did you see the way I looked at you at dinner?"

"I did, but I didn't think you'd want me to tell Bryce I needed to excuse myself so I could go service my wife."

"If you'd not arrived shortly, I might have gone down there and dragged you to our room by your ear."

"Mmm. Temptress. I think I would've liked that."

She laughed as he kissed her neck, but the laughter turned into a gasp and then ragged breathing as he moved to her breast and then lower. Soon he'd found her heat. She was whimpering and clutching at him, making it clear she wanted more. She even tugged on his ear.

He willingly scrambled up her body to do her bidding and join with her. "Shh," he said when she expressed her enjoyment a bit too loud. But even as he warned her, he smiled that she was unable to restrain her pleasure.

He had thrust into her only a few times when he felt her grip on him. She bit his shoulder, no doubt in an effort to keep from shouting. The pain pushed Liam to his finish quicker than he planned.

Panting side by side in the darkness, he smiled and kissed her hair. "That was over faster than I would have liked, but it seems I got the job done," he said.

She laughed and propped herself up to look down on him. "That you did."

"Might I ask what it was that stirred you so? Know I'm not complaining, but perhaps I may use it to my advantage at another time."

She laughed quietly but shrugged and looked away. "Sometimes when I see you with Gwennie it makes me want to bear you a child, and there's only one way for that to happen. I guess it's some kind of instinct."

He sat up and stared at her. "You want to have my child?"

She laughed. "Liam, surely you know how they come about."

"Yes. Of course, I thought it might happen. But to think you *wanted* it to happen. Or that you wanted a child from… me."

"Who would I have a child with if not for you? My husband. I would never—"

"I know. That's not what I meant. It's just…" He shook his head, too tired to find the words needed to explain it to her. But she was a bright lass, his wife.

She tilted her head as her brows came together. "Do you think a child of yours would be less for some reason?"

"Nay. Not *some* reason. For a very specific reason. I don't know my blood."

"Neither does Gwennie. Do you think badly of her?"

"No!" he nearly shouted and then quieted his voice. "No." He was the one who was put out now. "Gwennie is perfect."

"As will any child be from our union." She kissed him and brushed his hair back in a comforting gesture. "Being a good person is less about who you came from and more about who loves you."

His eyes went wide with surprise. Was she saying…? Could she…?

He might have pushed for an answer, but she settled up against him and let out a soft sigh before closing her eyes.

Did she think he was a good person?

He'd tried very hard to make up for his lacking. To atone for whatever he'd done that made his family cast him out in such a way that he'd sooner been eaten by wolves than make his way back to his people.

He glanced over at Gwennie, sleeping peacefully on the

floor, and imagined another child. With white-blond hair and a mischievous smile. His own blood. A child, like him, who wouldn't know his or her heritage but wouldn't know shame, only love.

He smiled and thought of how happy they would all be. He knew the danger of such things now. How the life he created in his mind might be nothing like the one that came to be. And after speaking with Bryce, he knew he wasn't the only one guilty of such things.

Creating a person down to their likes and dislikes was a dangerous thing. One sure to lead to disappointment. Instead, he focused on the person who was with him now. The people he was getting to know more each day.

Ev had fallen asleep quickly now that she'd been sated, and he joined her.

As soon as Gwennie was awake and dressed the next morning, Liam scooped her up to carry her down the cliffs. He made sure his daughter clung tight to his neck so he had a hand left to assist Ev.

"I don't know that I need your help to get down, but I may call on you to get me back to the top," she said while looking up from where they'd come.

Liam carried Gwennie close to the water and pointed at the seals lying about on the rocks.

"Do you see them?"

"Where?"

"They look like rocks, but softer." Liam rolled his eyes. That wasn't a helpful description for a child. "We'll get closer."

"Liam," Evelyn said, fear in her voice.

"I didn't come all this way to not show her the seals. We won't get too close," he promised. He'd just get close enough to toss a rock near them and wake them up a bit.

He didn't need to bother with a rock. When he took a few steps, one of the seals alerted and wiggled toward the water.

Gwennie's eyes went wide, and her fingers tightened in his hair, equal measures excitement and wariness. He'd seen the seals on a few occasions in the last year, but seeing them through Gwennie's expressions made them seem new and exciting once again.

He couldn't wait to show her other things and enjoy the discovery through her reactions.

"Children make things feel new and special again," he said as Ev caught up to them. He took her hand. "I hope we're blessed with many more."

She smiled and leaned her head against his shoulder. "I hope so as well."

...

Evelyn watched Liam and Gwennie play at the edge of the water as she sat on a rock in the sun. After Gwennie had seen the seals, she was happy to leave them behind. Evelyn couldn't blame her. They were bigger than she expected and didn't seem keen on having people close by.

"Watch out!" Evelyn called when a wave caught them off guard. Liam scooped up Gwennie, but it was too late; she'd gotten soaked.

"Don't worry, lass. You'll dry fast in the sun," Liam said, quickly calming Gwennie's fear over her dress. They collected shells and Gwennie was indeed dry by the time they made their way back to the castle.

Like the day before, they stayed with the children. Gwennie spent most of the time telling Rose stories about the bunnies. Evelyn and Dorie became good friends and Evelyn realized how much happier she was with all the people in her life when months before she'd wanted it to be only her and Gwennie. She knew Gwennie was better for it as well.

Early the next morning, Dorie and Bryce saw them off

on their way home.

"Did you enjoy your stay?" Liam asked her.

"Yes. But I'm looking forward to going home." Dunardry had become more of a home to her than Scalloway ever had. For with the MacKinlays she had friends and freedom, and perhaps even love.

...

Liam kissed his wife and moved to pull away, knowing she wouldn't welcome his addresses. Instead, she pulled him back to kiss him thoroughly. He stood and looked down as she tugged his shirt free.

He was quite happy to oblige her. In the two weeks since they'd returned from Baehaven she'd been with him nearly every night. Still, he knew this night would be different.

"Why are ye not helping, Liam?" she asked while struggling with his belt.

"Are ye not..." He held up a finger and dug into his sporran to find the scrap of paper he kept. He checked over the markings and shook his head. The air left his body. "You're late," he whispered as if speaking louder might bring on her courses.

"What is this?" She scowled at the piece of parchment.

"I was told wives don't accept advances from their husbands when they have their courses, so I've been careful to know when they are, so not to make myself a nuisance to ye."

She laughed. "Only you would be so considerate."

"You've not missed your time once since I've started counting. But ye should have started two days ago."

She considered and nodded. "It's only two days and could be because of the travel."

"Or it could mean you're increasing." He bent to pick her

up and spin her around before thinking better of it. He placed her back on her feet and bent to kiss her belly.

"We'll need to wait to see. I don't want you to get your hopes up this soon."

"I won't. But you should rest, just in case." He remembered Mari saying it was the scariest part. The early days. He understood better now why Cam didn't want Mari doing anything strenuous.

Ev laughed and batted his hands away. "I'll not be taking to my bed at this stage."

He knew he was getting carried away but couldn't help himself. They might have another child. He already felt a strong desire to protect Evelyn, but now that she might be carrying his child, he was mad with the desire to shelter her from any possible harm. Including him.

He backed away when she reached for his shirt again. "I don't think we should do this."

"Why not?"

"If there's a babe in there, I don't want to be... jostling it."

She laughed and he felt his ears grow hot from embarrassment. He liked children and bairns well enough, but he didn't know much about women carrying them. It wasn't discussed.

He felt he may need another trip to Cam's soon.

"You will not jostle anything. Besides, if it turns out I'm not yet with child, it will make it even later if we wait."

"Do you feel any different?"

She laughed again. "No. But I wouldn't feel anything this early on."

He nodded. "If you're certain I won't hurt anything."

Her only answer was to yank his shirt over his head and pull him down to the bed. He did his duty and soon she was gasping for breath as he rolled off her.

"Are you well? I didn't push too hard, did I?"

She laughed at him again. It was becoming a common thing. "Please don't get your hopes up. I'm only two days late."

He nodded, but it was too late. As they lay there, all he could think about was them having a babe.

Despite Ev telling him it was much too soon to know for sure, Evelyn joined him in his excitement, and at night when Gwennie was asleep they talked quietly about the possibility of having another child together.

When two days grew into four days and then five, he was overwhelmed with joy, which was the reason on day six when her courses came, he was devastated with disappointment.

He'd come into their chamber before the evening meal with that ever-present smile on his face and she turned on him with anger flashing in her dark eyes.

"I *told* you not to jump to conclusions because I was late. Now I have to disappoint you by telling you my courses came today." She walked in a circle. It was clear he wasn't the only one disappointed.

He thought perhaps it was more pain than anger that caused her to lash out. Pain he'd caused in his eagerness.

"I'm sorry, Ev. I'm not disappointed with you." Never her.

She let out a noise that might have been a laugh but was clearly not happy.

"No. Of course you wouldn't be disappointed in me. I'm some goddess who does no wrong and is not worthy of you. So you'll blame yourself. You'll think I didn't conceive yet because of some lack on *your* part."

He swallowed. It was true he had wondered if he was at fault. It wouldn't be a surprise for some new obstacle to be placed before him by Fate. And he *wasn't* worthy of her, though he was smart enough not to say that right now.

"I'm sorry I was overexcited by the possibility of a babe,"

he said, hoping they were the right words. Clearly, he'd misjudged when she stomped her foot and screamed.

"You don't need to apologize for wanting the chance to be a father to your own child."

"Perhaps you could just tell me what it is I should apologize for so I can do it properly. I'm afraid I'm not good with this." He came closer, thinking to embrace her.

She gave him a right sturdy shove and he stepped away only to have her come closer and wrap her arms around his waist. Her tears dampened his shirt and he held on as she cried. It was like being trapped in the winds of a storm, being pushed this way and that. Not knowing from which direction the next gale would blow.

"What did I do? I'm so sorry, Ev." He let out a breath and held her close. "I want to make it right. Tell me how to do that. I beg ye."

"You didn't do anything wrong." She calmed a bit, but he remained on edge, sure he would set her off again with his next words. Rather than risk it, he remained silent.

She went on, though her voice remained calm for the moment. "Seeing you excited made me rather excited and now I'm disappointed as well." She pressed her index finger to his chest. "But I'm not disappointed in you. These things happen when they're meant to happen."

"You're right. I'll be more patient."

"And don't track my courses, it makes me nervous."

"Yes." He pulled out the scrap of paper and threw it in the hearth. Since there was no fire burning in July, it just sat there on old ashes doing nothing.

Rather like he felt.

• • •

Evelyn clung to Liam and cried a bit. A bit was all she allowed, since there was no loss. There was nothing to lose. She hadn't been with child.

Still, her heart burned with sadness. Embarrassment for her outburst only made her angrier. Her poor husband didn't know what to do, but damned if he didn't stay there with her and try.

He was a courageous man. Or perhaps daft. She laughed at that, and he pulled back to eye her warily.

"I have to confess, Ev. You're jumping around so much it's like trying to get a drunken man into his bed. I don't know what to do."

"Just hold me. I feel many things right now and I don't feel I have the right to most of them."

"I'll not judge. Go on and feel whatever it is you wish to feel, and I'll just hold on."

"Being perfect isn't helping me right now."

He winked. "I'm afraid I know only how to be perfect. If you needed a flawed man, you should have looked elsewhere. Perhaps in another stall— Ow, woman!" he barked.

She knew she hadn't hit him hard enough to cause that reaction. He was trying to get her to laugh and feel better. And it worked.

She reached up and brushed his hair from his face so she could look at him closer. "You're beautiful."

"Are you sure ye haven't been drinking today?" His wide grin just made him all that more attractive.

"I'm sorry I was distraught."

"You don't ever need to apologize."

She'd ranted at him earlier. She'd said things she shouldn't have, but not everything was untrue or ridiculous. Liam didn't think he deserved an apology from her for mistreating him because he felt he should be lucky to have her.

He felt unworthy, and she didn't know what she might do to change that. She didn't like being held to standards she'd never reach in his eyes. She was bound to disappoint him time and time again.

She looked him in those icy blue eyes that held so much warmth. "I will apologize to you because I treated you badly and I'm sorry for it. It wasn't right to take my anger out on you. You are deserving of my apology."

He nodded but said nothing. She could tell he didn't agree. She'd take his silence as a step in the right direction.

Chapter Twenty-Six

By the next day, Ev was more herself and Liam relaxed again. He'd worried she might not forgive him. He knew Lach and Cam locked horns with their wives from time to time.

Liam hadn't expected he and Ev would ever argue. It was a strange thing to be relieved it had happened. It was easy enough to move on, though it had nearly killed him to allow her to apologize. Later, when he was alone, he thought it over and realized why it was important to her.

During drills in the bailey, Liam dodged out of Colin's way a bit too late and caught a hole in his shirt for his slowness.

"I'm sorry. Did I hurt ye?" the lad asked.

"If ye had, it would have been my own fault, not yours. I wasn't paying attention."

"I don't ever want to be married." The boy shook his head.

Liam remembered a time when he'd felt the same way. He didn't need to tell Colin he'd change his mind. Like any lad, he wouldn't believe it and he'd find out the truth of it soon enough.

He was about to make a move to take down the boy when one of the villagers interrupted. Liam listened carefully to what he shared and nodded. "I'll be there soon. Can you see that he doesn't go anywhere until we arrive?"

"He'll not. He can barely stand," the man assured him.

Liam frowned and told his men to continue while he went into the castle to find the laird. "We've some unpleasantness to deal with in the village," he said, his voice grim. He'd not go into more detail while they were in the solar with the women and children.

Ev looked at him with a smile, but it dropped when he couldn't offer her one back.

Liam selected a few of his men to join them and they left through the gates. "What is it?"

"I've told ye before that Robert has a heavy hand with his wife," Liam said. The man had been locked up for beating her and for threatening Evelyn when she'd tried to protect the woman. He'd promised he'd not touch his wife or child in anger again, but it appeared he'd not kept that promise in the worst way.

"I've spoken to him about what would happen if we were in this position again. I explained we don't hold with that treatment of our women. He's killed his wife."

It was rare a MacKinlay did something so heinous as murder his wife, but when a man gave in to his drink to the point it consumed him, he was no longer a regular man, but one possessed by a need that could never be met.

Lach let out a breath and nodded. "He'll need a swift judgment."

"Aye." That swift judgment would probably come at the end of a rope. They didn't have formal gallows, but a sturdy tree and a swift horse would do the trick.

The woman's body had already been taken away when Liam and Lach arrived. Robert was muttering and throwing punches at anyone who tried to come near.

Liam gave a nod to the warriors he'd brought with him, and they stepped into the fray, quickly overpowering the man and tying his hands behind his back so he could throw no more punches.

"Robert, do ye know who I am?" Lach said loudly, demanding the man's attention.

"Aye, *laird*." He sneered when he spoke the last word. In many clans that would be enough for him to be dispatched. Lach looked at the man with disgust and a bit of pity.

"It's a sad day when a man is so completely controlled by drink that he cannot abide the laws of his people."

"She was my wife, to do with as I pleased."

"Nay. She was a clanswoman, to be treated with respect and honor."

The man spat at Lach. "Worthless, she was. Gave me a worthless brat, too."

"His boy is but six years old and he's tried to put him out for work beyond his years while he sits and drinks," a woman said from the doorway.

"Shut up, ye bitch." Robert lunged at the woman but only stumbled and fell. Since his hands were behind him, he couldn't break his fall and landed on his face. His nose gushed a river of blood, and he moaned a bit before returning to his curses.

Lach frowned and shook his head. "We've warned ye more than once. No more warnings shall be given. You are charged with murder and the punishment is death by hanging."

Lach turned to Liam. "Have my order carried out." A scribe had been called to document the proceedings. Lach signed and stood out of the way with his arms crossed.

Liam didn't need to repeat the order to his men. With a nod, they pulled the man up and dragged him outside. Liam turned to follow but heard a whimper in the shadows of the room. He moved closer and found a small boy tucked into a ball in the corner.

"Ho there, lad. Do ye remember me?" he asked Sheamus.

The boy nodded.

"Have you been in the house all day?" Liam asked, praying with all his might the boy had just returned from one of those jobs his father had sent him on rather than having seen what had happened here.

"Aye."

"You saw what happened? With your ma?"

He nodded and sobbed. "She's dead. He killed her."

"He did, and he's going to be punished for it. He'll never hurt anyone again. The laird doesn't allow his clan to hurt one another. Do you understand why he must be punished?"

Sheamus nodded.

"Do ye have any aunts or uncles?"

The boy shook his head.

"I'll take you to someone who may look after you for a bit." He found the woman who had spoken up. "Might you be able to take him in?"

"Nay. I've no place of my own. I'm sure the Hardys wouldn't mind one more. They have so many children already."

Liam gave a nod. He knew where the Hardy cottage was. He knew his men would take care of the hanging without him, so Liam was able to see to the matter of the boy.

In truth, Liam wasn't one for watching someone die. He'd seen it many times and even caused his share of death on the battlefield, however, protecting yourself and your clan in battle was a very different thing than a hanging. It was too slow, too much thinking of it.

Knocking on the Hardy's door he rested his hands on the lad's shoulders, noticing how he shook. Liam crouched down to his level and gave him the wooden rabbit he'd been working on for Gwennie. She'd not mind if he didn't have one for her today, especially if he told her Sheamus needed it. The two had been fast friends when she'd lived here. "The Hardys are kind people. You don't have to worry about them hurting ye. Do you understand?"

He nodded and wiped at his dirty face. Something in Liam's heart hurt for the boy. Even if he was given food and a place to stay here, he was just another mouth needing fed. Another body. How would he receive any attention or love here?

Mrs. Hardy opened the door and looked down at the boy with a frown.

"Might you have room, mistress? This is Sheamus."

"Would it be temporary? I've only a spot on the floor." Mrs. Hardy had a big heart but unfortunately a small home and a brood of children.

"Aye. I'll try to find him a place with someone else soon enough."

Mrs. Hardy smiled and hugged the boy. "Very well. We'll see you safe for now."

Liam thanked her and turned to leave, but the boy didn't release his hand. He bent down again. "I must get back. I'll see you again soon."

Sheamus said nothing. Simply put his arms around Liam's neck and squeezed. "Thank you, sir."

Liam hugged him back and then stood to go. He turned back once to see the boy wave. Liam needed to do something better than find the boy a place to sleep and food for his belly.

Sheamus MacKinlay needed a home.

After everything was handled with Robert, Liam turned for the castle feeling determined and hopeful. He was certain of what he needed to do and thought Ev would feel the same as he did.

He couldn't wait another moment. Knocking on the door to the solar, all the women looked up. "Might I have a word with ye, Ev?"

She came out into the hall alone, leaving Gwennie to play with the other children. He led her to their room and closed the door.

"Is everything well? You looked so grim when you came for the laird earlier."

"It was not an easy morning. Robert beat his wife to death."

"Oh God. Madra."

"He was punished for it." Liam said sparing the details.

She rested her hand on his arm. "I'm sure that is unpleasant."

"It's easy enough to carry out the laird's orders. I'm sure it weighed on Lach to give them."

Ev nodded and wrapped her arms around him as if she knew he needed her touch to push away the darkness. He held her for a moment or so, enjoying the warmth of her body in his arms before he backed away.

"Poor Sheamus," she said.

"The lad saw everything. I found him hiding in a corner."

"He's a sweet child."

"Aye. A sweet child with no family. I thought we might bring him into ours. Give him a home." Liam was so excited he could hardly stand still. "He and Gwennie are already friends. He could be a big brother to help protect her. I daresay I'll need all the help I can get when she comes of age. She's sure to be beautiful like her mother. The lads will be persistent." He frowned at this thought.

"I am just learning my way with my own child."

Liam didn't like the way she'd said *my*, but he let that go. "I want him to be our son."

"Because I'm not carrying. You said you'd be patient, but my courses come and you're off to the village to find a child."

She threw her hands in the air.

"You know that's not how it is. I thought you would be as happy to help this boy as I am. You know I wanted a big family, I just—"

"Thought you'd take on others rather than wait for me to give them to you?" He knew she'd been disappointed that she wasn't increasing, and he'd not handled it as well as he ought, but this was not like her.

"I can see you're not in agreement with the plan. I've not spoken to him about it, so he'll not be disappointed it didn't work out." Liam bit his bottom lip. "But I want to know why you're against it, because I'm surprised it was not you who made the offer before I had the chance to speak of it."

"Liam..." She reached for him, but he stepped back.

"I want a reason we're not to be the boy's family."

Tears glistened in her eyes.

"Tell me why you can't love him."

"It isn't that," she said as her shoulders slumped.

"Then tell me the reason."

The tears escaped and she shook her head miserably. "I can't."

Rather than rage at her, Liam raced out of the castle and headed for the gate. He found himself roaming across the field where he'd been found all those years ago. A lost soul wandering alone. At times, he still felt that way.

He didn't want that for the boy. He didn't want him to grow into a person with a cold heart from a lack of love. It was clear he'd not been treated well so far. He'd seen far too much for someone so young.

Liam would have to hope some other family would take him in and give him the love he needed to grow into an honorable man. After all, the task of taking in orphans didn't fall solely on Liam's shoulders.

He was no savior, that much was clear.

Chapter Twenty-Seven

Evelyn was sobbing fully by the time she returned to the solar. Kenna and Mari were quick to come to her and offer comfort. Not that she deserved it.

"What's happened?"

She wiped her cheek with the back of her hand and sucked in an uneven breath to answer. "What's happened is I'm a horrible person and an even more despicable wife."

"That can't be true. You've made Liam very happy," Mari was quick to come to her defense.

She shook her head. "No. Liam would be happy with anyone, it's the way he is. He would be so no matter who he called wife. And I just..." She moaned as she sunk to the floor. "I hurt him horribly."

Kenna and Mari attempted to soothe her and get the whole story out of her, but Evelyn couldn't tell them everything. She knew she'd see the disgust in their eyes, and worse, warranted their judgment.

She hadn't been able to tell Liam the truth of why she didn't want to take another child into her heart. It would already be enough to have to walk away from Gwennie and Liam. But to become a mother to Sheamus—a boy whom she already cared for—would be another piece of her heart left behind if she needed to return to her father and do her duty. How could she do it?

"I was rash and selfish." She'd thought of nothing past protecting her already aching heart. "But I was wrong."

Mari and Kenna said nothing but continued to sit by her. Their hands on her back offering support, despite her words.

"I'm a vile person," she finally said.

"That's not true," Kenna said. "What you were was caught off guard. Your reaction may have been extreme, but Liam shouldn't have presented it to you in such a way and not given you the time to think it through."

Mari nodded in agreement. "You should think it through now. You know what Liam wants, but this is your family, too. You have to be sure. It will be much harder to bring the boy into your home and then realize you're not comfortable with such an arrangement."

"Yes. All right. I'll think about it seriously." She gathered herself and stood. "I'll be back. Will you watch after Gwennie?"

They smiled without the judgment she'd expected. Perhaps they had more faith in her than she had in herself. "Of course, take your time."

Evelyn left the castle, planning nothing more than to go for a walk by the loch to think, but instead she found herself in the village. It didn't take but a few questions to locate the boy Liam had thought to make their son.

He was even skinnier than he'd been the last time she'd seen him. His large green eyes had shadows under them, and his wheat-colored hair was filthy. Evelyn smiled to herself when she thought of how he offered yet a different set of features to their motley group.

Liam didn't seem to care what their children would look like as long as they were happy and there were plenty of them.

"Hello there. Do you remember me?"

"Yes, my lady."

"Would you mind walking with me for a bit?" she asked, feeling nervous. He was just a child, one she'd known before, yet she felt she might find herself lacking.

He agreed and followed along beside her, a silent companion as she talked about how lovely the day was. But, of course, it wouldn't be lovely to him. He'd lost his parents today. She frowned at her mistake and went about asking him questions about himself. He answered politely with short answers.

She bought them each a meat pie and handed the rest of hers over when he finished his eagerly.

"Is it good?"

"Aye." When he smiled, she noticed one of his teeth was missing; the new one was already growing in.

"I shall get you another pie. I know what it's like to be hungry." She brushed a piece of hair from his face so it didn't get into his food. He needed a wash and his clothes didn't fit properly. She imagined Madra had done her best and her heart squeezed to think of the woman Evelyn had assumed was safe.

She hadn't lied to the lad. She did understand hunger. When she'd been a prisoner of the McCurdys, they'd not spared a lot of food for her. "Being hungry is a horrible thing."

When he'd finished off the third, they continued on.

"I remember your mother called you Shea." Evelyn stopped to look at him. "I'm sorry about your mother. It must've been horrible. I hate that you had to see it, and I know you will miss her."

"My father beat her until she stopped moving." He said it as if it were nothing more than fact. As if he wasn't personally affected by this tragedy. Already he'd found a way to protect himself by distancing himself from what happened, much as she had done. He'd need someone to help him through this. Someone he could open up to so these memories would not haunt him the way hers did. "They hanged my da."

Evelyn rested her hand on her chest, hoping to keep her heart from breaking for this poor child.

"I understand it may be difficult, but I must say I'm glad for it, for what he did to your mother was very wrong."

"Aye." He nodded. "I won't miss him at all. A right bugger he was."

While Evelyn didn't approve of his language, she thought it was most likely the best description for the beast.

"I imagine he hurt you as well."

Rather than answer, the boy shrugged and looked away. His voice dropped. "I tried to help my mum, but I was too little."

Evelyn kneeled down to his level so she could look him in the eyes. "You shouldn't have needed to protect her. And I am sorry I didn't come back to check on you and your mother. I'll always regret that I didn't. But I am proud of you, that you tried to help. You're a very brave lad."

If any doubts remained about whether she could stop herself from loving this little boy, they were cast aside when his bottom lip quivered and his green eyes glistened with tears he was too proud to let fall.

Shea needed someone to tell him it was fine to cry when he needed to. And she wanted to be that person. She didn't know what would happen if her father came for her, but having one more person binding her to this place wouldn't matter. She couldn't save herself from the pain.

Slowly, she held out her arms. He didn't need a verbal invitation to take the two steps to slam into her so she could wrap him in her embrace.

"Liam and I would be honored to have a brave boy like you join our family. You could be a brother to Gwennie, if you would want such a thing."

"I would have to share my food only with my new sister?" he asked.

She laughed with tears in her eyes. "We will see to it you're not hungry."

His eyes went wide with surprise. "Truly?"

"I promise."

He tilted his head to the side. "Does the war chief drink much?"

She shook her head. "No. Not at all. He will see you have plenty of wooden rabbits." Not to mention his love and protection.

Shea's eyes lit up with recognition.

"Would you like to come live with us?"

"He doesna hit ye?"

Evelyn thought she might be ill to think what this child had lived with in his short life. The questions he asked made it clear he was worried of such a thing happening again.

"Never. He is kind and good." So much kinder than she.

He nodded. "Can I get my things first?"

"Of course. We can stop on the way home."

He put his hand in hers as they walked back to the Hardy's modest cottage. They were good people, just filled to the rafters with their own children. Evelyn explained that she was going to take him. Mrs. Hardy seemed relieved to have one less mouth to feed.

Evelyn watched as Shea collected the small wooden rabbits Liam had given him. They were all he had, and it tightened her throat to see the care he took in gathering them.

After saying his farewells, he and Evelyn continued to the castle. She couldn't stop telling him about his new home and the other children, reminding him of the short time he'd spent there as his mother had healed from her injuries. They'd stopped to give him a good bath in the bailey, and she'd gotten clothes from Kenna.

She couldn't wait to find Liam and tell him the news, but he wasn't at dinner.

When night fell, she began to worry about him. Lachlan told her he might stay out the night if he had a lot to think about.

After being captured by the McCurdys, she was much too afraid to go looking for him in the dark. Even on the MacKinlay lands, nasty things lurked in the darkness.

When she entered the chamber, she thanked the nurse for getting the children settled, but then she realized only Gwennie was in the small bed.

"Where's Shea?" She spun to look for the boy.

"He's there." The woman pointed to the dark corner of the room before leaving.

Evelyn moved the candle so she could see. There on the floor on the scrap of fabric he'd brought with him lay Shea, fast asleep.

"That won't do at all," Evelyn said as she bent to scoop him into her arms. Despite being taller, he was not much heavier than Gwennie. They'd see he was fed so he'd grow strong.

She nudged Gwennie over a bit so there was room for Shea and covered them both with the blanket. After placing a kiss on each of their heads she climbed in bed.

She left the light burning and turned on her side so she could watch her children sleep.

Chapter Twenty-Eight

A light was still burning when Liam entered the room. He'd considered staying out the rest of the night but wanted his bed. He also wanted to hold his wife. He would apologize in the morning now that he knew what he'd done wrong.

It had taken much too long to figure it out, but he knew now he should have approached the topic differently. Given her a chance to think it over. To discuss it with her rather than state it as if she had no choice in the matter.

As her husband, he understood it was his right to make decisions for his family but having the right to do something didn't mean it was the best way to go about it. Still, he was going to try again in the morning. Giving the boy a home was worth some amount of discomfort between him and his wife.

Evelyn slept turned away from him. The candle burned on her side of the bed. After removing his weapons, his boots, and kilt, he moved around the bed to give Gwennie a kiss and blow out the light.

He stopped short when he saw Shea tucked in next to his daughter as if he had always been there.

Liam covered his mouth to keep a sound of surprise from escaping and waking anyone.

"We've another child," Ev said from the bed.

Even in the shadows, he could see her smile. He sat on the edge of the bed close to her and leaned down to kiss her.

"Thank you."

"I don't deserve your thanks. I was awful."

"You did this to make it up to me?" he asked, hoping that wasn't the case. The last thing Shea or he needed was to be resented later.

"No. I was afraid of what the future held for me, Liam. I didn't want to love anyone else I'd be forced to leave someday. But I went to see him, and I couldn't walk away. I want him to be with us. Not out of pity, though he deserves plenty for the life he's lived, but because he belongs with us." She smiled.

"You can love him as your own?"

"It was an easy thing to do." She laughed. "I find myself excited for morning so I can get to know him better and see him smile. He hasn't had much reason for smiles before."

Unfortunately, they didn't have to wait until morning to learn something of their new son. He woke them with his screaming. Gwennie was frightened and wailing as well. It took a good quarter hour to get them both settled enough to speak.

Ev settled on the only chair with both children in her lap. "Shh. It was just a bad dream. Gwennie, you've had them before. Tell your brother what we do when we have bad dreams."

Gwennie answered with a small voice. "We sing them away."

"That's right. We sing a happy song to scare away the bad thoughts."

"I don't know any songs," Shea confessed.

Liam sat on the floor and took Gwennie into his lap.

"We shall teach you a fine song for such things," Ev said happily as if she wasn't the least bit upset she'd been woken from her sleep in such a way.

Liam could only watch in awe as she started to hum and then sing a jaunty tune that had the children laughing in no time. He'd never heard it and wondered if his wife conjured it up out of the air.

When they were all growing weary again, Ev nodded. "I believe for this first night we should all sleep together." She nodded toward Liam for his approval, and he smiled.

"Aye. I think that's a fine idea. Nothing can bother us if we're all together."

The children were asleep within minutes, but he knew his wife was not.

"He has terrors," Liam whispered.

"Did you think he could live the way he had and not?" she said.

"You have them, too," Liam said, remembering the few times she'd woken him by fighting off her demons. "I know who you fight. I'm glad they're long gone from this world. I wish they'd stop bothering ye in your dreams."

She sighed. "You have them as well. Ye yell out some woman's name."

"Moira."

"Yes. Who is she?"

"I don't know. She was an old woman when I was little. I think she was with me, but I lost her. Or maybe I became lost. I'm never quite certain. I call for her to help me. She doesn't come. She fell asleep and I could not wake her."

"Our pasts haunt us while we sleep, when we're not alert enough to keep them away."

"Perhaps if we all hold onto one another, we'll know we're not alone, even in sleep," he suggested, not needing a reason to hold on to his family.

"It would be worth a try," she said and reached across the children to rest her hand on his upper arm. He reached over and laid his hand over her hip.

This was another of those things he'd imagined that wasn't the same in reality. When he thought of his family, he'd thought he'd be able to save them from anything that would cause them unhappiness. But he was only a man. The best he could do was offer comfort and understanding.

As he nestled into the warmth of his family, he thought perhaps that might be enough.

...

Evelyn woke to whispering, though the two children doing the whispering didn't seem to realize it was supposed to be done quietly. Liam shushed them and then frowned when she opened her eyes.

"I'm sorry," he said with a wince.

"It's not your fault. I'm sure you didn't wake them so early."

Another wince. Even more guilty than the first.

"Liam! You woke them?"

"Well, not outright. But I may have disrupted them a bit."

She could only laugh. He was excited to see them, and she couldn't blame him really.

"We're at the part of the tale where the bunny gets on a leaf and goes to see the seals," Shea provided and turned back to Liam. "What is a seal? Like a selkie?"

"No, these would be regular seals," Liam answered.

"They look like rocks and sound like a dog," Evelyn helped as Gwennie made the sound and giggled.

Liam went on with the story, ending as requested with the bunny meeting up with the seal.

"What did they do next?" Shea asked.

Liam's brows raised and he looked at her as if for assistance. She shrugged so he knew he was on his own.

"After the bunny made friends with the seal...he uh..." His eyes lit and he smiled. "A gull came down and scooped him up from his spot on the leaf and flew off with him."

"Where did the gull take him?" Gwennie wanted to know.

"The gull took him to London and the bunny found work and a home there and was happy with the other bunnies."

Evelyn frowned but said nothing. She didn't understand why the gull would have taken the bunny to London of all places or why the bunny needed to find work. After all, being a bunny seemed to be the main job of a bunny.

She brushed it off and got out of bed. Getting two children ready and dressed took much longer than she would have thought. Gwennie and Shea were easily distracted as they dressed and washed their faces. Fortunately, Liam stayed to help. He carried Gwennie while Evelyn held Shea's hand as they went to the hall to break their fast.

Shea looked at his plate with big eyes and then looked up at her. "This is all for me?"

"Yes."

"I don't have to share it?" He glanced down at Gwennie sitting next to him with her own serving of food.

"No," Evelyn said. "We'll see that you're not hungry again." Tears of shame burned her throat and she swallowed them down as she looked at her husband. When he mouthed the words, "Thank you," to her she shook her head. She didn't deserve his gratitude. She should have checked on them after she moved back to the castle. With her husband gone, Evelyn had assumed Madra and Shea were safe. She'd been very wrong.

She reached across to him. "I'm sorry. I nearly missed this chance. I'm so blessed."

"We all are," Liam said.

After the meal, Evelyn took the children to the solar and joined the ladies as they sewed new clothes for Shea. They were always willing to stop working on the clothes for their own growing brood to help someone else.

Kenna smiled at the children. Shea was playing with her boys. "He seems to be settling in well."

"We had some issues last night, but nothing that wasn't to be expected. The poor lad. I must say, I love the boy as much as my own child already. I didn't know how easy it would be. The thought of not having them both…"

She shook her head and turned to Mari. "I've heard you tell the story of how you knew you would be hanged after you gave birth to Lizzy. I'm not sure how you did not go mad with the need to stay."

Mari smiled. "There was a time at the end when I considered running. But it was easy to grasp onto the love I felt for Lizzy and Cam and see what was before us. It is a far easier sacrifice than you'd think to give your life once you know those you love are safe and will go on." She laughed. "Don't get me wrong, I'm beyond glad I'm still here to love them myself. But if I were faced with the same decision today, I'd make the same choice."

Evelyn understood. If her father put her family at risk, she'd give them up if it meant protecting them.

Chapter Twenty-Nine

A few nights later, Liam was awakened in darkness by Gwennie nudging him and crying. "What is it, sweetheart?" He reached to pull her up onto the bed. If she'd been woken by one of Shea's nightmares, she'd settle quickly between him and her mother where she felt safe.

He was barely awake, but he noticed first that Gwennie's gown was wet and then he smelled the cause. Since he'd known the lass she'd not once had a mishap.

"What is it?" Ev asked, leaning over him.

"Gwennie wet the bed."

"Not me. Sheamus," she reported sullenly.

Without complaint his wife got out of bed. "I'll get Gwennie cleaned up and into a dry gown while you take care of Shea."

Liam nodded and got up, stopping when the lad wasn't in the bed. Ev lit a lantern and Liam searched the shadows for the boy, even checking under the bed. Finally, he found him crouched in the darkest corner, curled into a tight ball. He thought the boy might be embarrassed.

Liam sat next to him prepared to reassure him, but Shea flinched away, his head buried in his arms.

"It's all right, lad. Don't worry about it. It's happened to all of us a time or two." Liam had spent many nights sleeping in the hall and after the first mishap, he made sure not to shame himself again in front of the other men.

"Ye don't have a switch leaning in the corner. Do ye use your belt?" Shea mumbled.

It took Liam a moment to piece together what he meant. Liam tried to make the situation lighter with a jest. "Aye. I use my belt to hold up my kilt, so my arse doesn't stick out."

The boy turned his head. There wasn't a smile, but at least the tension eased a bit.

"You aren't going to beat me? I won't cry. Ye canna make me." The last words trembled despite his defiance.

"Nay. I'll never beat you. And besides, it would be a foolish thing to beat someone over something they didn't know they were doing because they were asleep, don't you think?"

He waited until the boy conceded with a short nod.

Liam gave him a friendly nudge. "You don't think me foolish, do ye?"

A quick shake of his head. After a moment he asked, "Will ye beat my new mum?"

Liam let out a breath and rested an arm over the lad's thin shoulders. "I understand—growing up how you did, and what you've seen—why you are worried about such a thing. But I swear on my blade, I'll never lift a hand to you, your sister, or your mum in anger so long as I live. I am the war chief of clan MacKinlay and my blade is my most valuable possession, so any oath I take upon it is true."

Shea didn't move. Liam thought perhaps he was thinking it all through. There was something else the boy needed to understand.

"You're part of my family now, Sheamus. I would give my life to protect you. You don't need to worry. You're safe with us."

His promise not to cry was broken as he leaned on Liam's side and sobbed.

"My da was beating me for being lazy. My ma tried to make him stop and he…he…"

"I know what he did." Liam hadn't realized the woman had been protecting the boy when she'd been killed. What the lad must feel. "Your da paid for what he did. He'll never hurt anyone ever again. And your ma is in a safe place now, too. And she's looking down on ye and smiling, happy that you've found a family to love you."

When he'd quieted, Liam moved away and stood. "Let's get you cleaned up and into dry clothes. There's room for us all in the big bed."

Gwennie was already tucked in and sleeping next to her mother. Ev smiled and helped pull Shea up into bed after he'd changed. He settled in next to Gwennie. There was still plenty of room for Liam as he shifted and turned down the lantern, leaving it burn just enough that no one would be frightened if they woke and didn't know where they were.

"Is he all right?" Ev said when Shea fell immediately to sleep.

"He's had a bad time of it, but he has us now."

"You're a wonderful father," she said with a smile. "To think you could have had this bed to yourself."

Liam laughed quietly. "From the moment I was given this room I could think only of having you in it with me. And children." He reached over and stroked a lock of hair from Gwennie's cheek.

He pointed at the space still left. "Do ye know who might fill this space perfectly?" He tilted his head as if measuring it up. He smiled at Ev who was biting her bottom lip, clearly a futile effort to hold in her own smile.

"Rose?" she whispered. He could hear a hint of hope in her voice.

Liam nodded, happy they were of the same mind on that. "Aye. I'll speak to Lach tomorrow about going and bringing her home to us."

"And what if we have a babe?"

Liam patted his chest and winked at her. "I've still a bit of room here for a tiny one."

She reached across the children and rested her hand on his cheek. He took it, placing a kiss on her palm. "Thank you," she said.

"Nay, it's you who has made us a family," he corrected. "Without ye, I'd just be a lonely soul." He paused and smiled before adding, "With this big bed all to myself."

...

With a kiss, Evelyn saw Liam off the next morning. Lach had given him permission to go get Rose and bring her home to Dunardry.

When he was gone, she and the children met the others in the solar so Evelyn could work on some dresses for their new arrival.

Mari tilted her head. "I believe that dress will be too small for Gwennie."

"It's for Rose."

Kenna was smiling. She must have already known and was eager to share the news. Before Evelyn had the chance to elaborate, the woman blurted it out.

"Liam left for Baehaven to retrieve a little girl and bring her home."

Mari turned to Evelyn with a big smile. "That's wonderful."

"Rose is a little over a year old, though not as big as Andrew," Evelyn nodded toward Kenna's youngest who was just a year.

"My boys are not to be used for gauging the size a child should be." The woman laughed, though it was true enough. The twins were only four and nearly the size of Shea, who was six.

"And wee Cam is the same size as the twins who are a year older than him," Mari pointed out. "We'll have to stop calling him *wee* soon enough."

They laughed and went on with their work. "And soon enough we'll have two more with Rose and my new niece or nephew," Kenna turned to Mari and reached out to place a hand on her stomach. She looked over at Evelyn. "Or three?"

Evelyn shook her head. "No. Not me."

"Not to worry. It will happen when it should. In the meantime, you've plenty of little ones to love."

"I do love them all." She was speaking of the children, but she couldn't help thinking of Liam and how she was beginning to feel for him as well.

...

"Thanks for joining me," Liam said to Cameron as they rode toward Baehaven.

"Aye. I wouldn't miss an opportunity to drop in and point out how Bryce isn't much of a laird."

"From what Lach has said, I thought Bryce was doing well."

"Oh, aye. But my job is to make sure his head doesna get too big to get through the gates."

Liam smiled. It had always been that way between the cousins. Despite the roughhousing and rudeness, they were like brothers. Many times, Liam wished he could join in, but he wasn't family. "I'm sure he'll appreciate your visit."

"I hear your words, Liam MacKinlay, but then I also hear what ye didn't say as well." Cam scowled.

"That he'll be glad to see you go?" Liam joked and Cam laughed heartily.

"I think your woman has changed you," he said.

"How so?"

"You seem more...sure of yourself."

Liam's smile faded a bit. "I have a family of my own now. I feel like I finally belong somewhere."

"Don't let Lach hear ye say that. He'd skin ye for thinking you didn't have a place before ye married Evelyn."

"I don't mean any offense." Truly, he didn't. The laird often said he was one of them, but they were words. The man was accepting like his father before him.

"Nay. You never want to offend." Cam made it sound as if this were a bad thing. Liam let it go.

A while later Cam shifted in his seat and squinted as he looked at Liam.

"What?" Liam asked, uneasy with the scrutiny.

"I figured Lach was sending ye to Baehaven to deliver something, but I don't see any packages."

"No. I asked Lach if I could go. He has a letter for Bryce, but a messenger had already taken the parcels last week."

"Then why are we going to Baehaven?"

Liam couldn't hold back his grin. "I'm adding to my family. I'm picking up a small girl we met on our visit. Her name is Rose. She's a brave mite. Many little children who don't know me are often standoffish, because of my eyes, I think. But not Rose. She walked right up to me and held up her hands for me to pick her up."

"Another child who isn't your own?" Cam said it without judgment. Just a fact.

"Aye. I wish I had room for more of them. There were

many orphaned when we took over the McCurdys last year. Dorie renovated the dungeon as a children's ward."

"They're keeping the children in the dungeon?" Cam frowned.

"You'll see. It's warm, dry, and pleasant."

"A pleasant dungeon." Cam sniffed. Though it was an accurate description.

They made camp and hunted for their dinners. Lach couldn't remember a time he'd been with just Cam without heading into battle.

"I can see how selecting a child can be far easier on one's nerves than waiting for your woman to give birth."

"Are you worried about Mari?"

"Always, but more so when she's increasing. She's so small. It's taken me some time to understand that small doesn't mean weak. My wife is the strongest person I know. Not just for birthing my large children, but for the things she's faced. The way she has moved past the darkness with such grace it humbles me."

Liam nodded. "I see it in Evelyn as well. Not just what she faced with the men who kept her captive, but having to give Gwennie up... I'm not sure how she survived it. I can't imagine a day without them now that they're in my life."

"We are lucky bastards indeed."

"Before when you said I got to select the children," Liam recalled. He shook his head. "It doesn't work like that. They select you."

Bryce rode out to meet them late the next morning when Baehaven castle was in sight. The new laird smiled and greeted them warmly.

"I'm glad to have ye visit. Or is there something that needs sent off on a ship?" Bryce eyed their horses.

"Nay," Cam said. "I've come to see what a piss poor job you're doing here. I hear you've locked up children in your dungeon. Liam has come to free a wee lass from your evil clutches."

"Is that so?" Bryce said, ignoring his cousin's other comments. "Dorie mentioned your daughter had taken a liking to one of the little ones during your last visit. I'm happy to see her find such a wonderful home with ye, Liam."

Bryce smiled a lot more now than he ever had when he'd lived at Dunardry. Liam suspected it had more to do with his wife than the location. Though being a laird and having his own clan seemed to set well with him.

"I'm happy to say we've found homes for a few more since you left. We may be able to turn it back into a dungeon soon. Not that we've been in much need of one. I'm happy to say the people who stayed on with us haven't caused much trouble. They've accepted me as laird quite easily."

"It wouldn't take much effort on your part to be a far better laird than the McCurdy," Liam said. "There was more than one McCurdy sword pointed back on their own warriors that day in the hope of freedom from their rule."

Cam laughed. "Aye, but the threat of being put on a ship with no return passage most likely helps with their loyalties as well."

"Ye make it sound like we throw them overboard." Bryce rolled his eyes at Cam's accusation.

Dorie was waiting to greet them when they rode into the bailey. She had their son Dorien on her hip and a smile on her face. "It's great to see you again so soon."

Bryce kissed her and took the boy from her. "You were right when ye thought they might want to take Rose. That's why Liam has returned."

"It's always a joy to hear when I'm right, but even more so when it's wonderful news." She looked at Cam. "And what about you?"

"Nay. I'm here to visit."

They were given a meal and stayed late into the evening with their drinks, talking about past battles like old times.

The next morning, they followed Dorie down into the children's ward. As Bryce had said, there were fewer children than before. Rose was still there and came running to Liam with her arms up as she had the first time. He happily swept her up and kissed her pudgy cheeks.

He was filled with joy to hear her laugh. His happiness was shadowed slightly when he noticed the four remaining children. Twin boys, probably five years, who had been playing with Rose. And two older boys maybe ten or eleven.

"The two older boys will be happy to join the grooms in the stables. The twins will be harder," Dorie fretted. "I do hope they can stay together."

Cameron crouched down to talk with them as Liam played with the newest member of his family. As happy as she was, he was surprised when he started to carry her out and her bottom lip pushed out and she reached behind him.

"Did we forget something?" he asked. When she wailed and squirmed, he put her down. On uneasy legs she tottered over to the twins.

"Where is it?" the boy said with a laugh. He brushed some straw aside. "Here it is. Hold onto it tight," he encouraged as he held up the little wooden bunny Liam had carved. The one Gwennie had given Rose when they'd visited.

Thinking she was settled now, he picked her up again, only to have the same thing happen, despite her grip on the rabbit.

She ran back to the smaller boys and crawled on the one boy's lap. It was clear his new daughter was attached to the twins. He rubbed his forehead. "I canna go home with three when my wife sent me for the one," he whispered to Dorie. She laughed and nodded.

"Boys, Rose has a new home. She needs to leave. Can

you walk her out with us?"

The boys were quick to comply, and each held her hand so she could manage the steps herself. "Your new da will be able to make you more bunnies, Rose."

Liam appreciated their help, but it wasn't enough for Rose to go quietly when he settled her on his lap once he'd mounted.

"You're all right, Rose. We will probably be leaving soon, too," one of the boys reassured her.

Liam could see the boy didn't believe what he said, and it hurt Liam's heart to have to leave them.

Just then Bryce laughed loudly and nodded. "Aye. I think we can manage that. Are you sure?"

Cameron let out a breath and nodded. "I may end up having to move here with ye if she doesn't like it, but I have to. I canna leave them here. Not when I have room in my house as well as my heart. What kind of man would I be?"

Bryce spoke to one of the older boys who ran off toward the stables. A few minutes later he returned with a small horse.

"Up you go, lad. I'm taking ye home with me," Cam said to the first boy. He eyed the one horse and then gripped his brother's hand and shook his head. "You'll both share the horse. Which of ye wants to be in the front?"

The boys looked at each other and smiled. Without discussion, they took their places. Liam had seen Lachlan's twins do the same thing, tell each other things with no more than a look.

Once they were seated on the horse, Liam pointed and spoke to Rose. "Seems they're coming with us."

Rose quieted and other than leaning out occasionally to make sure they were still there, she was happy the rest of the trip.

"I didn't truly understand until now," Cam mused as he

looked at the boys riding next to him while they pointed and exclaimed over Dunardry in the distance.

Liam laughed. "Did you think it was you who was saving them?"

Cam nodded. "Aye."

Liam had been just as mistaken when he'd wanted Sheamus to join their family. He knew the boy had been through a lot and wanted to give him peace and a place to call home. But it wasn't very long before Liam realized the boy wasn't just taking, he was giving so much by being part of their family.

He could only hope Cam and Mari would be as happy with their choice. Or rather Cam's choice. They would find out soon enough how Mari would feel about the situation.

They were met in the bailey by Liam's family, Kenna, and Lach. Of course, the laird and mistress would want to meet their newest clan member. Or members, as it turned out to be.

When Ev stepped forward with her arms up and tears in her eyes to take Rose, he realized he'd been mistaken on another thing—love wasn't something that was. It was something you did. And kept doing because you couldn't help yourself.

He swung down from his mount and held her as she wept with a smile on her face.

Chapter Thirty

When Liam had ridden into the bailey, Evelyn could see only the grin on his face and the tiny angel in his arms. She hadn't paid much attention to Cam and definitely didn't see the smaller horse behind him carrying the twins, who were alike in every detail, including the way they hunched slightly in their new situation.

"Liam?" Evelyn whispered as she took them in, nearly the same size as Shea. She recognized them from the children's ward at Baehaven when they'd visited.

She wondered how they'd all fit together in the one room but wouldn't scold her husband for bringing them. She would love every gift she was given while she had the chance and deal with how to handle her father if or when the time came.

Liam had a huge heart and she'd not break it ever again by telling him he couldn't help a child. Even if they were wall to wall with children.

Liam picked up Gwennie and ruffled Shea's hair affectionately, but he looked at her when she said his name. Together they turned as she watched Cam lift the boys down from the horse.

"Cam decided to bring the twins home with him."

Kenna and Lach must have overheard his explanation, for Lach chuckled as Kenna instructed a maid to go bring Mari right away.

"You may want to tell your sister to bring a fireplace poker," Lach said, referring to the fact Mari killed her first husband, small as she was. Kenna frowned at his inappropriate joke.

"I couldn't pass up the chance to have my own twins," Cam said, a hand on each of their shoulders. He winked at them, and Evelyn knew it wasn't Cameron's competitive nature that had made him bring the boys home.

Mari entered the bailey and smiled at her husband. The smile faltered slightly when she took in the boys. "Mari, we have some wonderful news."

Mari glanced over to where Evelyn was holding Rose and took a breath before turning back to the boys. "Are you to live with us, then?" she asked.

They nodded in unison and Cam leaned down to kiss his wife. "Thank ye."

"I'm sure it will be me who is thanking you," she said quietly, though Evelyn still heard it.

Two families had been enriched this day. And three children brought home.

"I'm starving," Liam said, putting Gwennie down. "I'm too weary to find food."

Gwennie and Shea laughed, each taking a hand they led Liam into the hall and toward a table, giggling when he veered to one side in his "weakened condition" as he called it. Rose even joined in with her own laughter and pointed.

Not long ago, Evelyn was alone facing a future she had no control over. And now she was blessed with this rowdy bunch that belonged to her. If the time came to go to war with her father, she might well take him down herself to keep what she had here.

...

"You summoned me?" Liam bowed before the laird in his study. Cam was resting against the window. It had been two weeks since they'd returned from Baehaven with the children. His family had settled in, and he knew Cam's had as well.

It was a surprise to see Lach and Cam looking so grim. Unease twisted in Liam's stomach.

"Aye. You know I sent the Stewart a letter telling him his daughter and granddaughter resided with us, and I made it clear it was where they would stay."

"Yes. Having you address it directly was the better approach. We've not seen any Stewarts this last month."

Lach gave a short nod and let out a breath. "As you well know, it's a father and laird's right to marry his daughter off for an alliance, as it's something bigger than just his child's happiness, but the strength of the whole clan that may depend on it."

"Aye," Liam said, his brows pulled together in confusion.

"This was the reason Evelyn had been promised to the Morgan clan, because the Stewarts needed cattle, and a match was made between their clans."

Liam's eyes went wide.

"I can see from your reaction you didna know she was promised elsewhere."

"Nay." Liam frowned. "I can't say honestly it would have mattered, but I would have prepared you at least. Found another place to live until we were certain we weren't a danger to the clan."

"I'm not sure if Evelyn was aware, either. But I doubt she would have said anything if there were a chance you'd not take her and Gwennie with you. It's clear she wanted only to be with her daughter at the time you married her."

His words stung Liam's heart. He knew it was true at the time, but he hoped, now that they were closer, it was different between them. He felt like a true husband.

"Her father has demanded her returned to him with a signed annulment so she can be married off to the Morgan heir as planned next month. They're coming and plan to take her either by force or by law."

Liam looked between Lachlan and Cam. "They're taking my wife?" He thought the man would bluster about but would give up. He'd known Evelyn still worried.

"Nay. I tell you only what he's demanded." Lachlan placed his hand on Liam's shoulder. "I made a mistake once when I didn't stand with Cam to protect his wife, and I'll not make the same mistake again. Evelyn will stay with us and, when they come for her, we will protect her as one of our own."

Liam shook his head and backed away. "I can't allow it. It's too great a risk. I'll take Ev and the children, and we'll flee. I can't put the clan in danger for me."

Lachlan and Cam exchanged a look and turned to him. "We'll not let anyone take a member of our clan from our lands."

"As you say, but she's not a member of the clan because... I'm not. Not truly. I'm not MacKinlay. Not by blood."

Lachlan's head snapped back as if he'd been struck, and his gaze narrowed in anger on Liam. "Take off your shirt," he demanded.

Liam didn't understand. "Laird?"

"That's right. I'm the laird you pledged fealty to when you could barely hold a sword. Now take off your shirt."

Liam tugged it from his belt and reached behind his neck to pull the garment over his head. Balling the cloth up in one hand, he stood before them bare-chested. He spared a second for the old embarrassment, but it was gone when he remembered he was a man now. He'd filled out in the last years and was no longer a scrawny lad.

Cam crossed his arms and studied him. "How many scars would you say he has on his body?"

"Forty or so," Lach answered as he stepped closer. He pointed at a larger one on Liam's shoulder. "Tell me, Liam, did ye bleed from this?"

"Aye." It had happened during a raid. Cam had been injured and Liam was so worried for his friend he hadn't noticed he was wounded until later that night.

"And whose blood spilled from this wound if not MacKinlay?"

"I—you know I do not know, my laird." Liam tried to swallow.

"All of these scars for a clan you do not wish to belong to?"

Liam shook his head. "It's not that I don't wish to belong. I've wished it as long as I can remember. But wishing does not make things so." How well he had learned this.

"I know it well enough, for I wish you to know in your heart you are one of us. You are my brother. Your blood has spilled on my land in protection of my people. If that doesn't make you a MacKinlay I canna say what would. Being born with the name is not enough."

"I didn't mean disrespect. I am beyond proud that your sire allowed me to use the name as my own."

"He didn't allow you to *use* it!" Lachlan shouted and gave Liam a harsh shove that nearly knocked him off his feet. "My father *gave* you the name MacKinlay because he found you honorable enough to have earned the right. I know you would give your life for any one of us here, yet you refuse us the honor of our protection for you and your family."

Tears leaked from Liam's eyes and his throat was almost too tight to speak, but he managed. "Forgive me, brothers."

Their hands came down hard upon his shoulders as they leaned close. "Whose blood ran from your wounds and consecrated the MacKinlay lands?"

"Mine," Liam answered fiercely. "Liam MacKinlay." He had no long list of names from his parents, just the two simple ones Roderick and Davinna MacKinlay bestowed on him as a child. The two names he was honored to have.

The laird nodded and offered Liam a smile. "If you dare say to me you're not a MacKinlay again, I'll make sure your lip is too swelled to say anything else. Do you understand?"

"Aye. I understand." Liam wiped the moisture from his cheeks and took a deep breath. He'd been overwhelmed by their generosity, but he should have known better.

He'd be upset as well if Gwennie or Shea ever said they weren't part of his family. Blood wasn't as important as love and honor.

"Thank you for standing with me to save my family," Liam said, humbled.

They thumped him on the back a few times, and the dramatic moment was over as they moved on to planning. A messenger was dispatched immediately to Baehaven to have Bryce's warriors sent.

Liam still didn't feel it his right to ask them to fight, but he realized now he didn't have to ask. These men didn't think twice about helping him as one of their own. It was time he accepted the honor they offered.

They split off to gather men and supplies. Liam took a moment to find Evelyn and tell her the news of what was happening. He expected her to be surprised and then to worry over what was to be done. He was the one surprised when she let out a soft curse and paced to the window.

"You knew your father planned to marry you to the Morgans?" His voice was flat. He'd read the man's early letter that spoke of duty, but Liam had not known she was pledged.

"Aye."

"And you said nothing?" He tried to keep the irritation from his voice but failed.

"I said nothing when I approached you in the stable because I feared you'd leave me behind if you knew. After we were married, I said nothing because it no longer mattered. I wasn't available to wed the laird's heir."

"I thought he was merely angry you'd disobeyed him when he sent for you. You've underestimated how badly your father wants this alliance. He's demanding an annulment so you're free to wed the Morgan as planned."

"Is there no other way out of this than battle?" she asked.

"Aye, there is. But it would take more cattle than we currently own. It's not a viable course of action." Liam and the others had already looked over every possibility. "You should have told me the truth. We would have had more time to leave. To travel to London or somewhere even farther away so your father couldn't reach you."

There was little time now. They wouldn't be able to get far enough fast enough with three little children slowing them down. The Stewart warriors wouldn't stop until they were found.

She nodded and paced a bit more. "I know. I wanted to. I planned to. But...I couldn't risk that you'd send Gwennie away." Eventually, she came to stand in front of him. "You'll care for Rose, Gwennie, and Shea as your own?"

He frowned, unsure why she would doubt him now. "They are my children. You know I will always see them safe and happy while there's breath in my body." Even if it meant providing for them while they lived in London if they managed to get there.

Another nod. "Then I'll go. Please let my father and the Morgans know I'll go peaceably, that you'll sign the annulment."

"Have you lost your mind, woman? I'll not give you up. You're my wife. You're the mother of my children and could be carrying another one right now. Handing you over to them was never one of the choices. It was either our family runs or our family stays and fights, but we're a family, Evelyn MacKinlay."

"When I married you, it was so that my daughter would have a loving home. I've done that. She's safe here with you. I'll not allow blood to be spilled for me. I'm but one person. Please tell them my wishes."

"You can't mean to do this." He shook his head.

"I do. Now that Gwennie is safe and loved, I can see to my duty. I knew it might come to this one day."

Liam stepped away as her words singed his heart. "I didn't know your duty was so important to you."

"I'm the daughter of a laird, to be used for alliances and traded for wealth."

"You would choose to be a laird's daughter over being the mother of my children and my wife?"

"I don't get a choice. This is what I must do, what I was born to do."

He'd seen the way she looked at him when he made love to her. He'd seen the joy in her eyes when she watched their children sleeping. She couldn't possibly mean to turn her back on them.

"Please, Ev. We need you here. We've sent to Baehaven for more men. We'll fight and we'll win, and you'll stay as my wife."

"All those deaths for me?" She shook her head and brushed away the tears. "No. I'll not live with that." She speared him with her dark gaze.

"Then we'll leave today. We can be on a ship three days from now. We'll go to London, I'll find work."

She gasped. "You've planned this? The story with the

bunny..."

"Yes. I didn't know what options would be available. I only wish there was more time."

She stepped away but came right back, shaking her head. "No. I don't want the children to grow up in London. I want them here, with their family where they belong. Where you belong."

"Our family belongs wherever we go."

"No. You promised me the day we were wed you'd never force me to do anything. Did you mean it, Liam?"

He let out a gust of breath as if he'd been caught in the stomach by a fist. She meant to use his promise, spoken in duty, against him now? Anger grew hot in the pit of his stomach as he bit out his answer. "Aye, wife. I'm a man of honor."

"Then you'll not force me to stay here." She would not meet his eyes now. He waited. He would not make it easy for her to walk away.

When she finally looked at him, she did not waver. "Will you give me my freedom, or will you keep me captive as the McCurdys did?"

His heart plummeted to his feet. "You can't mean to compare me to..."

He might have continued, but it was difficult to argue the hard coldness in her eyes when she broke his heart. She planned to leave and there was nothing he could say to stop her.

"What will I tell the children?" he asked, his voice barely a whisper.

"Tell them..." She shook her head. "It doesn't matter what you tell them." With that, she pushed by him and left the room that had been their home.

• • •

Evelyn managed to make it out of the keep and to the back

of the stables before breaking down. Tears poured down her cheeks as she gasped for breath. She thought she might die from the pain.

It was bad enough to have to leave them. Though Mari had been right that making a sacrifice to save the ones you loved was easy enough when you were certain they could go on and there were no other choices.

But seeing the pain in Liam's eyes... Pain she'd caused with her words. Words she wanted to take back. But she had to do this to spare him and the others who would fight and fall to protect her.

She couldn't allow it.

Even the thought of Liam dying for her, caused her stomach to heave. Any time men came to battle they fell. If even one MacKinlay was lost to save her from a fate she was destined to live anyway, she couldn't bear it.

This was better.

He'd hate her. She shook her head as more tears fell. No, he *wouldn't* hate her. Liam wasn't capable of hate. His heart wasn't made that way. He may have to raise his sword and kill to fulfill his duties as war chief, but it wasn't hatred that drove him.

She'd have to dig deep for the strength needed to carry through with this plan. She wanted so much to stay here with her husband and children. Have more children—either by birth or by love—and watch them grow. But the risk to fight was too great. If Liam were lost and she was forced to marry the Morgan heir, who would take care of Rose, Gwennie, and Shea? She'd have won nothing if the Stewarts and Morgans outnumbered her new clan.

What if Lachlan or Cameron were struck down in her defense? Kenna and Mari would be alone to raise their children. They would despise her, and rightfully so.

Evelyn would never regret marrying Liam or coming

here. The last months had been the best of her life, and she would rely on those memories to get her through whatever was to come. But she was leaving. She'd play the part of the laird's daughter and face her duty in order to protect the people she loved.

An hour had passed before Evelyn pulled herself together and could continue with her plan without risk of faltering. She'd have to hurt Liam to save his life.

Maybe one day he could forgive her.

...

Liam felt empty as he went back to the solar to tell the laird of Evelyn's decision. Cameron was still there so Liam would be spared from having to tell it more than once.

He wasn't certain he'd manage the one time.

They looked up at him when he stepped closer.

"What's wrong? Your skin's near the same color as your hair," Cam said with wide eyes.

Liam's vision fluttered at the edges in the way it did when he'd taken a particularly sharp blow to the head and was about to lose consciousness. He almost hoped he'd be lost to the darkness for a bit.

He knew from past experience when he left this realm there was no pain until he returned.

And one thing he knew, he would need to return. He had three children to care for. Three small people who weren't going to understand why their mother chose to leave them.

Since he didn't understand himself, he'd never be able to explain it.

"Evelyn has decided to go peaceably. She wishes to take the annulment and marry the Morgan heir as the Stewart laird has commanded." He swallowed past the lump in his throat. He'd already gone to tears in front of them once today.

"You can't be serious."

"She said it is her duty. Being a laird's daughter, she knew it might come to this. Now that she found a home for Gwennie, she'll go in peace and take her place as wife to the Morgan heir."

"Don't you see what this is?" Cam said with a harsh laugh. "She's doing the same thing Mari did. These bloody women think they need to protect us." He threw his hands in the air and rolled his eyes.

"She wasn't interested in running so we could stay together. She didn't even consider it."

"Mari didn't consider it, either. Running is no way to raise children. They're not wrong on that."

"What do I do? I made her a promise I'd never force her into anything. How do I break that promise? How do I make her stay when she's determined to go?" It was almost too much to hope they had an answer. She'd seemed so clear in her choice.

"You do nothing," Lach said as he walked to the window to look out over the rolling hills.

Liam opened his mouth to protest, but Cam was nodding in agreement. "Let her think we have conceded. We'll still have Bryce and his men join us. We'll say it's in case they decide to raid us while they're here."

Lach nodded. "It would be a prime opportunity when the two clans were here to stand against just us. In the meantime, allow her to think we're going along with her plan. Eventually, she'll realize it's not feasible and allow us to do what we're meant to do. Protect our families."

Liam didn't see the harm in preparing; he could only hope they were right, and that Ev would eventually change her mind and decide to stay with him.

Now he would need to win her heart and make her see the only choice was to stay with him.

Chapter Thirty-One

All conversation stopped when Evelyn took her seat at the table next to Liam for the evening meal. Mari sat next to her and reached over to pat her leg. That small kindness almost broke Evelyn into tears again, but she bit her bottom lip to make it stop trembling and went about her meal.

Rose climbed into her lap and patted her face. "Mum, mum, mum," the baby babbled, and Evelyn pressed a kiss to her hair, breathing in her scent. As was normal, the lass squiggled back over to Liam, and he bounced her on his knee and held out a bit of food for her. He'd already seen to cutting Gwennie's food so she could manage it on her own. Shea's food was long gone and he was waiting for another helping.

Without a word spoken they'd shown her the little things that make up being part of a family. A family that would go on without her.

"Mama, look what Papa made." Gwennie reached across Liam to hold out a piece of wood.

Evelyn took it expecting it to be a rabbit, but it wasn't. "A seal." She smiled as she turned it about. She let her thumb glide over the smooth flipper. "You did it," she said to Liam.

He said nothing back. Just allowed a sharp nod.

"You'll be fine," she whispered, desperate for him to understand.

His glare stole her breath. The icy blue of his eyes had never seemed cold until that moment. "I will never be fine." With that, he placed Rose in her lap and left the table.

Evelyn didn't cry. She didn't deserve it. After what she'd done to Liam, she had no right to seek comfort with tears. She was a horrible person leaving him like this, but she knew one day he'd move on and see why she had to go.

Shea scooted over and finished the food on Liam's plate. She brushed his hair back from his face.

"Why are you sad?" he asked.

She managed a smile. "I'm not sad. I love you all too much to be sad."

Liam didn't come to their room that night or the next. She thought it was for the best, but she wished she'd have the chance to love him one more time. To hold him, to feel his touch.

When she left Dunardry, she'd have only memories of this life. The man she was pledged to marry would probably want children. She'd have to lie with him, but the thought brought only distaste.

Liam would remarry if for nothing else but to have someone to help with the children. She couldn't help but hope he'd find happiness with his new wife. There was no time for being petty or jealous. She needed to hold on to the love and happiness every minute she could.

For too soon it would be gone.

• • •

Liam had stayed away from his wife for fear his anger would

get the best of him and he'd truly become a beast. She'd asked him if he planned to hold her captive like the McCurdys. He'd thought the idea impossible, that he could ever be like those monsters, but he felt like a monster now.

Three days since he'd touched her and already he felt cold and inhuman. What would happen when she was truly gone?

"Papa, look, rabbit." Gwennie pointed at a live rabbit hopping in the grass by the stream.

"Do you think he's going to jump on a leaf?" Shea asked.

Liam did his best to show Rose the rabbit, but she wasn't looking in the right place. Shea lost interest and went back to his own carving.

While Liam was doing his best to avoid Ev, he'd made it a point to spend time with the children so they'd not see how upset he was. After all, if Evelyn got her way, it would just be the four of them soon enough. He should get used to managing their care on his own.

He knew how to feed them and get them bathed and dressed. He knew how to make them laugh and how to settle them for bed and deal with unruly behavior. He was their father in every sense of the word except by blood.

He'd see them raised well and loved, but he didn't know how he'd deal with their questions and tears about their mother who left them. Maybe one day they'd all look back and know she did it out of love for them. But at the moment it didn't feel like love at all.

She lacked faith in him.

Or perhaps it was something else altogether. The thought was but a fleck of doubt, but it sprouted and grew until he had no choice but to seek her out.

They all returned to the castle and, with the children playing in the solar, he asked to speak to Ev with a sharp request. She was quick to join him in the hall and follow him to their room where he closed the door behind them.

Without a word, she launched herself into his arms. His own arms were trained to pull her close despite the agony in his heart. She reached up and kissed him. Her soft lips on his felt like home, and he gave in to the feeling for a moment before he remembered why he had brought her here and set her away.

"Do you wish to slum about with a commoner up until the last minute you're given to the laird's heir?" He didn't recognize his own voice, so full of contempt and anger. "Perhaps you plan to go to him with my babe in your belly. It would be a grand thing for a child from a bastard like me to be a laird someday."

He was ashamed of his words as soon as they were out. Rather than apologize, he leaned against the wall and slid down to sit, letting his head hang.

"In truth," her voice wavered, "I do hope I'm carrying your child. Maybe the Morgans wouldn't want me then and I'd be able to stay. And if I find out later when I'm already gone from you, I'd be happy to have a piece of ye with me."

"I'm sorry for what I said. It's just easier to be angry with you than try to understand why you would walk away from our family."

"Even if you can't understand, you must know I don't want this. I'd stay if it were possible without endangering so many others."

She reached out her hand to help him up. It seemed almost humorous that someone so small would offer to assist a warrior of his size to his feet. But as Cam had said, these women were stronger than they gave them credit for. She had certainly broken him, sturdy as he was.

He stood without touching her and turned for the door.

"Liam."

He paused, hoping with all his heart she would tell him she'd changed her mind. Instead, she said in a faint whisper,

"Forgive me."

He left her with her useless apologies and went out to the stables to throw things about.

• • •

"He is so angry," Evelyn said when she returned to the solar. She'd thought perhaps they could move forward and enjoy the time they had left. But it was clear, Liam was filled with rage.

"Do you blame him?" Kenna said while glaring at Mari. "I know well what it's like to have someone leave you for your own good. It's unpleasant and unforgivable."

"I thought you said you forgave me when I did not end up hanged by the English," Mari said with wide eyes.

"Fine. I did forgive you, but I'm still sore over it."

"I wish Liam was only sore with me. I think he may hate me. He said the most horrible things."

"Cam called me a coward," Mari said. "I was facing death at the end of a rope, and he said I wasn't brave enough to live for him and Lizzy."

"That seems a bit unfair," Kenna said, focusing on her knitting.

"Oh? Is it more unfair than a letter from my younger sister saying it's better the English do it because if you were there, you'd choke me to death yourself?"

Kenna waved a hand. "I've always been one for dramatics. I was trying to make you mad. When a person is angry it means they haven't given up."

"Do you think that's what it means for Liam as well? Perhaps he doesn't hate me?"

"He surely doesn't hate you, and they've not given up," Kenna said. "The men are up to something, I feel it. Best to let them to it."

Evelyn shook her head. "I'll not let there be a battle and risk your men. They are husbands and fathers and not to be sacrificed for the likes of me."

"And what does that mean?" Kenna tilted her head curiously.

"I knew when I left my father that he had plans to wed me off. I disregarded them because I wanted to be with my daughter. And now I must pay the price for my disobedience."

"Disobedience? Is that what you call wanting to live in happiness? I call that determination," Kenna said. "I call it strength. And courage." She patted Evelyn on the knee. "I'll stand next to ye no matter what you decide to do."

"Thank you."

"I have an idea," Kenna said while tapping her chin.

"Is she not facing enough trouble already than to deal with whatever idea you've conjured up?" Mari said.

Evelyn was desperate for any way to reach Liam and mend things between them. Even if she had to use one of Kenna's ill-fated ideas to do so.

Chapter Thirty-Two

Liam sat in the hall watching the stairs for his wife and children. It was always one of his favorite times of day when they spotted him and smiles lit their faces. Gwennie and Shea often ran ahead, the quicker to get to him. Rose reached for him as soon as Ev got close enough. And his wife would greet him with a kiss no matter how many others were gathered in the hall; she didn't care who saw.

But today it wasn't his wife who led his children to him. They came among the other children with Mari, Kenna, and a nurse herding the brood.

Liam stood and went to meet them. "Where's Ev?"

"She's not feeling well. I believe she has a fever."

"Have you sent for a healer?"

"Oh, aye," Kenna was quick to say. But Liam had already kissed his children and told them to stay with their aunties.

He took the stairs two at a time and rushed into their room to find Ev abed. Her hair was down, and she was wearing only her shift.

"Kenna said you were sick. What is it?" He placed his

hand on her head to feel her skin was much too hot.

"You're burning up," he said, while going to get a cool cloth. When he turned around, she was naked except for the saucy smile she wore on her lips.

"I do burn, Liam. For you."

"My God." He dropped the cloth and stared at his wife as she reached for him. She was a temptress with her hair flowing and her breasts plumped up in her own hands.

He'd fallen completely under her spell. He didn't even realize he'd tugged off his boots until he heard them thump to the floor. His shirt was off as he rounded the bottom of the bed. His belt and kilt dropped next, and he crawled onto the bed next to her.

"You're so hot," he said as his hands touched her skin. "Are you ill?"

"Nay. I just stood close to the fire before you came in. It was Kenna's idea. She did the same when she was little and wanted to get out of her lessons."

Liam laughed. "I can imagine it." He shook his head. "What were you trying to get out of?"

"Sitting at the table with my husband who hates me."

He let out a shaky breath as she placed a kiss on his neck and another lower. Her tongue traced his nipple, and he was shocked to find it made him jump with pleasure. She nipped him with her teeth and he groaned.

He'd not wanted to give in to this. He knew she wanted them to go on as if nothing was wrong so they could have a few grand memories. He'd refused, wanting her to see now how destroyed they would be when she left. But he couldn't resist her any longer. Not when she looked up at him with those dark eyes and licked the length of his cock.

"Christ almighty," he cursed and twitched.

"It is amazing how much pleasure can be given with one's mouth," she said as she took another swipe with that pink tongue. He'd been wrong. This would end him. She was giving mercy by killing him before he had the chance to miss her.

When her warm mouth captured him, he cried out. He was too weakened by her sorcery to put up much of a battle against it. He lay there receiving her attentions, and when he was so close he feared he'd spend, he pulled her away. It was one thing to allow her to put her mouth there, another entirely to do *that*.

But she wasn't to be stopped. Rather than continue with her mouth, she straddled him. A groan left his throat as she slid down on him. Unlike the temperature of her skin, this heat was expected.

"Ev, I'll not last. You're too…I'm…"

She smiled and leaned close to kiss him. "This is for you, husband. We've all night to share our pleasures together."

"All night?"

"Aye. That was the other part of Kenna's plan. She and Mari will keep the children tonight."

True to Ev's word, they spent the whole night in each other's arms. A tray of food was sent up and left for them outside the door. They ate and made love and eventually they spoke.

At first, they strayed from the subject of their future; instead they spoke of their childhoods. They'd shared stories with each other before, but this was different. This was all the feelings that went with it. How she was afraid of disappointing her father. He could see she wanted much the same thing he did. To be loved and wanted. He thought of their children and how badly they needed those things as well.

They rested and woke again reaching for each other. He couldn't get enough. He thought he might convince her to stay, but she had instead convinced him to give her the memories she wanted.

When the sun was rising, they woke and stared at each other. He wanted to tell her how he felt. That he loved her. Not the idea of her, as he'd mistakenly told her before, but how he loved Evelyn and every bit of who she truly was.

But he couldn't say the words and have her leave him, so they went unsaid.

"I don't want to ruin this moment by speaking of things that will come, but I must. It's very important." She turned only her head toward him. When he didn't move, she turned to stare at the ceiling and went on.

It was easier when they weren't looking at each other. She rattled off her instructions. "I don't want to lie to the children. I don't want to tell them I'll return. It will only breed distrust between you and, while it might be easier in the beginning, it will cause more damage later."

"Aye," he agreed.

"I don't want you to force memories of me upon them. Rose won't remember me. Gwennie will for a while…"

"But she'll forget as I forgot my family," he finished. "She'll be haunted by snippets of memories. If she asks, I'll not lie. It's hell not to have someone to ask."

She sniffed and nodded. "She'll be all right. She was used to having me in and out of her life with quick visits."

"Yes." He pressed his lips together. "She was worried of you leaving her and I promised her you never would. It seems I've already lied to her." How was he supposed to explain this to his children? That their mother didn't want to fight for them.

"I'm sorry for that. Sometimes I still think it may have been easier if I'd never married you, but I can't regret it when I think of how happy I've been the last months. I'll forever be thankful for the time we had. The family we made."

He nodded again, unable to speak.

She cleared her throat and with that strength that

continued to surprise him, she went on with her instructions. "Shea may be the most difficult. He will feel betrayed, since I told him I wanted to be his mother and now I won't be. He won't want to cry, and he'll hold in his anger."

Liam thought he was likely to do the same thing.

"You must make him talk of it and get it out, so it doesn't fester and destroy him."

"Aye." Another reluctant agreement. She was killing him with each word. With each plan she made for a future without her.

Once again, he found himself wondering what he must have done to deserve yet another punishment. He didn't know how much more he could take.

"I know I might sound cold, as if this doesn't bother me much, but it's not true. I'll have time to grieve once I'm away from here. I'll not waste a single moment for it now."

He let out a breath and pulled her close. He knew he'd never change her mind. He also knew if their roles were reversed, he'd insist on doing the same thing she was preparing to do.

...

When Evelyn entered the solar the next morning, she noticed a few extra people. Dorie and wee Dorien were visiting. They stopped speaking when she entered and offered strained smiles.

"Did everything work out as you wished?" Mari asked as Evelyn sat next to her.

"It seems a waste of a wish to want a single night with my husband. Wishes should be used for far grander things like a way out of this blasted nightmare."

Mari patted her hand. "Don't lose hope. Things may still work out. I'm sitting here as proof of it."

Evelyn offered a smile and turned to Dorie. "It's so nice of you to come for a visit."

The women exchanged glances and Evelyn realized her mistake. "You were accompanied by an army?" she guessed.

"Yes. Bryce said the plan was not to engage, but to defend if the Morgans or Stewarts decided to leave with more than what they came for."

Evelyn nodded. She knew that was the plan. She didn't want the castle to be at risk of being overthrown, but she couldn't help but think the lairds and her husband were planning some grand battle to save her.

Her faith was in Liam. He'd promised. He'd not go back on it. He was a man of honor. No matter what he might want, he would put her first.

"There's still a chance," Dorie repeated Mari's words. "After all, I had moved to England with my father, and Bryce had signed an annulment, yet we are still wed and happy."

Evelyn lifted her chin and swallowed. "I'll place all my remaining wishes on my miracle then."

The women leaned in and piled their hands on top of one another in a show of strength.

Evelyn hugged her children and laughed with them. She slept in her husband's arms pretending she would have the chance to do so all the rest of her years. But she was granted only two more nights to continue the dream.

Reality came by messenger on the third day.

Chapter Thirty-Three

Liam knew before he answered the door the knock brought bad news. He was right. The messenger whispered the information and hurried away. Liam didn't need to tell Ev what word he brought. They simply exchanged a look.

She gave a stern nod and turned to the children.

"Let's get you all dressed," she said as she did any other day. For herself she put on her best dress and planted a shaky smile on her lips.

In the corridor, the women were gathered at the solar. "We thought perhaps it'd be better to break our fast in private this morning."

Ev looked at him and he saw a tremble in her lip. "I can't eat a thing," she whispered to him. "I'm afraid I'll be sick."

He nodded. "My lady, would you see to the children? Ev and I are going to get some air." When Kenna nodded, he turned his wife toward the steps that led up to the battlements.

"It's lovely up here, is it not?" she said. He couldn't agree, for his view looked out into a field full of soldiers ready to take his wife from him by force if necessary.

"It is," he agreed. "Ev..." He let out a gust of air. "If ever your new husband dies and you're found free to marry again, I hope you'll write to me so I can send for you and bring you home."

"And if you've married another?" She made it sound like a reasonable thing, but he couldn't think of it. He'd only ever thought himself with her. He'd not find happiness with someone else while Evelyn lived and could possibly come back to him. He'd wait for her the rest of his days. "I'll not marry again."

"But the children need—"

"I'll see that the children get what they need, that they're loved and cared for. But I have only ever wanted you, Ev. When that seemed impossible, and your father rejected my suit over and over, I never wavered. I knew I'd not take another to wife as a substitute for you. I'll not do so now, either."

He shook his head and laughed once. The coldness of it carried off in the breeze. "I thought Bryce a fool for not allowing himself to love again after his first wife died. But I understand now. As long as you live you will be my wife and have my heart, and I'll not have it to give to another."

"I may have to give my body to another man and take his name, but my heart is yours, Liam MacKinlay. No one else shall ever touch it."

They held each other tightly, but Liam knew it was time to go.

"You'll stay in the castle until we've returned and it's assured there will be no hostilities."

She nodded. "Aye. I'll remain in the solar until you return."

"Very well."

With that he left to join the men gathered in the courtyard.

Liam waited in the bailey until the last moment, watching

the door to the hall, hoping Ev would rush out to tell him she'd changed her mind. When she didn't, he nudged his horse and rode out to join the others.

Lach, Cam, and Bryce were heading across the field at a leisurely pace. Liam didn't mind the slow progress. He was in no hurry to have this done.

"I can't believe it's come to this," he said.

"These women and their damned stubbornness. Why must they sacrifice themselves for us?" Cam complained. "We're supposed to be the strong ones."

Lach laughed at that. "You've seen them give birth. Do ye really think you're stronger than them?"

Cam winced and shook his head. As Cam had admitted to him before, they all knew how strong their women were. What they were willing to give up to keep those they loved safe.

"Whatever bugger came up with annulments should be drawn and quartered," Bryce grumbled and shook his head. He'd signed one once, only to have Lach hold it so it never got to its destination.

"I believe that was the church, Bryce," Cam bit his lip.

Bryce crossed himself. "They seem like the work of the devil to me."

"I can't believe I was so wrong about what was between us," Liam continued in a daze. This felt like a nightmare. One he'd never wake up from.

"I doubt you're wrong," Lach said with a sigh.

Cam nodded. "I know it sounds impossible, but it's because she loves you, she's able to leave you."

"That makes no sense at all." Liam looked at Cam as if he were daft. "And she doesn't love me. She accepted me as a means to get what she wanted."

The men glanced about one another. Lach was the one to speak. "Love doesn't often make sense. And I doubt Evelyn would be going through this if she didn't love you."

When they cleared the rise, Liam looked down at the army waiting for them. Two banners waved in the breeze. One he recognized as the Stewarts', the other had to be the Morgans'.

The Morgans wore helmets as if they were expecting to do battle instead of accept the MacKinlay's surrender. Did they think the MacKinlays dishonorable? Anger welled up, making his skin hot. It was all too much.

"I can't do this. I can't give up my wife."

"Let's speak to them, face-to-face. Maybe something can still be done," Lach said and nudged his horse.

They stopped in a line in front of the other clan. The four of them against an army. Liam glared at the men across from him. One older, one younger, no doubt the laird, and the man who would marry his Evelyn. His fist tightened as he itched to reach for his claymore and end them.

Evelyn's new bridegroom looked to be younger than Liam by a few years. Still lanky with youth. He'd be easy to take down. He looked back at the older man, who was more formidable. The larger man looked shocked as he stared at Liam.

Lachlan addressed the Stewart laird as friends and Evelyn's father sneered and accused them of stealing his daughter away against her wishes. As the two argued, the Morgan laird continued to stare at Liam, not in anger but something else.

Liam refused to look away first. He may not get to keep his wife, but by God, he'd not give the man the satisfaction of winning at this.

"Stop!" the Morgan laird shouted when Lach and the Stewart began to argue more fiercely over the accusation. Everyone quieted as the man moved closer. His horse's nose was close enough for Liam to touch. Not that he would. "Who are you?" the man asked.

Liam stood straighter in his saddle. "I am Liam MacKinlay, husband to Evelyn Stewart MacKinlay."

"Who are your parents?" the man demanded as he continued to look him over.

Liam was startled by the question but wouldn't be shamed. The Stewart laird must have told him Liam's history. If he thought this would make Liam back down, he was wrong. He held no disgrace for his past. Not when clan MacKinlay had taken him in and made him one of them.

"I don't know who my parents are, but it doesn't matter. I am a—"

"How old are ye?" the man interrupted with another question.

"I don't see what any of this matters." Liam was seconds away from pulling his sword and ending the questions.

The man swept off his helmet, his pale blond hair shimmering in the sunlight. This close, Liam noticed his light blue eyes. The same color as his.

"It matters. Now, how old are you?"

"I—I'm not sure exactly. I think twenty," Liam answered.

"Why do you not know? Tell me where you came from."

"I was found wandering in this very field when I was a boy."

"Do you have a scar on your foot?" the man pushed, eagerness clear in his eyes.

"I have scars everywhere." Liam tossed up his hands in frustration. While he was glad they hadn't launched into battle, this man was acting absurd with his questions.

"Let me see your left foot. Right now!"

Liam looked at Lachlan, who seemed just as confused but nodded. Slowly Liam dismounted. The other man did as well and came to stand before Liam as he took off his boot and stocking.

The man gasped and muttered a curse while pointing at the small scar on the top of Liam's left foot. Like most of his marks, Liam couldn't be sure where he'd gotten it, but this one had been there for some time. As long as he could remember.

"Alexander. It is you." The man grasped him tightly, pulling him into a firm hug. "My son."

• • •

When the Morgan laird released Liam, he took a step back. Studying his face, Liam saw similarities to his own. His smile was broad, and a dimple pulled in his cheek, opposite of Liam's.

"Father, it isn't him," the younger man said while sliding down from his horse.

"The hell it isn't. It's like looking at a younger version of myself."

"Forgive him," the younger man said. "He lost my older brother when Alexander was a young boy. His body was never found so he thinks he still lives."

"David, I tell you true, this is Alexander. This scar. He lifted my dirk when he was barely old enough to stand and dropped it. The mark goes all the way through. We thought he might lose his foot, but he recovered."

Curiosity made Liam stand on one foot so he could see the bottom of his sole. Sure enough, the man was right. Lach and Cam saw it, too, for they'd come to stand next to him.

"How did you lose your son?" Lach asked.

The man's face turned grim. "My dear wife Anna died when Alexander was born. I assigned a nursemaid to look over him and had no intention of ever marrying again. I had my heir and just wanted to settle into my grief."

"Seems a reasonable request," Bryce mumbled.

"I certainly hadn't planned to remarry only a year after my wife died, but I was seduced by a witch of a woman who bore my second son." He glanced toward David.

David shook his head. "Father, this is ridiculous. Alexander couldn't have come this far at such a young age on his own."

"I wasn't alone at first. Someone was with me," Liam said, not sure if he believed this tale.

"Alexander was my life. He was my piece of the woman I loved. And Janet became jealous when I didn't pay enough attention to David when he was born. It wasn't that I didn't love David, it was just he was a babe, and Alexander was three and a half. He liked to play."

"Did you carry him on your shoulders?" Liam whispered.

"Aye. All the time. He—"

"Held onto your hair as tight as I could. It was fun, but scary being so high." Liam swallowed, noticing he was taller than the man who may or may not be his father.

"This proves nothing. All lads are carried about on their father's shoulders," David said with wide eyes.

"Janet hated that her son was not the heir, and hated me for loving Alex. In a fit of anger, she sent Alexander away with her maid. The woman had a few days lead, since I was away to collect rents. When I returned, Alexander and the woman were long gone. I went into a rage, demanding to know where the woman had taken my son, but she swore she didn't know. She told the maid not to say where she was heading so she couldn't be forced into telling."

"But you forced her anyway," David said with a sneer.

"I would have if it had been you as well. I know you've never believed it."

David looked away and nodded without further argument.

"I wouldn't have killed her. She was the only link to my son." He let out a breath. "But I was angry when I approached her. I yelled and threatened. When she ran from me, she tripped on the stairs and fell, and any clue as to where Alexander could have been taken died with her a few days later."

Liam glanced over at David, who had set his gaze on a distant spot, his jaw tight.

The laird continued the tale. "I sent trackers in all directions looking for the maid who took my son, but we never found her." He shook his head. "Bloody Moira."

Liam's head snapped up and Lach, Cam, and Bryce nodded. "We've all heard you yelling her name in your sleep," Cam said.

It seemed to be the last piece of the puzzle. The final fact that proved he was this man's son. He was Alexander Morgan.

"Moira said she needed to lie down. We were hiding in the woods. She went to sleep. I'm not sure how long I waited for her to wake up—time is different when we're young—but she never woke. I grew hungry."

Cam laughed and patted his shoulder. "You're always hungry."

Lach hugged him. "You told me once you thought you were bad and that was why your parents sent you away," he said, resting his arms on Liam's shoulders. "I told you then it wasn't true. I'm pleased to tell ye I was right."

Liam laughed and turned to his father. "I do remember something else. A wooden horse, I think."

Tears filled the man's eyes as he reached into his sporran and pulled out the horse. Liam took it and allowed the man to pull him into his arms. They hugged and laughed and cried for a few moments.

Liam noticed David was still staring off. He understood why he might not want to celebrate, but he was Liam's brother and would be part of Liam's life now whether David wished it or not.

"I'm sorry about your mother. You must not remember her," Liam said.

"You can't miss something you never knew," he answered stiffly.

"I would argue with you there. I've long wished to have a family of my own. Which is why I'm pleased to call you brother." Liam turned to his father and father by marriage.

"And it is why I'll not agree to give my wife to ye. I do not wish to fight you, but I'll not sign away the woman I love."

Hugh Stewart frowned but said nothing.

"Bloody hell," David exclaimed. "I've lost my birthright and my bride today." He mounted and rode off.

Liam opened his mouth to offer to go after the lad, but their attention was drawn away by the thunder of hooves and a high-pitched war cry. Everyone turned to see the MacKinlay warriors from both clans coming at them. In the front, Liam made out three women, one with hair of golden fire.

"My wife better not be with them. She's carrying a babe," Cameron grumbled.

"It appears only three of our women have decided to launch an attack," Lach said with a resigned sigh.

• • •

Evelyn's heart was beating so fast she could feel it over the pounding of her horse's hooves as she descended on the group. She thought she'd made out Liam but then realized there was a second man with white hair. She spied her father and slowed.

She'd never been in a battle before, and her emotions were shifting with every inch they grew closer.

She was scared yet determined. While she didn't want to have to draw a dagger against another person, she'd fight to stay married to Liam. Instead of mounting to face off their attack, the men remained rooted to the ground and stood calmly next to one another.

She slowed again and the warriors following did as well. Were they too late? Was the document already signed? Had she lost Liam?

They slowed to a stop and Evelyn was the first down from her horse. She rushed toward the group. Her hair had come undone during her siege and fell over her shoulders.

"Who is this Valkyrie who descends upon us?" the man next to Liam asked.

"That would be my wife." Liam smiled and came to greet her with a kiss. His eyes were bright as he rested his hand on her cheek.

"Am I still your wife?" she asked. "I'm not too late? I was a fool to say I'd go with them. I can't. I belong with you, Liam MacKinlay. I love you. I'll not leave you. Not ever."

Tears had started to fall as she reached for him. She pressed her face to his neck, breathing in the soothing scent of him. Sunshine, happiness, and loch water.

He set her down and looked over his shoulder before turning back to her.

"I'm afraid you are destined to be the wife of the Morgan heir," Liam said. His words didn't match his easy tone and wide grin. Perhaps she'd misunderstood.

She stepped back and shook her head. "Please, Liam. I want to be with you."

"And you shall. You're my wife and will be for the rest of our lives."

"But you said…"

She glanced to the man standing beside Liam, and noticed how similar their smiles were. Their eyes were the same pale blue.

"Father, may I introduce my wife, Evelyn? Ev, this is my

father, Gaven Morgan."

"You're his heir?" she whispered, putting it together.

"Aye. It seems you'll still be able to do your duty as the laird's daughter." Liam cocked a blond eyebrow at her, but the smile remained.

"I didn't mean anything I said. I was only—"

"Trying to protect the men," Cam interrupted. "Why do they think they should protect us?"

"It's wonderful to meet you," Evelyn said to the laird of the Morgans. "I apologize for not wanting to marry into your clan before."

He raised his hand, halting her apology. "As Alexander said, you've married the Morgan heir as promised."

"Alexander?" Evelyn tilted her head at the unfamiliar name.

"'Tis the name I was given at birth," Liam said.

Evelyn was grateful no blood would be spilled; however, she was still uncertain what this meant for her family.

"It seems we have much to discuss," Kenna said, ever the mistress. "Now that we're all friends, may I welcome you to Dunardry to eat and drink with us as our honored guests?"

"Thank you for your kindness. I accept," Gaven Morgan said.

The men mounted and moved toward the castle. Liam stayed back and walked over to her father. She followed him, ready to come to his defense if her father said something cruel. Apparently, she was still set to protect her husband.

"Laird? A word if it pleases you?" Liam said.

Her father stood impassive and silent.

"I ask your forgiveness for the way I married Evelyn."

"You mean the way you stole my daughter when I told ye you couldna marry her three times already?"

It was just like her father to bring up a person's shortcomings. How long had she lived like that, listening repeatedly to all the ways she'd failed him? She'd wanted only to make him proud. She'd wanted to be loved like he'd loved her when she was younger, before she'd been ruined. But the man couldn't see past it.

It was strange how different she felt now. She'd thought the laird a good father once, but seeing Liam with their children changed that impression. She knew without a doubt that Liam would love their children no matter what trouble they found themselves in. He would offer support instead of harsh criticism and judgement.

Liam had been a father only a few months and he was so much better suited for it than the man who had claimed her the majority of her years.

Liam didn't falter from her father's accusation. "I'll have you know she married me willingly."

"She would've married anyone to defy me."

"Perhaps, but it was me she married, and I'll be forever grateful."

"It doesn't matter now. Your father is the Morgan and he's said he'll honor the contract and give me the cattle I require."

Liam wrapped his arm around Evelyn. She thought he was shaking, but it was her.

"Is that all you care about, Father? The cattle? You care nothing about my happiness?"

"I care about daughters who are honorable and see to their duties." Her father didn't even look at her when he spoke.

She stepped back, sagging slightly against Liam.

"You are a guest of clan MacKinlay, so I'll thank ye to treat my wife with respect or you may leave our lands, since your alliance is complete."

Her father's eyes went wide. "You think to send me away? Your laird may have something to say about your arrogance with his guests."

"My laird is like a brother to me, and I know he'll support my decision to send you from here if you upset my wife."

Her father stormed off and mounted to follow the other men to the castle. No doubt he would tell Lachlan how he'd been mistreated.

She placed her hand on his chest. "It's all right, Liam. He doesn't matter. I'm your wife. To him I was just livestock with which to barter." She offered him a smile.

"Is it enough to be my wife?"

"It's more than I could have ever hoped." She'd wanted only a way to be with her daughter, and Liam had given her that and so much more.

Chapter Thirty-Four

Liam kissed his wife as the men prepared to move the festivities up to the castle. They'd be together the rest of their lives, but he couldn't seem to get enough. Eventually, he managed to pull away and smile down at her.

"Will ye go help Kenna to see the men settled? I'm off to talk with my brother." He laughed. "That seems a strange thing to say."

"Your brother," she said with wide eyes. "The man I was to marry."

"Aye. He wasn't as pleased to meet me."

She placed her hand on his cheek. "It's his loss. You're the most wonderful man I've ever met." After another long kiss, she pulled away. "I'll see you when you get home."

Before she got away, he pulled her close once again, his lips by her ear. "Make arrangements for the children. I plan to have you screaming my name all night."

A beautiful blush tinged her cheeks. "And which name will I be screaming? Alexander or Liam?"

He shrugged. "As long as I'm inside you, it makes no

difference. I'll not be confused who you mean." He winked at her.

She gave him a playful smack and shook her head.

"Perhaps if my two names are confusing, you could just call me the greatest lover in all the lands." Another painless slap, but he wasn't near done teasing her and making her blush. "If you could really belt it out, so the whole castle knows— Ow." She'd found his weakness when she gave his nipple a pinch.

They laughed together and he pulled away only far enough to rest his forehead against hers. "I'm someone, Ev."

"You were already someone."

"Aye. But now I have a title—heir—that makes me someone worthy of you."

Her smile dropped away, and she shook her head. "I don't care about any title aside from husband, or father of my children." She gave him a naughty smile. "Perhaps, greatest lover in all the lands."

He laughed at her jest.

"I love you, Liam—or Alexander. You." She poked him in the chest to make it clear.

"Perhaps tonight when I'm loving you, you could scream out my newest title."

She rolled her eyes. "And what is that? These names get longer and longer, I'll not be able to remember them."

He brushed a lock of hair back from her face. "Luckiest man in all the world."

Her smile turned shy. "I'm happy you think so. I wasn't pleasant when we first married."

"Aye, that's why I came up with a title for you."

"I don't think I want to hear this."

"It's fine. I plan to tell ye anyway." He rubbed his nose against hers. "The feisty wench I love above all others."

"Ooh. I do like that last part."

• • •

Evelyn couldn't help laughing at her husband. She'd thought today would be the worst of her life, but it turned out to be one of the happiest.

"You said you loved me," Liam said smugly.

He didn't seem in any hurry to leave, and she'd gladly spend the rest of the day right there with him. The men heading for the castle held no interest. Especially the laird of the Stewarts. Liam was most important to her.

"I should have told you long before now. Telling you today makes it seem like I'm trying to outshine the event of you meeting your father for the first time."

"I don't know him. I don't know what he'll want from me. But I know that whatever it is, I can handle it better because I know you love me."

His smile faded as he looked up at the sky. "I have many decisions before me." He squinted into the sun.

"I have no doubt at all that you'll do what is best for our family. I will stand beside you."

He linked their fingers together and kissed the back of her hand as they made their way to their horses.

"Still, I'd rather we discuss our options and make the decisions together."

"Good, because I don't know how I'll feel if you force me to call you Alexander."

He lifted her into her saddle. "I said I'd never force you to do anything." He frowned before looking back to her. "I'll have another vow from you, wife."

"What's that?"

"You'll never do something foolish to protect me." He mounted and pulled his horse up next to hers.

"I promise you, Liam Alexander Morgan MacKinlay, to always be honest. Even when I'm terrified that the truth will put you in danger. I'll trust you—us—to make the right decision. Together."

"Thank ye." He paused and turned his horse. "Now I must go have a talk with my brother. I'll see you up at the castle." And with a kiss he was gone.

She watched him ride off with a contented smile on her face.

"I got my miracle," she whispered though no one was there to hear.

...

Liam had seen the direction in which his brother had ridden off and knew he'd probably not cross the stream. He found David not far from Liam's usual spot for thinking.

He walked loudly enough not to sneak up on the man, but David didn't look toward Liam.

"Might I have a word with ye?" Liam asked.

David looked surprised when he finally turned to see it was Liam. Clearly, he expected someone else to have come after him. Was this a common scenario between father and son?

Liam remembered the way Shea went off when he was upset and how Liam would give him time to calm down before going after him. But David was much older than Sheamus.

"Did Father send you?" he asked.

"Nay. He went ahead up to the castle. There will be a feast. You'll not want to miss it."

"I lost my birthright, and a bit of mutton is supposed to make me feel better for it?"

It was an odd situation. One man raised to take over as laird one day, while the rightful heir had been an orphan with no idea where he belonged. He would be patient with his brother, since they were both coming to terms with their new situations.

"I'd hoped maybe you'd consider that you gained a brother to make you feel better, but perhaps I'm not as valued as mutton."

It was a fine joke, but David only frowned. With a deep breath, Liam went to take a seat on the fallen log next to his younger brother. Liam couldn't help but notice the similarities between them. Their fingers and hands were alike.

"Do ye hate me?" Liam asked him.

"I don't even know you. You've been nothing more than a ghost who has haunted me all my life," David said and let out a breath.

"I'm sorry for it. I would have liked to have been a big brother to ye. I'm sure we would have gotten into our share of trouble together."

David seemed surprised. "I never thought of that. It might have been nice to have someone take half the punishment."

"I thought of it many times. At night, I wondered if I might have a family out there somewhere who missed me. Brothers and sisters. I imagined what they would be like and what we would say. In truth, I made up an entire imaginary family. They were perfect and happy." He frowned and tossed away a bit of moss that had stuck to his plaid before going on.

"I did the same thing when I thought of having a wife. I met Ev some time ago and over the years I created a life for us." He laughed. "It turned out not to go that way at all. I had imagined her happy to be my wife and dote on me, pleased to have my affections."

He nudged his brother. "I must tell ye, the real marriage did not start off at all how I'd thought. She disliked me for some time. And even now it's not like I'd envisioned, but it's better because it's real. We've had our share of obstacles, but she loves me, and I love her."

Liam didn't know why he was rambling on. He'd hoped

to make some kind of bond with the man. He would need him when called up to be laird.

"My point is that I hope you and I can be friends if not really brothers. I have no idea how to be laird. I take it you've been preparing for it ever since I was taken away."

"No. It took many years for Father to give up hope and accept that I was his heir. He didn't want me."

"That must have made you try doubly hard to impress him."

David nodded.

"Which means you're even more prepared than I ever would have been."

"I would never let down my father or my clan."

"Of course not. I understand. I'm the war chief here. I know about duty and honor."

David nodded but didn't look at him.

"I'm sorry things worked out the way they have. Not the bit of meeting you or my father, but the order of our birth. I'm more than a little worried of embarrassing myself in the role of heir."

David looked at him for a moment and let out a breath. "I will help you."

"Perhaps we could work at it together. Father seems strong and healthy. I daresay neither of us will need to worry over it for some time," Liam said.

David agreed and held out his hand. "I apologize for my behavior. It was such a shock, and I didn't react well."

Liam shook his hand only to pull him into a brotherly hug. "I don't know that there was a proper way to manage finding out you have a brother you didn't know. You did it well enough."

When David smiled, Liam saw more of the likeness between them.

"I'm sorry you've had such loss today when I have gained

so much. It doesn't seem fair."

"Well, I did get a brother," David said. "Better than mutton."

Liam laughed. "Come. Let's get back to the castle before all the food is gone."

"Are ye already bossing me about?" David said with a grin.

"Perhaps I'm meant to be an older brother after all. I just fell into it naturally."

They continued joking and teasing each other. When Liam and David got back to the castle, the festivities had already started. David instantly caught the attention of one of the maids.

Liam searched the hall for his family and noticed Ev and the children heading toward the stairs where the Stewart laird was entering the hall.

Ev carried Rose and held Gwennie's hand, who was in turn holding Shea's hand. Liam thought his heart might burst with happiness. He had everything he'd ever hoped for.

He stepped up, placing his hand on Ev's back as she smiled at her father. "This is my son, Shea, and my daughters, Gwendolyn and Rose," Ev said.

The laird shook his head. "I don't know where this boy came from, and you've not been here long enough to birth a babe of this size."

Liam paused, giving the man a moment to puzzle it out on his own. When he didn't, Liam explained. "They're not from us, but ours all the same."

"Ah." The laird snorted in understanding. "Bastards," he whispered.

Without a thought, Liam pulled his dagger and grasped Hugh's collar to pull him close. "If you speak that word in front of my children again, you'll lose your tongue for it, father-in-law or no. Do ye understand me?"

The man glared at Liam but offered a reluctant "Yes." He was quick to add an apology when Liam pressed the tip of his weapon against his skin.

When Liam felt he'd made his point, he released the man. He was bright enough to move out of reach and then rush away to the head table ahead of them to take a seat far from the spaces left for Liam and his family.

"I'm sorry. I shouldn't have bothered with him," Ev said, clearly shaken.

"It is not for you to be sorry to want to introduce your children to your father. I hope we shall have better luck with mine."

Shea tugged on his arm. "I'm no bastard, am I? My da was a bugger but he was married to my ma."

It was sad that someone so young knew how these things were.

"We'll not use that word." Liam frowned. "Either of those words," he added when he remembered "bugger" wasn't suitable for a child. "They don't mean a thing in our family. We are all loved and happy, yes?"

Shea nodded.

"Good. I would like you to meet my da."

"Is he a bug—uh."

Liam winked at the boy. "Nay. I don't think so."

Chapter Thirty-Five

As they walked to the head table, Evelyn was sure to keep her wits about her as they passed her father. She was careful not to look in his direction, instead, smiling at the women who were waiting on the other side of the man whose heart was filled so with hatred.

She followed Liam to stand beside his father. Liam was carrying Gwennie, whose face was tucked in Liam's neck. Evelyn didn't want her children to be subjected to any more harsh words. She could only hope Gaven Morgan had a kinder soul than her father.

"Ah, Valkyrie," Gaven addressed her with a wide smile earning a laugh from her. He leaned in and kissed her cheek. "Who are you, little one?"

Rose reached out to the man, fearless as usual. To Evelyn's surprise the laird took her and held her up as people did with little children. Rose squealed and patted his face.

"These are our children, Rose, Gwendolyn, and Sheamus," Liam said.

She noticed a glimpse of confusion from David for a

moment before he offered a smile. She loved her father and brother by marriage for the kind way they held their tongues.

"Children, this is your grandsire and your uncle."

Gwennie peeked out and Shea offered a bow. Rose called Gaven, "Papa." Then pointed to Liam and repeated it. They did look so much alike.

"I have a sword," Shea said to David. "My papa made it for me."

"I shall love to see it," David replied.

"After dinner," Evelyn said when Shea turned to her. David laughed and pulled Shea up on the bench between him and Gaven.

She reached to take Rose, but Gaven patted her back. "She's well enough here for a bit longer."

Gwennie sat between Liam and Evelyn, but soon enough she was on Liam's lap chatting with Gaven, her earlier shyness forgotten. Kenna patted Evelyn on the leg.

"I'm so glad everything worked out," she said.

"Was Lachlan very angry at ye for helping me wage a battle without his permission?"

Kenna laughed. "Nay. In fact, he told me it was the most rousing thing he'd seen in some time. The children will be staying in the solar with the nurse tonight."

At that, the MacKinlay laird stood and raised his voice, demanding quiet throughout the hall.

"Let's raise a drink to our guests. There's no greater thing than family, and we're blessed to call the Morgans such. Welcome!"

Evelyn couldn't help but notice her father's sour expression during the toast. Obviously, family wasn't important to her sire. She kept her smile in place, but Liam must have noticed, for he leaned over and kissed her cheek.

"I'm sorry, love. I wish there were a way to make him see what he's missing."

"I know." She patted his hand. "We'll not worry over it now. We have wonderful things to celebrate this night."

She couldn't allow her father's hatred to ruin this evening for her husband and his family.

...

They continued on into the night. More toasts were made to Liam's good fortune of finding his lost family. Lach, Cam, and Bryce toasted to his success as heir. Liam watched them closely to see if any of them had the same reservations he had. But their smiles seemed genuine.

They didn't look the least bit upset to see him go away to join another clan.

Gaven Morgan detailed many of the responsibilities Liam would face when they got back to Stromemore Castle—the place he was born. Liam nodded but wasn't sure if he'd be good at any of it. He'd been trained to fight.

It wasn't that he would neglect his duties, it was that he'd not been prepared for any of this like David had. Liam worried he'd make a muck of it.

As the men in the hall grew heavy with drink, he felt Shea tense and Liam excused himself and his family for the night.

"We'll talk more in the morning," Liam said.

"Aye." His father agreed. "We'll make plans to head for home in a few days." He laughed. "I daresay, once we get back, there will be more celebrating before us."

Liam forced a smile and led Evelyn and the children from the hall. They were stopped by Hugh Stewart. "If I may have a word."

As to remind the laird to watch his tongue in front of the children, Liam stepped in front of Gwennie and Shea. Rose was asleep in Ev's arms.

He'd not let this man get too close if he planned to spit

more of his venom.

The man cleared his throat, his face red and splotchy from drink. "I'm glad you've found happiness," he said to his daughter. "I was so angry when you returned. Angry at myself for not protecting you better. I didn't want to look at you because it made me realize how much I'd failed ye. But now I see I'm still failing you."

"What happened wasn't your fault. I ran away, but even still I know now it wasn't my fault, either. It was their fault. Those men who took me and hurt me. I'll not let them take my life. I'll live it with love and happiness." Liam's brave wife lifted her chin, but he noticed a wobble in her lip. He loved her all the more.

Hugh nodded and held his arms out. Evelyn waited so long to step into them Liam thought she may not do it. But she did and both she and her father broke down in tears.

"Mama sad?"

"No, love," Liam bent to comfort Gwennie. "She's happy."

When Hugh released his daughter, he held out his hand to Liam. Once he repositioned Rose, he took the man's hand.

"I'll see that you receive Evelyn's dowry. You've made her a fine husband."

"Thank you, but we don't need—"

The man put up a hand to stop Liam's rejection of the money. "You have a growing family. Perhaps it's time you built a home so there's plenty of room for everyone."

Liam had spoken to Cam about a plan he'd drawn up for a cottage, a room for just he and Ev. And plenty of space for more children. But now that he was heir, he'd be living in Stromemore Castle.

"Thank ye," Liam agreed.

While he thought it didn't matter what the man thought, he did feel relieved to have his blessing and acceptance. Liam was confident the man's blessing and acceptance were offered only because the Morgan laird had honored the contract between them.

After the children were settled in their own beds, Liam climbed in next to Ev. He'd wanted to speak to her alone, but the day caught up with her and she fell asleep only a few minutes into their conversation.

He kissed her hair and tried to calm his mind, but it was no use. If only his father had found him shortly after he'd arrived here as a child. He would have happily gone home to resume his life. But now, as a man, with a family of his own, he'd made Dunardry his home. It felt as if he was giving up as much as he was gaining.

When dawn was near, he slipped from their bed and went out. He needed to clear his mind, so he went to one of the places on the MacKinlay lands where he'd always felt at peace.

He settled cross-legged on the grass in front of the stone marking the old laird's grave. The laird's wife was buried next to him, and Liam leaned over to drop a few flowers on her grave. He'd liked giving her flowers—weeds really—as a child because she was always so pleased.

He'd spent most of his youth doing all he could to please these people. Even into manhood, he'd continued in that vein. To be the man Roderick MacKinlay would be proud of, so he'd never regret his decision to give him a name and a home.

Hearing footsteps approach, Liam didn't need to look to know he was being joined by his current laird. Lach pressed a kiss to the stones and sat next to Liam.

"I come here when I'm not sure what to do about something, or I feel overwhelmed and in danger of making a poor choice. Sometimes I ask him straight out, most times I don't need to say the words to hear what advice he would have given me," Lach said.

Liam nodded. "I do the same. I want him to be proud of me. Sitting here somehow makes it easier to know what to do."

"And do you know?"

Liam let out a breath. "Nay. Not yet."

"Perhaps if the old man canna guide us, we may be able to work it out together," Lachlan suggested.

"I have a great opportunity before me," Liam started. "I'm the son of a laird. I never coveted a position of power, though I'm honored to be the war chief. I only ever wanted a family. It seems now I have two. One I know, that belongs to me. And one I don't know, that I belong to."

"Kenna said it would be selfish of me to ask you to stay, but I fear if I don't, you'll not know how I feel. I'll not stand in your way if you decide to go. But it's important you know you're wanted here."

"You'll not tell me which choice I should make?" Liam laughed and Lach joined in, slapping him heartily on the back.

"You're a man. You'll make your own decisions. I just want it to be clear you do have a choice."

"Thank you, Lach. Truly."

"Ye shouldn't thank me. I considered letting all the horses run off so there was no way for you to leave."

"Let me guess…Kenna forbade it."

"That she did. It's a blessing to have a wife by your side to tell you when you're acting like an arse. Or to just be there when you're facing something difficult. Someone who will listen and support you as you make a hard decision."

"Perhaps I should be speaking to my wife about this rather than a stone?" Liam understood the laird's message.

"My father would be proud of you no matter what you decide to do. He loved you. I think the only reason he never claimed ye as his own was out of worry that your family would show up and it would break his heart to have to let you go." Lach cleared his throat. "I have to say, facing the possibility now myself, I don't blame him for wanting to avoid such a thing."

He stood and hefted Liam to his feet. With their hands still clasped across their chests, they embraced with the other arm.

"Go to your wife. Don't spend too much time with me. I'll try to sway you and earn the ire of my wife."

"I'll not tell Lady Kenna how much I appreciate that you wish to sway me. Last night I thought you were happy to see me gone."

"It took great strength for Cam, Bryce, and myself to hold those smiles on our faces. We did it for you."

"Thank you, brother."

Liam rode back to the castle and went up to his room. Stepping inside he smiled. He recalled the first time he'd entered this room. When he'd taken the position as war chief and was given his own quarters.

He'd rejoiced at the possibilities having a room had opened for him. The ability to have a wife and a family. Now he had everything he'd dreamed of.

He was content where he was, but he knew he'd be content at Stromemore Castle. He'd be happy wherever his family was. He didn't want to give up the opportunity his birthright afforded simply because it was unknown; he would not be too cowardly to take the chance. But he didn't want to give up what he had already for something that would never truly be his home.

Gwennie and Shea had climbed into the big bed and were snuggled in next to Evelyn. Kicking off his boots, he scooped up Rose and settled in next to them to watch them sleep until the sun woke them.

Gwennie demanded a story, and Liam told her of a rabbit who had been lost and found a grand home with wonderful friends. And how one day the rabbits who had been looking for him found him.

"The rabbit had two different homes. And two different families?" Shea asked, no doubt seeing the similarities in his own life. "I had two different homes and two different families," Shea said. "But I like this one so much better."

"Papa, the leaf. And the seal." Gwennie didn't care for deviations in the story.

"Right. I almost forgot that part." He finished the story in the normal fashion, not sure how the leaf and the seal played into his own story.

When Ev ordered them to get dressed, they scurried off the bed.

"If you thought they were going to tell you what you should do, it didn't work." Evelyn smiled and gave him a kiss.

"Will you tell me what I should do?"

"I'll tell you what *I* will do, and that is I'll go or stay with you."

"You're much too accommodating."

"I'll remind you of that when I'm not accommodating at all."

"I'm frightened," he whispered. In that moment, he was the little boy in the large field all alone.

Except he wasn't alone.

Even now, his daughter was tugging on his kilt asking him to pick her up while his son sat on Liam's foot struggling to put on shoes he would soon outgrow. His other daughter was tucking her rabbits under the covers.

And his wife held both of his hands in hers. "It's fine to be afraid of things we do not know, but you should never fear facing them alone. We'll be right next to you. Always."

Together. The way a family was meant to be.

Epilogue

A year later...

Liam was nearly brought to his knees when his wife screamed from behind the heavy wooden door. How many times had he supported other men as they waited for their children to be brought into the world?

He should've known what hell it was and done his best to avoid such a thing.

"I should have kept to collecting children who were already born," he told his father while dragging his hand through his hair for what was probably the hundredth time that night.

"Aye. If we told the women how difficult it was for us, they'd laugh us out of our homes." His father shook his head.

Another scream rent the air and Liam crouched by the door clenching his hair. Strong hands landed on both of his shoulders. He looked up to see Cam and Lach.

"Mari and Kenna will come for ye soon enough. You'll need to be ready," Cam said.

He stood and took a deep breath in a futile attempt to steady himself.

"Try not to shame yourself by swooning." Cam nudged him in the arm.

David's face turned pale. "You're going in there? While the babe is still…"

"It would be better than staying out here not being able to do anything," Gaven said.

David's eyes went wide. "And what will he do if he's in the room?" His pale skin had taken a greenish tint. "I'm going to check on the other children." He rushed down the corridor.

"He'll need to get over his squeamishness before he becomes laird," Gaven said.

Liam smiled at his father. "He has plenty of time. You're still hale and hearty."

"Aye. But your dear wife is aging me today." Another cringe as Evelyn screamed.

"Thank you for coming all this way," Liam said.

When he'd told the man his decision to stay at Dunardry, he worried the Morgans would hate him, and he might lose his family by blood.

It had been a difficult decision for sure, but he knew David would be a fine leader. A better leader than Liam would be. Gaven had agreed with Liam's choice but still wanted both his sons and grandchildren to live with him at Stromemore.

Fortunately, it was only a week by ship. They'd been able to visit one another before Evelyn shared she was increasing.

"Riders approach the castle," a messenger said. "Flying a Stewart banner."

"The man is going to miss it if he doesna hurry," Gaven said.

Liam didn't mind if Hugh was a bit late. At least he was going to be there to see Evelyn and his newest grandchild. He'd visited once since he'd gotten word he was to be a grandsire again. He'd brought gifts for all the children as well as a few men to help with the building of Liam and Ev's new home.

"Liam, do ye wish to come in?" Mari's voice interrupted his thoughts of his new home where everyone would be happy and not in fierce pain as they pushed his child from their body.

"Aye," Liam answered, though what he wished was that the babe was already out.

Lach and Cam moved to block his way.

"Don't look…down there." Lach pointed down.

"Keep your eyes on your wife's face the whole time. It's not for a man to see his favorite place used as such. Trust me on this." Cam's voice held sincerity and Lach nodded slowly.

Liam swallowed and gave a curt nod. He turned back to his father, who was smiling.

"Give my best to the Valkyrie," he said.

With his family behind him, Liam went in.

•••

Evelyn tried to smile, but she was panting and breathless and had no idea what she might have offered. Liam walked determinedly into the room and took his seat by her side. She noticed his gaze didn't wander from her face as he walked to her.

Gripping his hand in hers, he used the other to brush sweat-dampened hair from her forehead. "Valkyrie," he said softly with a smile. "My father has the right of it. For ye are the fiercest thing I've ever seen."

"I don't even carry a sword," she said in a moment of stillness. She could already feel her body ready itself for the next attack.

Liam pressed a kiss to the back of her hand as she strained

against him and screamed. When it was over, she saw tears gathered in his eyes.

"I wish I could do more to help ye than hold your hand."

"When I gave birth to Gwennie, I was all alone. Scared. Angry." She licked her dry lips. "Having you here with me. Knowing what awaits us, gives me the strength needed to go on. Thank you, Liam."

He laughed through his tears. "Thank ye, Ev." He gave her a nod and turned serious. "Now. Let's get on with this. Ye have no idea how difficult it's been for me. The children asking if the babe is here every few minutes." He winked, then whispered. "Finish this, my warrior queen. Bring this little one home to us."

She gripped his arm, squeezing with all her might as the child slid free at last.

"A son," Liam said with a smile. She knew very well he would have looked every bit as happy if it had been another daughter. A few moments later, Liam carried the babe to her and placed him in her arms. "Are you sure of the name we chose now that you've met him?"

She nodded and wiped at her tears.

"I am." She kissed her son's puckered forehead as he settled from his first wailing cry and opened his eyes. Blue eyes like his father, and a fiery halo of hair like hers.

"Welcome to our family, Alexander Roderick Morgan MacKinlay," she said.

Liam kissed her and smiled. "None of us shall ever face the world alone."

About the Author

One very early morning, Allison B. Hanson woke up with a conversation going on in her head. It wasn't so much a dream as being forced awake by her imagination. Unable to go back to sleep, she gave in, went to the computer, and began writing. Years later it still hasn't stopped. Allison lives near Hershey, Pennsylvania. Her contemporary romances include paranormal, sci-fi, fantasy, and mystery suspense. She enjoys candy immensely, as well as long motorcycle rides, running, and reading.

Don't miss the Clan MacKinlay series...

HER ACCIDENTAL HIGHLANDER HUSBAND

HER RELUCTANT HIGHLANDER HUSBAND

Also by Allison B. Hanson...

WITNESS IN THE DARK

WANTED FOR LIFE

WATCHED FROM A DISTANCE

Discover more Amara titles...

HIGHLAND CHAMPION
a Children of the Mist novel by Cynthia Breeding

Lorelei Caldwell is elated about her first Season in London without family interference. Until her best friend's very handsome, yet too-protective, brother arrives. Lorelei sets out to distract Alasdair by setting him up with a duke's daughter—all so she can have her freedom. Except that backfires when Lorelei realizes that *she* craves Alasdair's attention and it may be too late.

THE HIGHLANDER'S PIRATE LASS
a The Brothers of Wolf Isle novel by Heather McCollum

Highlander Beck Macquarie has never met a woman like Eliza Wentworth. He hasn't met many women, thanks to the blasted curse set upon Wolf Isle decades ago. To save the clan, he needs a wife and bairns, and rough-around-the edges Eliza is anything but wife material. She has no intention of staying once she's able to set sail again. He should let her go. But the desire between them is impossible to ignore.

THE BACHELOR BARGAIN
a Secrets, Scandals, and Spies novel by Maddison Michaels

Olivia Haliford is tired of seeing women being abused by rich and powerful men and so decides to expose them by starting an anonymous paper. She strikes a deal with Sebastian Colver, London's king of underground crime: he helps her, she helps his sister become a lady of society. Though they risk danger in exposing the secrets of London's upper class, they risk even greater danger when they begin to fall for each other.

Printed in Great Britain
by Amazon